Carter

A blonde, a brunette, a redhead…he can have his pick of them all on any given night and he knows it. They wait, hoping he looks up and gives them his signature smirk, choosing them over the others because that's his game.

Except now he's signed the contract of a lifetime, one with a pesky little clause that says his zipper must stay up and his playboy image has got to tamp down. It'll be fine—a piece of cake, even—he can do this and he's almost convinced himself of that … and then she walks in the room

The new PR girl whom they've hired to change his image, she's the star of all his dreams, but there's one tiny little problem … she can't stand him and all of his player ways.

He knows he only has thirty days to show her why they call him Hollywood's Prince. He's up for the challenge, so game on.

PRAISE FOR NATASHA MADISON BOOKS

If you've been looking for a HOT and HILARIOUS new book to fall in love with then you have to read this book!!!

Aestas Book Blog

This is how rom com is done! Hilarious. Sexy. Witty. I couldn't get enough.

Aly Martinez *USA Today* Bestselling Author

A heartwarming, breathtaking, sinfully delicious read that I seriously cannot recommend high enough.

Gayle Williams Blogger From Down Under

This is one of the funniest books I have ever read! I didn't want it to end. Natasha Madison gives us readers what we need. Brilliant!!!! - Dirty South Book Blog

A fantastic read and hit all my sweet spots. It's why Natasha Madison continues to be a instant one click author for me.

Melissa Teo Book Smacked

Natasha Madison's trademark push-and-pull romance is on display here with many angsty and hilarious moments.

Jess Moro USA Today HEA

Cover Design: Jay Aheer
Editing done by Jenny Sims Editing4Indies
Proofing Julie Deaton by Deaton Author Services
Content Editing By Elaine York
Interior Design by CP Smith

DEDICATION

To my cousins Lydia, Sabrina, Stephanie,
Marissa, Victoria, Juliana and Shelly
for always having my back!

Hollywood PRINCE

NATASHA MADISON

One

Erin

"HEY, ERIN." I HEAR my name come over the speakerphone as I sit in my cubicle brainstorming for the up-and-coming movie premiere.

"Yes, Sylvia?" I answer right away.

"Come to the conference room please." She doesn't give me a chance to answer before she hangs up. I take a deep breath and stand. The clicking from my stilettos echoes down the long hallway as I exit my cubicle and head to the conference room where I've been summoned.

For the past five months, I've been an intern at Hillcrest Production Company, and I have one more month to go until I officially graduate at the top of my class, which is why Hillcrest chose me. I was brought n in the marketing department to bring fresh ideas for promoting their movies. I knock on the closed brown wooden door and hear someone say to come in.

Turning the silver handle, I open the door, surprised to see five people sitting around the conference table. Sylvia, head of the Public Relations department, sits next to Ryan, the owner of Hillcrest. The rest of the department heads, from the CFO to the COO, fill the other chairs. It's the who's who in the movie business. Not the actors and actresses but the ones who build the movie from the ground up. From set design to filming to producing to marketing, it all takes place under one roof.

"Erin," Sylvia says, "have a seat." She motions to one of the empty chairs, and I nod and sit down. The nervousness of all the eyes on me makes my mouth dry. I put my hand on top of the table and look around. Ryan looks at me and smiles.

"Relax," he says, "you haven't done anything wrong." His words make me breathe out a sigh of relief. "In fact, I've heard only good things."

"That's good to know," I say, and then he leans back in his chair.

"I'm going to cut right to the chase," he says and then looks over at Sylvia, who just nods at him. "For the past five months, we've been watching you, and we love the ideas that you have brought to the table." I look over at Sylvia and wonder where this is coming from. She hasn't exactly welcomed me with open arms, so it's no surprise she's rude because it was evident from the first day I started interning here. Hillcrest Production Company is a dream for anyone who wants to work in the PR field. There is no sugarcoating, and I know I have a month left before the contract expires. "We have a job for you, and well . . ." he says. Sitting up, he puts his hands on the table. "If you can actually do this, I'd love to hire you for a full-time position either here or in the New York office." Not only does Hillcrest run L.A., but it runs New York also.

This must be a joke, right? "I'm not sure what to say," I answer, trying to find my words and not sound like an idiot. To be in charge of a whole PR team is hands down one of my biggest dreams.

"Don't say anything yet. Wait until you see what you need to do," Sylvia says, and I swear she hides a snide smile.

"It's not that bad," Ryan says and then looks at me. "What do you know about Carter Johnson?"

I look at them. "The one who just signed on to be the Loyalist?" HillCrest is going all out on their next movie. You don't have to live under a rock to know that their last movie starring Tyler Beckett killed it at the box office. You also don't need to know the who's who in Hollywood to know that Carter Johnson is the next big thing. Word going around says this is his biggest contract yet.

"That's the one," Ryan says, and he looks at me, tapping his fingers on the table.

"Um …" I try to think of nice words to say, but I don't get a chance.

"He's the biggest gigolo out there," Sylvia says, "and he's a PR nightmare. He was just shown on TMZ walking into a hotel with two women and then walking out six hours later with a smile on his face and a cigarette hanging from his mouth with his shirt unbuttoned. I think there were even scratch marks, and I saw at least one bite mark." I don't say anything. I can't say anything because it's actually all true, and it wasn't just on TMZ. He headlines every single gossip site at least once a week as he literally fucks his way through Hollywood. Last week, he walked out of the same hotel at two different times with two different women. Both of them draped all over him.

"I have heard of him," I say to Ryan and then look at Sylvia, hoping she gives me something.

"Good," Ryan says. "Now here is the job. We need you to recreate his image." The minute he says the words, my mouth hangs open.

"What?" I ask him. Surely, I didn't hear him right because there is no way I, or anyone else, could recreate his image.

"I don't think that's humanly possible. His image is so far down in the gutter that even the rats have a better image than he does right now."

"Well," Ryan says, getting up and pushing away from the table, "then you have your job cut out for you. You have one month to make it happen. Basically, you are going to have to live through a nightmare in order to get the job of your dreams." He nods his head to everyone at the table and looks back at me when he gets to the door. "Thirty days. We meet with him tomorrow."

I sit here in shock, wondering how the hell I'm going to do this.

Two

Erin

THE WALK BACK TO my cubicle is slow, and the clicking of my heels is now dull, considering I don't hear anything else because my heartbeat is so loud in my ears. "There has to be a mistake." Mumbling to myself, I sit down in my chair and stare at the list I was working on before I got called into what I'm going to call my life-changing career moment.

"So what are you thinking?" I hear Sylvia's voice, and I turn in my chair to see her standing at the entrance of my cubicle. She is wearing a black pant suit with a pink ruffled shirt under it and peep-toe shoes. Her short blond hair is curled under perfectly, her blue eyes with just mascara, and her red framed glasses sitting on her nose.

"I'm thinking it's an impossible task," I tell her honestly. I'm expecting her to agree with me, but she crosses her arms over her chest instead.

"I'm not going to lie, so had you asked me that five months ago, I would have said you didn't have the balls to do it," she says, and I'm wondering if she's ever actually given anyone a pep talk. "When you started here, I have to say I had bets you'd leave within the first three weeks. But you didn't; you came in, day in and day out, and worked harder than anyone else in the department." She smirks. "Except me, that is." I chuckle. "We meet with him tomorrow at four. How about we sit down before that and go over strategies and see what we can come up with?"

"I would love that," I tell her, "because I'm going to be honest. I have nothing. There is nothing I can think of that will change his image. I mean, besides him changing his name and starting over. And maybe plastic surgery. There's always plastic surgery." I try to instill some humor into a humorless situation.

"That will be hard for someone who has been in the game since he was ten," she tells me. "The good old *Mickey Mouse Club*." Her phone beeps in her hand, and she looks down at it. "I have to run, but tomorrow, meet me in my office at ten. Obviously, do your research beforehand and detail some of his biggest scandals and what they involved so we know *exactly* what we are dealing with."

"I will," I tell her and then look down and then up. "Thank you so much for the talk."

She doesn't say anything else as she turns and walks away. Leaning forward, I look at the list I started before

I walked into the meeting and crumple it, throwing it in the garbage, and then I start gathering information on Carter. A list that I started this morning that will no doubt be shoved into someone else's workload now that I have my next assignment.

By the time I look up, the sun is long gone, and no one is left in the office. With my stomach growling at me, I grab my jacket and make my way home to grab some dinner and go to bed, hoping upon hope that tomorrow looks a little brighter than it does today.

The next day, I walk into the office before anyone else. I gave up on sleeping at four thirty this morning and decided to start the day early. I'm just hoping I don't crash before the meeting. I even went to the gym and put in an hour and a half on the treadmill. I press the button in the elevator to take me to the thirty-seventh floor. Looking down at my black Louboutin stilettos, I take a deep breath. How ironic that I'm dressed for a funeral. I'm just praying it's not my own. My black pencil skirt falls right below my knees, and I paired it with my black long-sleeved shirt with white polka dots. The wrists are tight, making the sleeves flow a little.

When the elevator doors slide open, I'm not surprised that no one is here yet because it's only seven thirty in the morning. I put my Starbucks coffee on my desk and then take off my black jacket and put it on the back of my chair. Pulling out my chair, I have a seat and start the computer. I grab my notes and the reports I did on him yesterday, and the first thing I do is google Carter's name and then set up a Google alert for him on my phone.

I scroll and see that he was out and about last night. The picture of him leaving a Hollywood hotspot three hours ago fills the screen. I scroll through them, seeing him arriving in gray jeans and a red, white, and blue plaid shirt with a blue jacket. Then there is a picture of him leaving the hotspot wearing a white T-shirt, holding the jacket and shirt in one of his hands while his other hand holds a redhead's hand. Her skirt is barely there, and her shirt looks as though it's buttoned wrong. He smirks at the camera guy, making me groan.

"You're here early." I hear Sylvia behind me. I turn and see that she is wearing another pant suit, this one gray with capris, and she is wearing a white shirt with a pink jacket. "Let me put my things down, and we can start right away," she says. Turning around, she walks into her office and puts down her big Louis Vuitton purse in one of the chairs facing her desk. She opens the shades in her office, allowing the sun to come shining in. "We should use the conference room and get things set up," she says loudly. Sitting behind her desk, she picks up her stack of messages. She is still old school. She wants all messages written on little pink papers, and right next to her desk is a shredder that she uses as soon as she finishes with the message. My phone buzzes on my desk, and I pick it up and it's Sylvia. "I have to return a couple of calls, so I'll buzz you when I'm ready," she says and hangs up. I start on another list of things that we should do. When she finally buzzes me, I grab my coffee, my pen, and the folder that I started for him.

We walk to the conference room together, and she pushes open the door. We sit down at the table and toss ideas around until it's a little after three. "You really did your research," she says, leaning back in her chair. I stare at the notepad in front of her. She's taken so many notes that she filled four sheets.

I shake my head. "I had to see what I was up against." I tap my pen on my own pad. "Honestly, I don't think this will ever happen."

"Define this?" Sylvia asks, then doesn't wait for me to answer. "If you are referring to you being able to tame the biggest social risk we've ever had, I am ready to bet you that you will not only make it happen, but you will also have him eating out of the palm of your hand."

My eyebrows come together in confusion. "I don't understand."

"Do you know you've been here for five months, and you have everyone under your spell? You are social, you are nice, and you make people come to you and respect you." She laughs. "I was on the fence with you, but when I saw the way you were with everyone here, I knew if anyone could do it"—she points at me—"it would be you." She shakes her head, laughing a bit. "Now me, on the other hand, I would not do well. I would lock that asshole in a room and bring him out only when I needed him."

I laugh silently. "You saw all that." She has been the

hardest nut to crack since I've been here. I've befriended everyone but her.

"I did." She pushes away from the table. "I see everything. Now go get something to eat and get ready because he isn't going to cave easily. The saying a leopard doesn't change his spots means you have to be ready to prove them wrong." I nod at her, and she walks out of the conference room, leaving me alone with my own notes.

I get up and run down to grab another coffee. Carter will be here at four and Sylvia will buzz me when it's time for me to come in. I don't know why I'm so nervous. Maybe it's just the biggest opportunity of my life. Maybe because if I actually achieve this, it will put me up there and my name on the map. I'm walking back in when my phone rings. I look down at it in my hand and see it's my mom.

"Hey, Mom." I answer the phone, walking back to the office and enjoying the little heat that I've had today.

"Hey, sunshine." I smile when she uses my childhood nickname. "Just calling to check in." My mother was a single mom, always. She and my father were never together really. They had a relationship of sorts, but nothing that would stick, and they were both okay about it. When my mother found out she was pregnant, she said she was keeping me, and it was up to my father if he wanted to be involved because she was not going to force me on him.

I guess I got lucky because my father accepted it with an open mind. He was always in my life, and he supported my mother and me very well. At first, we grew up in a two-bedroom condo near the beach in Florida, and slowly, we moved up to a house, which she refuses to leave. It's right on the beach, and she wants to keep it in case I want to move home. Was I close to my father? I mean, I was as close as I can be to a person who would visit on the holidays. He was there for some birthdays and some not. I was always okay with it because my mother made sure I never doubted I was loved. Not for one minute. Growing up, she would date but only casually and in passing and never brought any man home.

When I got accepted to the college of my choice, it was bittersweet. I would be leaving her, and I dreaded that, but she never made me feel guilty about it. My father ended up covering my whole tuition and still paid my mother every month. He also never had any kids, nor did he have women. I mean, I know he had women, but none that he brought home to me or introduced me to.

"Mom, you don't have to keep checking in with me," I tell her with a smile. She wasn't just my mother; she was really my best friend. "You could just call to see what I'm doing."

"Okay, fine." She laughs. "What's new?"

"Have you spoken to Dad?" I ask her, knowing why she is calling. "I spoke to him last night so I know that you know."

"I do know, and I did," she says. I hear the waves in the background, so I know she's sitting out on the deck watching the sun go down.

"Sorry, it got late, and by the time I looked at the clock, it was already midnight your time," I tell her. I smile, walking into the lobby. "Mom, I am not sure I can do this."

"Oh, please," my mother starts, "if anyone can do anything, it's you."

"You are saying that because you are my mom," I tell her, pressing the button to the elevator.

"No, I'm telling you this because it's the truth. If you want it, you will get it. You have never backed down from a fight." Her voice is calm, and I suddenly miss her.

"Mom, this isn't high school where someone called me a name," I tell her and step in the elevator. "It's a big deal."

"I know it is," she says. "It's a dream job, and one you've been talking about since you decided this was what you wanted to do."

"I just don't want to let anyone down," I say, my voice low even though I'm by myself in the elevator.

"Honey, as long as you give it everything you have, there is no way you can let anyone down." The elevator pings, and I walk out, almost crashing into a man who walked out of the other elevator. His hands hold both of my hands before I crash into him and spill the coffee.

"Oh my gosh," I say softly. The warmth of his hands on my arm makes me look up, and I think I stop breathing. His smell of musk hits me right away. I can't see his eyes because he's wearing aviator glasses, but even with them on, I know who this man is. His brown hair looks like he just stepped out of the shower and ran his hands through it, and I think he actually did. A smile starts to come over his face; the famous smirk that graces all the magazine covers.

"Sorry, sugar," he says, and his voice comes out smooth.

"Erin, are you okay?" I hear my mother's voice through the phone that is still up to my ear.

"I have to go," I say to her and bring my hand down. He slowly lets my arms go. "Sorry, I wasn't watching where I was going," I say and then turn to walk away before I openly gawk at him.

"If you weren't a sight to see from the front, you're an even better sight to see leaving," he says when I walk away, and I halt in my steps, turning now and taking him in. Twelve hours ago, he had a redhead on his arm, and now he's looking for a date tonight. He's wearing blue jeans rolled at the hem that fall over his brown boots. A tattered leather jacket covers his black shirt. "Listen, I have a meeting, but how about we take off when I'm done?" He walks to me as I stand here watching him. "Why don't you just sit here and wait, and when I come back out, we can take off?"

"Are you asking me to leave with you?" I ask him, shocked but definitely not surprised. When he smirks, I bite down hard to block my mouth from telling him to fuck off. And before he says anything, I hear Sylvia behind me.

"Carter, good, you're here," she says, coming to us.

"We are just waiting for you."

His smirk disappears, and he takes off his glasses. It's the wrong move because now I can see his green-blue eyes. "I'll be out in ten minutes, fifteen minutes the most," he says, and I just look at Sylvia.

"Let me know when you need me," I say and then turn and walk back to my desk. I keep my shaking hands in check. I sit down and literally count to ten in my head. My heart beats faster and faster and then slowly calms. And just when it's finally beating normal, the buzzer on my phone goes off.

"Erin, we are ready for you," Sylvia says.

"I'll be right in," I say and look up at the ceiling. "I can do this," I mumble to myself. "How bad could it be?"

In the back of my mind, I am almost afraid of the answer.

THREE

Carter

I SLAM THE DOOR shut behind me and walk straight to the winding staircase that takes me upstairs to my bedroom. When I make it up to the landing, I come face-to-face with the wall of floor-to-ceiling windows and a view of the blue ocean outside. The sun shines high in the sky, making it perfect. This view made me dish out twenty million dollars. That, and well, it's right on the beach and gives me the privacy I deserve. I've been in show biz for the past twenty-five years, so basically most of my life, after being chosen at an open casting call my parents brought me to at the mall when I was eight.

We lived in a trailer, and some months, we were lucky to have water. The minute they cast me on *The Mickey Mouse Club,* I was my parents' golden ticket. Almost like in *Willy Wonka and the Chocolate Factory*.

They loved it so much that when I turned eighteen, I was happy to say I had not one penny left. My father had spent it on five homes that he paid for in cash while my mother jetted around town with a chauffeur.

So I started from the bottom when I legally became an adult, crossed them off my list forever, and then went on with my star-studded life. They tried to sue me for back royalty. Can you believe they claimed to have managed my career? Luckily, I had a shark lawyer who went toe to toe with them and even presented proof of all the money they embezzled from me. I've been on my own since I was eighteen years old, if not younger, but I have one person to think about, and that is me. I don't have time to have any strings attached to anyone. Unless it's for the night.

I pull a black shirt over my head and walk to my bedroom on the right. The open curtain gives a view of the ocean again. I toss the shirt in the laundry, taking off my shoes at the door and then make my way to the bathroom to shower. I woke up thirty minutes ago and snuck out of my latest conquest's house. I look in the mirror and see the nail marks down my chest. Why do these women feel it's necessary to leave a mark as if I'm actually going to remember them in the morning? I mean, don't get me wrong, I've dated women but just casually and sporadically. Besides, in my line of work, why eat the same food every night when you can feast at a buffet?

I open the glass door to the huge walk-in shower. Even though it's fitted with a bench, it's never seen any action. I've never brought a woman home. Actually, that's a lie. I brought one girl home seven years ago, and she stayed a fucking week. I literally had to send one of my friends to escort her from the house because she thought we were in love. Love. Like I'd be stupid enough to fall in love with anyone. Love was for fools, and I wasn't a fool. I only had to depend on myself and no one else, and I loved myself. I loved my life.

Grabbing my brown leather jacket and sliding my sunglasses on, I run down the stairs and straight to the garage, then get into my black Ferrari. I make my way over to Hillcrest where I'm meeting my manager to sign the biggest contract of my life. The engine purrs every time I rev it. I pull up to the valet and toss him my keys. Grabbing my phone, I check to make sure I'm not late, and I see I have one minute to spare. I press the button for the elevator and then make my way up to Ryan's office. I got a message from Jeff, my manager, that he's already in the conference room.

I look up, and I swear the earth stops, or I think it does. My arms come up as I try not to run over the woman with long auburn hair walking out of the opposite elevator. If you put glasses on her, she'd look like one of those sex kittens. I don't even know what I say to her, but I think I just asked her to wait for me. She turns and walks away from me, and then I give her my trademark smirk. A smirk that makes sure I don't go to bed alone. I watch her walk away, and I was not wrong when I said it was a good view. Her tight ass in that tight as fuck skirt causes my cock to spring to half mast. Her long hair is swinging side to side. I'm going to bury my hands in her hair, wrap it around my fist, and slam my cock into her.

"Jeff is waiting for you," Sylvia says to me. I've met her twice before when I came for meetings here. I nod at her, and she turns to walk away, but the view is definitely not the same as the sight of heaven I just witnessed. We walk down the hallway to the conference room, and when she opens the door, Jeff looks up and sees me. He gets up, coming over to me, and he's wearing a business suit, like always. When I turned eighteen and found out I had nothing left, I went to his office. I had seen him around on set when he visited other clients. Sitting in his office that day, I told him everything. Every little detail. He sat in the chair beside me facing his desk. He got up and then slapped me on my shoulder and said, "Let's get it all back and then some, yeah?" And from that day on, he was like a brother to me. I even spent holidays at his house with his wife and kids, no questions asked like I've always been there.

"Hey, you are right on time," he says to me. He isn't giving me his regular smile. No, his look is bleak, and my stomach falls. Fuck, did they cancel the deal?

"Right on time," I say, looking at him. I'm trying to read his eyes, but I see nothing. When he turns away, I see Ryan sitting at the table in a suit without a tie. The top two buttons are open. He sits at the head of the table with two other suits next to him—I can't remember their names—and then Sylvia sits beside them. Jeff takes a seat in front of them, and I pull out the chair next to Jeff.

"So," Jeff starts, looking at the contract in front of him, "there is an adjustment to the contract." His thumbs tap the table, so I can tell he's nervous about it.

I put my glasses on the table, trying not to show that I'm irritated or better yet pissed. "Really? Exactly what kind of adjustment?" I ask, leaning back in the chair and putting a hand on the armrest.

I look at Ryan, and he looks back at me. From what I heard, he took a chance and started this production company when he was twenty. The first couple of movies were literally handheld equipment that he filmed himself, and now he's the richest person in Hollywood. He has his hand in everything that has to do with Hollywood. He is a key player, so bottom line, you want him on your side.

"Let's cut to the chase. Your last release didn't kill it like we wanted it to." I sit up now, and I'm about to say something, but he puts his hand up. "It did great. I'm not saying that. What I'm saying is it could have done better." I'm about to say something, but Jeff puts his hand up so Ryan can finish speaking. "With that said, we think your reputation is what is stopping you from going from here," he says with his hand halfway up, "to here." He raises it higher.

"Reputation?" I ask, confused. "I come to work each day on time, and I do my job. I don't pull any stunts, nor do I sit in my trailer and pout until I get my way," I say of another actor that is known to do that. "So I'm confused on why my reputation isn't getting me here," I say, putting my hand up to where Ryan just had it.

"It isn't your reputation on the set," he says, leaning back in his chair more to one side. "It's your reputation out there." He points his thumb at the window. "It's the partying every night. It's the girls. That kind of lifestyle really turns people off, which translates into people not wanting to go see your movies."

"Wait a second." I'm annoyed now. "I've never been drunk or on drugs," I tell him, and I'm not. When I was nineteen, I blacked out more times than I could count, so I stopped drinking. Period. Cold turkey. "I have no idea what you're talking about." I mean, I do, but so what if I get laid every night or twice a day?

He looks over at Sylvia, who opens her folder and takes out a picture from last night and then another one from the night before and before then and a couple from last week. "This is just in the past couple of weeks."

"So I like to date," I tell them. "There isn't a law against that."

"You're right," Ryan says, "but it pushes a huge chunk of your fan base away—specifically, the female audience—from the movie if they think you're a douche." I roll my eyes. "If you want a sampling, we actually did a survey on video, and we asked a hundred women what they thought of you and your movies."

"This isn't *Family Feud*," I snap back, and now Jeff talks.

"Okay, Ryan, we get it." He folds his hands on the table. "I haven't had a chance to talk to Carter, but he's going to do whatever is necessary to make sure that this movie kills it."

"I am glad you said that," Ryan says, looking over at me, and I look at him and then at Jeff. "Who is going to tell him?"

Jeff smirks and then looks at me. "For the next sixty days, you need to live the life of a monk, so you can't have sex."

"What?" I shriek. "What in the fuck?"

Ryan laughs. "And for the next thirty days, we are going to rebrand you." I shake my head, hoping I heard wrong. Surely, I heard wrong.

"I don't understand," I say, looking at Jeff and then finally snatching the contract from in front of him. Surely, they can't stop me from having sex. Is there a law against stopping someone from having sex? That's not actually a thing, is it?

"Well, we are going to be working with you on how to polish your image like a shiny nickel," Sylvia says. "And we have Erin, who is going to work with you on doing just that."

"Before we do that," Ryan says, "you need to sign that contract." I look over at Jeff who nods his head and then leans over to me.

"This is the deal of a lifetime. We are talking multi-movie deals with royalties," he whispers. "Don't let your dick fuck it up."

I nod at him and grab a spare pen lying on the table to sign on the dotted line. I toss the pen on the table. "There, I've signed it."

Ryan looks at Sylvia and nods his head. She leans over, picks up the phone in the middle of the table, and says, "You can come in now." She hangs up the phone, and then she looks at me. "She is the best that we have, and if anyone can rebrand you, it's her. We were working on this all morning long, and she has some great ideas." She stops talking when there is a knock on the door. When she walks in, I suddenly know that I'm most definitely going to be in breach of this contract.

"Erin, I believe you've already met Carter."

She looks at me, and I was wrong before. She isn't hot; she's smoking. Not only is she smoking, but she's hands down the most beautiful woman I've ever met. And let me say I've met a lot of them. Her perfect and round eyes look like they are blue with a splash of green. Her perfectly plump lips have a coat of just clear gloss on them. But fuck that her body is so fucking smoking has my cock already hard. I look down and then look up with a smile. "Erin, what a pretty name," I say smoothly and hear Jeff groan beside me.

FOUR

Erin

MY HANDS SHAKE AS I walk back to my desk. I knew he was good looking. Okay, I'm lying; he's not just good looking, he is so far past that I can't describe it. But I get it now with the smirk and the smoldering look. I can totally see why the ladies flock to him . . . and why he allows them to flock. That smirk speaks volumes.

Placing the coffee cup on my desk, I sit down and look at the computer screen. Counting in my head slowly, I breathe in and breathe out. I lean back in my chair and stare up at the lights. This is a bad idea. I have a feeling this whole thing will be a failure before I start. When the phone buzzes, letting me know it's time for me to be introduced, so to speak, I get up. Grabbing my own folder that I prepared, I walk down the hallway. Almost like you are walking to the principal's office . .

. or like the movie *The Green Mile*. I'm not sure which ending would be worse at this point. I swallow and take a deep breath, then I knock on the door and walk in.

Sylvia is the first one I hear speaking. "Erin, I believe you've already met Carter." I look over at him, and his smirk stretches into a full-blown smile on his ridiculously perfect face.

"Erin, what a pretty name," he says, and I hear the guy beside him groan. Carter reaches over, extending his hand, and I automatically reach out and shake his hand. His hand grips mine, and he slowly moves it, then stops and just holds my hand.

I look over at the other people sitting in the meeting. Ryan just shakes his head when the guy next to him gets up and pulls our hands apart to introduce himself. "I'm Jeff. I'm Carter's manager."

I smile at the guy whose beads of sweat forming on his brow and upper lip are becoming awkwardly apparent. "Nice to meet you," I tell him. Walking over to sit next to Sylvia, I try my best to control the pace of my beating heart. This is a big meeting with the biggest Hollywood player and all his people, and I'm sitting at the table feeling very out of my element. But I know it's my go big or go home moment.

"We were discussing with Carter the ways to change his reputation," Sylvia starts and then looks at me, then at Ryan. "Erin will be taking the lead on this, and she will be reporting back to us."

"Basically," Ryan says, "if she says do this or do that, then there is a reason, and I need you to respect it."

"I have no problem doing whatever Erin suggests I do for her," Carter says, leaning back in the chair.

Jesus, that fucking smirk is on megawatt charge right now, and it's becoming harder and harder to avert my eyes from his mouth.

"So what are you suggesting exactly?" Jeff asks, and Sylvia looks over at me and just nods her head. It's enough of a diversion that I'm able to focus so I get ready to pitch my ideas.

"Well, for one, we need to work on his Instagram," I start and take out some of the pictures that I pulled from his account. "He has twenty million followers, and the only pictures he is posting are of him partying with different women, multiple times a day, coming and going out of different hotels and bars . . . so a lot of female adoration from a personal standpoint, but not so much from the followers on your social media accounts."

"Twenty million is huge," Jeff says, and I nod.

"It is, but it has gone down a million over the past six months." I take out proof of this, handing it to them.

"There has to be a reason," Jeff says. "Some of the accounts must have been fake or closed."

"One million accounts are gone. That's roughly fifty-five-hundred followers per day. He's bleeding followers, so it could be that people aren't interested in seeing who he is sleeping with today," I tell him. "We'll use Tyler Beckett as a recent example. He grew to forty million followers after he started posting about his wife and kid. Not so much his kid but his home life. He became more personable, someone the masses can connect with, can celebrate their success with, can support. It's a unique algorithm that works with the female population. It gives the average woman an idea that 'hey, the love of his life is just like me and maybe someone like him could fall in love with me' when they see that he's posting pictures of a normal Sunday morning making pancakes with his wife and child. It's all about image and the impression, and the debauchery and a partying lifestyle that you have been posting about lately are not something your followers can relate to."

"Well, considering I don't have a wife and a kid, everything that you are saying could be a huge problem," Carter says, and I just look at him.

"Well, considering that you can post about anything else—literally anything—except for how much traffic a certain body part of yours gets on a daily basis, then yeah, maybe it might change." I'm about to apologize when Sylvia interrupts.

"What she is saying in a nice way is no one wants to know who you are going home with. They care about what you do during the day." I watch Carter as he takes in all the information.

"They want to know that you are the guy next door," I say. "They want to see that you get up and you have coffee. You have a dog or a cat. They want you to be like them, and the girls want to see that you have a soft side also."

"Trust me, honey, there is nothing soft about me," Carter says, and Ryan slaps the table, getting up.

"This, right here, is why you need her," Ryan says.

"I think you can be the biggest there is, but if you can't get the people to come to the movies because of your fucking attitude, then it doesn't matter." Ryan looks over at me. "I want to be included on this all the way."

"Not a problem," I tell him, and then he looks at Jeff.

"I trust you will explain to him how important this is," he says while the other guys stand and start to walk out. "If you will excuse us, we have to get on a plane." He looks over at Carter and points a finger, and says, "SIXTY DAYS, Carter . . . don't disappoint." No one says anything while the other guys walk out of the room. With the click of the door, it's suddenly just the four of us in the room.

"Okay," Carter says, the smirk now missing from his cocky demeanor. "I'll do whatever you want."

"Perfect," I say. Maybe I can actually do this. I mean, maybe he can be a civil person to work with.

"Let's meet tomorrow," he says. "Ten a.m. at my house."

"Um." I start to stutter and maybe suggest we just meet here when Sylvia answers.

"That is a great idea," she says, and I look over at her, trying not to make my mouth hit the floor. "You two need to be on the same page."

"I couldn't agree more," Jeff says, and then he starts to get up. "So we will see you tomorrow at ten a.m."

He said we, so I kind of breathe a little sigh of relief. "That sounds great." Carter gets up now, grabbing his glasses, and just smiles at Sylvia.

"It's great seeing you again." When he turns to me,

his eyes change and his smile changes, but I'm the only one who can see the shift. He's the hunter, and I'm his prey. "Erin, see you tomorrow," he says and turns to walk out of the room, and it's only then I notice that I'm not breathing. I was holding my breath, for what I'm not sure. Maybe hoping he wouldn't notice me at all.

"I don't know why we couldn't have the meeting here." I look at Sylvia who just leans back in her chair.

"He isn't going to be himself here," she says, and I know she's right. "He's going to have a chip on his shoulder, but if he's in his home, he's going to be open more. The guy was just told via a legal and binding contract that he cannot have sex at all for the next sixty days. A man of his proclivities will more than likely have more than a chip on his shoulder. If not now, then in the very immediate future."

"This is true." Gathering the pictures, I get up and push my chair under the table. "How long should I expect to be at his house?"

She looks over at me, and I see her smirk. "Thirty days." I don't say anything when she walks past me out of the room, leaving me by myself.

I pack the stuff in my bag and walk out of the office at five, dragging my ass since I've been up for twelve hours and my brain is finally catching up to everything that just happened. I make my way home and sit on the couch, catching up on my DVR. I fall asleep with the remote in my hand and wake up to the blue screen. I see that it's two thirty in the morning, so I make my way to my bed. Sinking into my king-size bed, I fall asleep again just as fast. When the alarm rings as the sun is coming up, I grab my phone and go through my routine.

I check Facebook to see what everyone was up to, then I slide over to Instagram to go through my stories there, and then I see that Carter made a personal story. I click the round circle with his picture, and it shows him sitting on a couch with a smirk. A movie playing on his screen.

There is a movie screen with the caption "Thursday night movie."

See, that wasn't so bad, I think to myself as I roll out of bed. I debate whether to make the bed. My mother is a stickler about making the bed. Something about a post she saw in the news about how the day just starts off better if one makes the bed. I just toss the covers over and pretend it looks done, and then I start my day. I take a quick shower while my coffee brews, then fix a to-go cup after I finish getting dressed. I have no idea what the dress code is for my meeting this morning, so I decide to go with pants. I grab the pink capris with black lines down and across them. Grabbing my black long-sleeved shirt, I toss it on. I pick up the same black Louboutins I wore yesterday and decide to wear my hair loose. Grabbing my bag and my to-go cup, I walk out the door.

I grab my phone once I get in the car and punch in the address to Carter's house that I got from the file. It shows that it's about forty-five minutes from me. When I get to the gate for the neighborhood, I tell the guard who I'm here to see. After he checks that I'm on the list, he tells me it's the second house on the right. I thank him and drive through the gate once it's opened. I pull up to the driveway and see the house. Stepping out of my car, I grab my bag and walk up to the house. A low concrete wall blocks off the house, but you see a huge window and little balcony. Once I walk closer, I see that it's the second floor and that you have to walk down a staircase to get to the front door. I walk down the steps, holding the cast-iron railing, and see the wall of the house is different shades of brown rocks. The big window from the top is the same on the bottom, and the house now looks like an L. A wooden bench sits beside the glass door, and a little cast-iron white table and two chairs are in the corner next to a small rose garden. It's such a romantic location, and I can't help but envision a social media post of Carter outside in this element and what sort of impact that would make on his image. My brain is always in work mode.

I reach out and press the bell and then turn to look at the different layers of his garden and how it hides his front door from all the passersby. I hear the door unlock and turn to see Carter open the door. Dressed in sport shorts and a plain white shirt, he has bare feet and a coffee mug in his hand. He hasn't been up that long, his hair is still sticking up all over the place from sleep, and his eyes are still a bit sleepy. He looks amazing dressed up, but like this, he just looks so much hotter.

"Good morning," he says, smiling at me and then moves out of the way for me to step inside. "Come in."

"Thank you," I say, walking into the house and

stopping in my tracks. Because two huge windows cover the back wall. The one on top doesn't open, but the bottom one is fully open with a panoramic view of blue ocean that is his backyard. After the huge infinity pool, that is. The sound of the waves crashing into the shore can be heard faintly in the distance.

"I don't know if you wanted to do this inside or outside," he says, and I look around to see who else is here. The house is an open concept, which is my favorite type of home. Following him past the staircase, I enter the living room. His big brown leather couches have throw pillows all over them. The stone wall fireplace faces the couch with a huge screen hanging above it. Behind the couch is the kitchen. The whole side wall has the fridge, stove, and dishwasher, and in front of it is a long counter like you find in diners with brown pendant lights hanging over it. Eight stools sit side by side, and seven fruit bowls sit on a lower counter. Two brown pillars stand between the living room and the dining room. I can see that the wall in the kitchen is also windows, and it's open also.

"I'm good with whatever everyone wants to do," I say to him, hoping that they want to work outside.

"Well, considering it's just me and you," he says, and I turn to look at him with surprise on my face. "Let's start outside because it's not too hot yet, and then we can come back inside," he says without giving me a chance to respond. He walks toward the big open window, and I follow him. Once we get outside, I see five lounge chairs right in front of the pool with different colored tables between them. He walks to the right where I see a table set up with six chairs. I walk behind him and take in the little pathway to the stairs that lead down to the beach. "Do you want to face the ocean or the house?" he asks. When I just shrug, he pulls out a chair at the head of the table. "You can have both," he says, and I sit. Putting my bags next to me, I take out my papers, then turn and see the back of the house. There are two balconies on the second floor each from a side of the house.

"Shouldn't we wait for your assistant before we start?" I ask him, knowing full well assistants run their lives.

"I actually don't have an assistant. Like I said, it's just you and me," he says, and I look over at him. With us outside and him facing the ocean, the sun hits his eyes, making them bluer than they were yesterday. The scruff on his face makes him that much more of a heartthrob.

"What do you mean you don't have an assistant?" I ask him, confused by this.

"I mean, I don't have an assistant," he says, his voice husky as he drinks another sip of coffee.

"But how do you manage?" I ask him. "You are very busy, and there is so much to do."

He pulls his phone out of his pocket. "This has a calendar, and if you enter your schedule in it, it tells you where you have to be."

"I know what it does," I tell him, "but how does it get on your calendar?"

"Jeff gets all the contracts, and his secretary puts it

all in there. I don't know how it happens, but it just tells me where to be and when to be there." He pulls up his calendar. "See, this afternoon I have a photoshoot here. Then tonight I have a dinner with the director and then tomorrow I have . . ."

I put up my hand to stop him from talking. "I get it. I just figured you would have someone who comes in and makes sure you do all that."

He puts his phone on the table. "I think we got off on the wrong foot." I turn and look at him. "I've never not shown up for a meeting. I've never shown up on set drunk or high. Fuck, I've never, ever even been late. I'm professional when I have to be, and then at night, I want to just be me, and if that is what gets splashed across the tabloids, then I can't really prevent that."

"So the me you want to be—and the one you want the rest of the world to know—is the one who goes home with a different girl every night?" I ask him, and I don't know why the question bothers me.

"What difference does it make if I fuck two different girls in the same night? We are all consenting adults. It has nothing to do with how I work or the work that I produce," he says, and his flippant attitude just makes me sick to my stomach. I knew he got around, but he isn't even ashamed to flaunt it. "For the next couple of months, I just have to be on the down low. It's in my contract now, so I have to sprout fucking angel wings, or at least somehow cover up my devil horns, and keep all my dirty little sins out of the tabs," he sighs. "I'm going to do what I need to do in order to make the film a success, but in no fucking way am I going to change who I am."

I put my hands on the table. "And who exactly are you?" I ask him, and I know right then the real Carter is gone. The Carter who answered the door with the smile on his face and the softness in his eyes is gone, and now I'm playing with Carter, the actor.

"I'm exactly who the Hollywood bigwigs pay me to be," he says and then drinks the last of his coffee. "I'm going to grab another cup. Do you want anything?" He pushes away from the table, and I shake my head. When I got here and saw him at the door, I was scared that I was in over my head, but now, with this Carter, I know I'm going to do my job, do it better than I've ever done it before, and I know, in the end, that nothing is going to change him.

FIVE

Carter

I WALK INTO THE house, squeezing the mug so hard. Her question still plays in my head. *Who are you?* I shake my head, not ready to answer that question. I'm a guy living his best life, and that is what I'm going to give her. I grab another cup of coffee and watch her from the kitchen. I see her open the folder and flip through some papers.

When I walk out and sit next to her, I notice the change in her right away. She isn't the same girl who asked me that question. I can see it right away with her eyes.

"So let's talk about your social media presence," she starts off, moving papers in front of me. "This is your Instagram. These shots are okay, but I want to create that boy-next-door image for you."

"I'm so far removed from the boy-next-door

persona," I tell her.

"Trust me, I know, but since they are *paying you to be that,* you need to pretend you're the boy next door." She throws my comment back in my face, and I don't say anything. "Take a picture of you taking a run. Take a picture of you pretending to be anything and everything that you are not. Treat it like a movie role if that's what it takes."

"So it's a fake account of sorts," I tell her. "Like a fan page."

She ignores my comment and then starts with other questions. "Do you have a Snapchat account?" I nod.

"How often do you use it?" She starts writing notes.

"I get up to three hundred tit pictures a day, so I go on there . . . occasionally," I tell her, and she looks up.

"Do you reciprocate?" Her pen is in midair while she waits for my answer.

"Are you asking if I've sent a dick pic?" I try to keep my smirk from forming but fail. "I mean, not lately."

"Great." She shakes her head. "If you can refrain from sending any out in the future, that would make my job a little easier. Or better yet, just use that platform to make dog videos."

"Aren't you exaggerating just a little bit?" I say, and then I know I shouldn't have said that. I should have just smiled and nodded like a good little indentured servant.

"Can I have your phone?" she asks with her hand outstretched.

"Are you going to put your number in it?" I ask her, leaning back in the chair, and her hand falls.

"Fine, keep your cell. We can use mine," she says. Taking out her phone, she opens her Instagram page. I see she's on her own account and make a mental note to go and check it out. She presses the little search button and types my name and then clicks tags. When she clicks on the first one, I'm a little shocked when videos of me out pop up. Like I knew they were there, but I didn't think they would still be passed around.

"This one is a good one," she says, turning the phone to me. On the screen is me sitting at Tao in Vegas, but I'm not sure. It's on a red couch. I'm wearing jeans and a button-down shirt, but the shirt is halfway open. Two girls are on each side of me, and my hands are outstretched. I smile at the camera, then turn and make out with one and then turn to the other. I press the arrow back and go through a couple more, and they all have a different girl in them.

"If you want, we can even search the hashtag CarterBigJohnson." She takes the phone and types it in. The first video is a girl, and she is describing my penis like she is on Yelp. There are a couple of pictures with women who have their hands down my pants. One video is of me and some random. Hell, they are all random now that I think about it. We are in a bathroom stall, and my head is back against the wall. She slides her tongue into my mouth, and you know or I know from the look on my face that she is giving me a hand job. The sound of me moaning makes her grab the phone away from me.

"That is exactly who you are?" She just shakes her

head. "Look, I don't know what to tell you." She gathers the papers, then puts them away, closing her folder. "I'm tying to work with you, but I can't do it by myself. I can't be that little white angel on your one shoulder when I'm in direct competition with the devil on the other side." She pushes away from the table and bends to put the papers in her purse. "I obviously can't do this job. I thought I could, but I can't." She picks up her purse and then turns to walk away.

I watch her, and the words that Jeff said yesterday replay in my head. *"Don't fuck this up."*

"Wait," I say to her, and she stops right before she walks into the house. "Listen, I don't know what to say."

"Yeah, you are pretty good at not knowing what to say or how to act," she says, and she isn't wrong. "I don't care what you do and who you do it with. I care that I was given a job. A job that is huge for me right now."

"How so?" I ask her, and she turns to me, shaking her head.

"Doesn't matter," she says and then turns around to walk into the house. I wait for the door to slam before my feet move, and I run around the side of the house. Taking the side steps two by two, I get to her car the same time as she is opening the door.

"Wait . . . please, Erin," I say, panting. When she looks at me, I can tell she is either upset or pissed, and I feel like a jerk for doing that to her. "Just . . . we might have gotten off on the wrong foot."

"The wrong foot?" She shakes her head, and I know

she's pissed. Her tone is that kind of "I want to kill you" tone I get quite often. I mean, often enough to know it, but usually, I shrug it off. This time, though, it does something.

"I'm sorry. I should have just listened instead of trying to justify every sordid moment of my past that's been captured on video," I say, and she crosses her arms over her chest.

"Do you know they have a nickname for your penis?" She doesn't wait for me to answer. "Do you know there is a website that has the number of women you have slept with on a ticker? Do you know the names of half the women you have slept with? Have you ever slept with the same person twice?"

"Yes?" I say to her on the last one. I mean, come on.

"I don't mean twice in the same night. I mean, twice in the same week?" Okay, now she is getting picky. "There were pictures of you last week. You are pictured with ten different women."

"So?" I say to her now, crossing my arms over my own chest.

"There are only seven days in the week." Okay, fine, she got me there, but it isn't my fault.

"I have a high sex drive," I tell her, not even sure why I have to tell her details that are really none of her damn business.

"I don't give a shit," she says, and the way she swears makes me want to laugh. "I don't care if you fuck up to five times an hour. What I care about is you doing it and it being on an Instagram or in a Snapchat video for the world to see."

"I'm confused. Do you care or not?" I try to make a joke, but she just glares at me, so I hold up my hands. "Okay, how about we go back in, and we can talk about things?" I see that she isn't falling for the old Carter Johnson charm. In fact, I think it's the opposite. Can she be immune to it? "Grab your bag, and we can do all the brainstorming you want."

She looks at me, and I can see that she doesn't trust me. "I swear. I promise to be on my best behavior, and if I'm not, you can leave."

"Fine," she says, grabbing her bag and turning to walk back down the side stairs with me. We sit down, and I'm ready for whatever she throws at me. We go through all my Facebook accounts, and that one isn't as bad as the rest are. I don't tell her it's because Jeff takes care of that one. Heck, she was actually excited about the state it was in. When we finish that, I look at the time and see it's almost lunchtime.

"I need to eat since I have a photo shoot in two hours," I tell her. "Why don't you come inside, and you can sit at the counter and talk to me while I make us some lunch?"

"You are going to cook for me?" she asks in shock. "Like food, food or . . .?"

"I can cook," I tell her, pushing away from the table and walking inside. She grabs her stuff and comes into the kitchen with me. Pulling out a chair, she sits as I open the fridge and grab a water bottle to hand to her. "You haven't hydrated in at least two hours, so drink that," I tell her, and she grabs the bottle and finishes half. "Why didn't you ask me for water if you were thirsty?" I ask her, grabbing a red pepper, an onion, and a green pepper. I walk to the counter in front of her and set the ingredients down, then grab a cutting board and a knife. She doesn't answer, and instead, she is straight back to business.

"How many times a week do you cook for yourself?" she asks me and grabs her phone and snaps a picture. "That is going to be your first 'I'm a good boy on my best behavior' Instagram picture."

"You can even use that as a caption." I wink at her, and she rolls her eyes at me. I begin to slice the vegetables. "I cook whenever I have a chance."

"How did you learn to cook?" she asks me as I grab the chicken breast from the fridge. I drizzle some olive oil in the pan and sauté the veggies, turning to her.

"Is this an interview?" I joke with her, slicing the chicken into strips.

"No, but it's good for me to know, so I can spin this into a positive thing."

"My parents were really never parents, so I had to fend for myself," I say, and I want to take it back. The last thing I want is to open that side of me up to her scrutiny. "They worked long hours." I toss the chicken in with the veggies. "Are you a vegetarian?" I look in the pan and stir it with a wooden spoon. "I guess I should have asked before." I look over my shoulder at her, and she snaps another picture.

"Nope, I eat everything," she tells me, and I wait

until the veggies and the chicken are done before I throw some salsa into the pan. After grabbing some tortillas and two plates, I place one plate in front of Erin on the counter and another next to her. I walk back to the fridge and grab some fresh guacamole and some pico de gallo.

"It smells so good," she says, and I look over my shoulder at her and take in the moment right there. She is the first woman to step inside my new house, apart from my house cleaner. She's the first woman I have cooked for in my house that is my haven.

I take the pan and put the food in a big dish, then bring it over to the counter. Sitting down, I place it in the middle of us. "This is my version of chicken fajitas," I tell her and get up.

"Where are the utensils?" she asks, and I look at her as she casually walks in the back to grab them. I point at the drawer, and she comes back with four spoons and two forks. "Do you think I can have another water bottle?" she asks me, and I fumble with my words. "I can get it. Please, you did do all the cooking." She walks over to the fridge and grabs two water bottles and then comes back.

I wait for her to serve herself, and then I go on the attack. She moans when she takes a bite and then looks at me. "This is so good."

"This is the first time a woman has moaned in my house, and it had nothing to do with my Big Johnson." I wink at her, and she throws her head back and laughs.

"Liar." She shakes her head and takes another bite.

"Nope," I say to her, grabbing another bite. "I never,

ever bring anyone here. My last house, yes, but this is my space and mine only."

"Oh, I get it," she says. "The whole smash and go."

"Smash and go?" I ask, confused.

"You have sex with them at their house or a hotel, so they don't linger?" she says, taking a sip of water. "Smash and go." I shake my head, thinking that is exactly what I do. The rest of the meal is quiet. When she's finished, she gets up, rinses her plate off, and then opens the dishwasher to find it empty. "You cook; I clean. It's the universal rule."

"Wow, I'm just learning all kinds of things with you," I tell her. Laughing, I pick up my plate and place it in the dishwasher. The doorbell rings, and I look at her and then at the time. Walking to the door, I see it's the photographer for the shoot today. "Hey, come on in," I tell him, and he walks in.

"We lucked out with the weather," he says to me and then walks in the house and stops when he sees Erin in the kitchen. "Was I interrupting anything?"

"Nope. She's my PR girl," I tell him, then look at Erin. "Want to stay and take pictures for my Instagram?" I ask her. For some reason, I'm hoping she says yes and am shocked when she nods her head.

Six

Erin

I SHOULD GO. I should make an excuse and get out of here because my nerves are all over the place. I'm okay with him being an asshole, but I'm not okay with him being that nice guy who cooks for me and then tells me I'm the only woman who has ever been in his house. Why? I'm rinsing off my hands when I see a man walk in carrying two huge bags in each hand. I hear him talking to Carter who just smiles at him. I can tell right away from the look in his eyes that his guard is down, and this is the real Carter.

"Was I interrupting anything?" the man says, looking at me and then looking back at Carter.

"Nope. She's my PR girl," he tells him, slapping him on the shoulder. He looks at me with a genuine smile on his face. "Want to stay and take pictures for my Instagram?" I should say no. I should take this as my cue to leave, but instead, I nod my head.

"Great," Carter says. "Ralph, this is Erin. Erin, this is Ralph, my main man."

Ralph laughs. "Not main man. I'm the one who makes his ass look super sexy in pictures. It's a hard fucking job, too. I mean, look at this slob." He points at Carter who just flips him the finger. "I'm going to get set up. You still want to take the pictures on the beach?"

"Yeah," he says, nodding his head. "I'm going to get my stuff, and I'll be right back." He turns and jogs up the stairs, and I see him walk into what must be his bedroom.

"So you are the new PR girl?" Ralph asks me, walking toward the back door, and I follow him after grabbing my phone.

"You coming on the beach with those?" He motions with his head at my stilettos. I kick off the shoes and follow him down the paved path toward the stairs leading down to the beach. We come upon a metal gate, and he presses the button and you hear a click as it unlocks. He walks out onto the beach, and I realize how windy it is when my hair blows in my face. My feet sink into the hot sand, and even though it's sunny, the wind makes it a bit chilly. I walk beside Ralph.

"Who do you work for?"

"Hillcrest," I tell him as we walk closer and closer to the water.

"No way," he says. "So are you here to make sure we get some good shots to use?" He stops right before the sand gets wet.

"No." I shake my head. "We are rebranding him."

"Jesus, that almost sounds like you are herding in cattle." He laughs while he starts setting up his stuff.

I laugh. "Not that bad." Pushing my hair back, I say, "Just revamping his image."

"There is not enough time and money in the world to accomplish that impossible feat," he mumbles. "It's just who he is."

I don't bother answering him. Instead, I sit on the sand and watch the waves crash against the shore. *I wish I had brought my sunglasses*, I think to myself. I put my hand over my eyes and see that just a couple of people are in the water.

"Hey." I hear Carter next to me and look up and see him in black swim trunks and a white shirt. His hair looks like he wet his hands and brushed it back and aviator glasses cover his eyes. He throws down his stuff next to me, and I see he brought three towels and two pairs of jeans.

"What do you want to shoot first?" Ralph asks, and Carter just shrugs. "Let's do the dry photos first, then we can do some in the water."

"Great," he says, and I watch him just pull off his swim trunks, and I swear I hold my breath, thinking that his cock is just going to be dangling in the air in two seconds, but he's wearing black boxers under it. I try not to focus on the package part and whip my head around to give him some privacy. He grabs the jeans and puts them on.

"I'm ready," he says just like that. No muss, no fuss.

But then I have to remind myself that this man has shown his cock to countless women in situations that are most assuredly less private than this, so it's nothing for him to strip down to his skivvies and change in front of his PR rep.

"Lose the shirt," Ralph says as he takes some test shots of the water, adjusting something in the lens. I look up, and holy shit, I have seen him on covers shirtless before, but I think he's been hitting the gym harder than ever because he's sculpted. His shoulders are wide, and you see the exact way the muscles form when he tosses the shirt down. His pecs are perfect, and his abs are outlined. There is not one ounce of fat on him. His waist goes trim, and you see his side v muscle. He has a soft dusting of hair on his pecs and then a little around his belly button. It trails down to a sight that's been seen by plenty . . . but not by me, and I'm feeling a little more than flushed. "The glasses also," he says, and he squats down beside me now.

"Here," he says, putting them on my face. "It'll help with the sun." Then he hands me his phone. "Do you want to take a couple of pictures of Ralph getting shots of me with the beach backdrop, and we can post it?"

"Um, yeah," I say, holding out my hand. "Actually, why don't you do a video on Snapchat showing them what you are doing and then do a short one for Instagram? Tell them pictures will follow."

He grabs the phone back, going on it and pressing things.

"Hey, Snap land, I'm shooting some beach today.

Stay tuned." He stops talking and then posts it and must pull up his Instagram. "Hey, Instagram, I'm at the beach . . . wishing all of you were here with me." He turns the camera. "Ralph, say hi." Ralph looks at him and waves. "Stay tuned for some shots of this man working his magic with a camera." He then hands me the phone. "Good?"

"Very!" I smile at him, and then he walks over to Ralph. As they discuss what they are going to do, I get up, dusting some of the sand from my pants, and then watch as he gets into place. I watch him turn into the heartthrob right before my eyes. The smirk comes out, and his eyes even twinkle. His gaze stays on the camera as he walks to Ralph, and Ralph snaps away. I take a couple of shots of him smiling at the camera and then one with his hand up covering half his face, giving the camera his famous half smirk. I zoom in, and his eyes land on me, making the picture perfect. I'm looking down at the picture when a text comes in with no name attached to it, just a number.

Unknown: We can totally fuck on the down low. Just name the time and place.

Looking back up at him, I feel the heat rushing up my neck. I just shake my head. His whole talk was for nothing. The meeting was for nothing because he isn't going to change anything. I toss the phone on his change of clothes and try to contain my rage. "Is there a code to get into the gate?" I turn, looking over at him posing, and Ralph tells me the code.

"Three, two, four, one," he says, and I turn and walk

toward the gate without even a goodbye. I get to the gate and punch in the numbers, and I'm walking up the steps toward his house. I'm so pissed—no, beyond fucking pissed—as I walk to the table. I don't even bother putting on my shoes. Instead, I squat down and pick up my shoes.

"Hold up . . . are you leaving?" I hear him behind me and notice that he must have run all the way here to catch up with me.

"Yeah. No use wasting time here," I tell him as I walk back into the house to grab my purse.

"Wait, what?" he asks, and I turn around and look at him with the confused look on his face.

"I'm so stupid," I mumble, "thinking you were actually going to listen to my advice and turn this shitshow of your life around." I don't let him answer as I take off his glasses, tossing them on the table. "Take care." I turn and walk out the door, then get in my car and take off. I look at the time and see it's almost four in the afternoon, so I take out my phone and call Sylvia. She answers after one ring, her voice filling the car.

"So how did it go?" she asks me, and I have no idea how to answer her.

"How do you think it went?" I ask her sarcastically, my voice going louder. "He's an asshole who is going to lead with his dick," I huff, and then count to ten and finally calm down. "The morning went, well, to hell."

"Okay," she says and then waits for me to finish.

"I went over a couple of things with him. I have no idea if he is going to listen or not." I tell her the truth but not about the text.

"Well, if he has any sense, he will. Ryan is at his wits' end, especially after the video from last night."

"Which one?" I ask her.

"The bathroom stall one," she says, and I shake my head. "We called Jeff, and he assured us it's an old video."

"Who knows," I tell her, just in case any possible pictures from tonight come out. "It's like he needs someone to hold his hand the whole time to make sure he doesn't do anything he shouldn't."

"That is what I mentioned to Ryan, especially with him going on the road to film for the next two weeks. He starts filming on Monday. They have two weeks to shoot the first half of the movie up in Montana."

"Well, to be fair, how much trouble can he get into in Montana?" I ask her, and she laughs.

"Don't discount geography, Erin. He had a semi orgy when he was in Utah," she says, and with that revelation, I think I'm going to be sick. How does one person just have sex like that as if it's nothing? Just a motion like scratching an itch. I'm no virgin, but the people I have slept with weren't people who I just met in a bar and went home with. I had a connection with them. I went out on dates and talked on the phone. "Anyway, have a great weekend. We will touch base on Monday unless something happens over the weekend that blows our plan all to hell."

"Fingers crossed it's smooth sailing," I say and disconnect. Making my way home, I feel like rough waters are ahead for us. I pull up to my little condo that my father bought me without me having a say. I walk up the steps to the second floor and see seven boxes in front of my door. I shake my head, knowing my father sent them, and by the time I carry them all inside and read the note, I know it's from him.

Congrats on a job well done!

Dad

I'm about to open a package when my phone rings, and I see it's Sylvia calling me again.

"Hello again," I answer right away.

"Sorry about that." She laughs. "So change of plans. We have a dinner tomorrow night with Jeff and Carter," she says, her voice a little irritated.

"Does that mean I have to come?" I ask, not sure why she is telling me this.

"Ryan is requesting that we both be there," she says, and I hear a beep in the distance and then a car door close. "Tomorrow night eight p.m. We'll send a car."

"Great," I say, and she disconnects. I open my packages and see that he's sent me five pairs of Louboutins that I don't need. A box of clothes from Neiman Marcus. I grab my phone and call him. He answers on the first ring.

"Honey," he says, and I hear people in the background and then it goes quiet.

"Dad, you didn't have to buy me all this," I tell him, sitting on the couch.

"Please, it's a big deal," he says. "It's not every day you get the chance to move up in the company."

"Yeah, well, let's not celebrate just yet. I don't think I can do it," I tell him, my voice going quiet.

"Baby girl," he says softly, and if he were here, he would put his arm around me and drag me to his side, "as long as you give it your all, there is nothing you can't do."

"You and Mom really have to stop with the matching pep talks," I tell him, and he laughs.

"I have to go. I'm in the middle of a meeting, but how about you come over on Sunday, and we can spend the day on the beach?"

"Yeah, that sounds amazing and exactly what I need after the week I've had," I tell him. I haven't been to his new beach house yet.

"Love you," he says quietly.

"Me, too," I say, and he disconnects. I toss my phone down and then get up to clean the mess. My phone pings a couple of times, but I don't bother with it. It's probably the Google alert that I set up for Carter letting me know his penis is on the loose. Opening my fridge, I see nothing to eat and don't find anything in the freezer either. I grab the phone on the counter and press the dial button, ordering in some Chinese food. I go and undress, sliding into some yoga pants while I wait for the order to arrive. Once it does, I get comfortable on the couch and turn on the television, eating my Chinese on a TV tray. *This is the life*, I think to myself sarcastically.

Seven

Carter

I WATCH HER WALK out of my house, and I'm dumbfounded. What the fuck happened? She was on the beach with me watching me do my thing. I looked over at her and saw her with her hair blowing in the wind, and it was something. I don't know what was going through me.

Then just like that, she tossed my phone down and walked away. I turn to go and finish my shoot on the beach. After I change into my swim trunks, I go into the cold water, and it wakes me up. "I like you all angry and shit, but can we get one smile out of you?" Ralph says. I nod my head, and it's go time. Smirk's on, dimple out. I stay in the water until the sun starts to set, and he snaps one more picture of me walking out with my hands in my hair. "That right there is going to be the shot," he says, and I just nod, walking to the towel and wrapping it around my waist and another around my shoulders. Picking up my clothes, I grab my phone when it falls, then walk to the gate while Ralph packs up all his equipment. I press the code and then walk in the sand even though it's stuck to my feet and itchy. I think about just walking up the stairs, but then it would make a mess, and the cleaning lady isn't coming until next week. I do the next best thing. Stepping into the pool, I move my feet under the water to clean off the sand. The phone rings in my hand, and I see it's Jeff.

"Hey," I answer. "What's up?"

"How's the reformed and somewhat virginal bachelor?" he says, laughing, and I roll my eyes.

"I'm still a bachelor," I tell him. "I just finished shooting with Ralph."

"Yeah." I can hear cars in the background. "You ready for Montana?" he asks me, and I dump my stuff on the couch, then walk up to my room. I'm leaving Monday to go film for two weeks, and I can't wait.

"As ready as I will ever be," I say to him, and then the call disconnects. I look down and see that I have a couple of text messages. One catches my eye, and I groan when I see it.

Unknown: We can totally fuck on the down low. Just name the time and place.

"Fuck," I hiss out. This is the reason she took off. While I was changing to go outside, I got a picture of her tits. I have no idea who it was who texted me, and I was stupid enough to answer her.

Me: If you're down to fuck on the down low, I'm

game.

It was stupid of me to respond, and the minute I pressed send, I forgot about it, and then I handed her my fucking phone. I don't have time to do anything when my phone rings again in my hand, and it's Jeff.

"Sorry, my phone died," he says. "Don't make plans tomorrow night. We have dinner with Ryan," he tells me, and I sit on the couch. "Hello, are you there?"

"Yeah," I say, wondering if I should tell him or not. "Sorry, just thinking."

"Okay, listen, I have to go, but I'll pick you up tomorrow at seven. The dinner's at eight," he tells me and then disconnects. I send him a text.

Me: Do you have Erin's number?

He answers back right away.

Jeff: I don't, but I can ask Ryan.

I pick up the phone to call Ryan myself, and he answers on the second ring. His voice sounds angry, and I wonder if Erin told him anything.

"What can I do for you?" he says, and I hear people in the background.

"Hey, it's Carter. I was wondering if you had Erin's number. She was over here today, and we were going over a couple of things, and I wanted to get her take on a couple of pictures that I took."

"So today went okay, then?" he asks me.

"Yeah, we went over a couple of things," I say to him. "I don't want to keep you. We can talk about it tomorrow."

"Yeah, I'll send over her number," he says. "Stay out

of trouble." He disconnects, and then my phone pings with Erin's number.

I send her a text right away.

Me: Hey, it's Carter. I was thinking of posting this on my Instagram. What do you think?

I attach the picture that she took of me. I look down and see it's been delivered. I get up and walk upstairs to take a shower. When I get out of the shower, I look at my phone and see that she hasn't answered me. I put on some sweatpants and head downstairs to look in the fridge. When nothing catches my eye, I order Chinese food and then look back at my phone again. She still hasn't answered.

Me: Should I post it or not?

I open my phone and go to Instagram. Searching for her name, I see that her account is private. My Chinese gets here and still no answer, so I head to the couch and turn on the television. When my phone pings, I lean over to get it with a smile on my face because I think it's her but it's not. Instead, it's the chick from this afternoon, and this time, she sends me a picture of her full frontal.

Unknown: Waiting for your call, and really ready for whatever you have in mind.

My finger hovers over the keyboard, itching to reply, but if I really think about it, I don't have the faintest interest in going out. I throw the phone to the side and flip through the channels. The whole time, I'm thinking about Erin. She probably isn't getting back to me because she's with her boyfriend or her fiancé. Well, not fiancé because she isn't wearing a ring, and if she were mine, and I was getting married to her, she would be walking around with a ring so big her hand would be dragging on the ground. Holy shit, I sit up in shock. Did I just picture myself married? I must be coming down with something. I get up, turn everything off, and walk up the stairs, thinking about the last time I actually slept in my bed. Or when was the last time I actually stayed in and went to bed at eleven on a Friday.

I take my pants off and slip into bed naked, and the minute I do, I remember how fucking comfortable my bed really is. It takes me maybe a minute to finally fall asleep, and by the time I turn over and open my eyes, I'm shocked to see that it's almost ten a.m. I grab my phone and see that she hasn't answered yet, so I just call her.

She answers after five rings. Five. Who waits to answer after five rings? "Hello," she says, and she sounds out of breath. Shit, maybe she's having sex. Should I hang up? What if she has Caller ID? Fuck, why is she answering her phone while having sex? Who does that? "Carter?"

Shit. "Um, hey," I say, trying to sound cool. "What's up?"

"I'm on the treadmill," she says. "What's wrong?"

"Nothing," I tell her, then turn to look out the window. I curl up to press a button, and the shades open and then the window, and I see it's a sunny day again. "I sent you a couple of messages yesterday."

"Yeah, I got them last night," she says, and that's it. Nothing else.

"Why didn't you answer me?" I ask her, now irritated that she got them and didn't answer me.

"Were you out with your boyfriend?"

"Were you even home last night?" she counters. "What happened to the down low girl?"

"I knew it," I say out loud. "That is why you left." I get up and go downstairs. "You were jealous."

"Jealous?" she says, almost screaming. "Jealous? I wasn't jealous. I was pissed you wasted my whole afternoon listening to me go on and on about how we were going to rebrand your image when all along you were just going to do your own thing anyway."

"I didn't go out," I tell her. "I stayed in. I also don't even know who that person was who texted me. I answered a random tit pic text with my old bad habits, but I didn't follow through with anything. I knew that was why you left."

"Do you want an award?" she asks me, her sarcasm coming through the phone. "One day without sex. Your dick just may fall off."

"I think it's funny you are thinking about my dick right now." I start my coffee. "You should come over, and we can talk about *things*."

"You're disgusting," she says, and I don't know why this conversation is suddenly more fun than I've had in a long, long time.

"I may be disgusting, but you are still picturing my dick." I laugh.

"Post the picture. I have to go. My boyfriend is here," she says and hangs up. I'm stuck in place in the middle of my kitchen while the coffee brews. Shit, she has a boyfriend, and I was trying to flirt with her. I shake my head, thinking about how wrong that was. I can be a total asshole, but I never, ever fuck with someone else's territory. That is a line I won't cross, no matter how good the pussy looks.

Erin: I just followed you on Instagram to see how your picture does. Post the second one I just sent you.

She attaches the one she took of me cooking. My phone shows me she sent me another text.

Erin: Put the caption "What are your weekend plans?"

I go over to Instagram and post the picture and then add her as a friend. If she can follow me, why can't I follow her? Besides, I really want to see what her boyfriend looks like. I spend the day in my home gym and then finish it off with a run on the beach. Getting back home, I see a brown box at the door. I pick it up, going inside and making a protein shake, while I open the box and see a brand-new iPhone. I set it up right before I get ready for dinner tonight.

I grab a pair of ripped jeans and slide them on with a short-sleeved V-neck T-shirt. I put on my white Converse, then grab my jacket hanging on one of the hooks and run downstairs. The doorbell rings as soon as I get to the last step. Opening it, I see Jeff standing there wearing a suit. "I'm ready," I tell him, grabbing my phone and keys and my glasses.

"It's nighttime," he tells me when I slip my glasses on and then my jacket.

"Well, if the paps are there, I'm going to get blinded so," I tell him, following him out of the house and pulling the door closed. "Why are we having this meeting with Ryan?" I ask as I get into his Bentley.

"He called me last night," he says, pulling out of my driveway and making his way to the restaurant, "and wants to make sure everything is okay and understood."

"Jesus," I say to myself. "I think I can go without sex and not die."

"Can you? Because, dude, your past history tells a different fucking story," he asks me with a huge smile on his face, and I give him the finger. I open my phone and see that four million people have liked my picture, and I have seventy-five thousand comments. I don't bother reading them. Instead, I click on the search and type in Erin's name. I see that I'm still not accepted, and mine still says requested.

When we get to the restaurant, the flashes start going off immediately, and I look over at Jeff. "This is why I wear glasses." He grabs his own pair. "I could have held your hand going in if you wanted," I joke when he mumbles to fuck off. I get out of the car and make my way to the door, pulling it open. "Why the fuck are we at Spago on a Saturday night?" I ask him as we walk into the Bel Air hotel. When we walk into the restaurant, the hostess looks over at me, and her whole face lights up. Her shoulders go up straight, pushing her tits out.

"Oh, God," I mumble, and then Jeff takes over.

"We have a reservation for Hillcrest," he says, and she looks down and then looks up.

"You are the first to arrive." She grabs the menus and then looks over, tossing her blond hair over her shoulder. "Follow me." She turns and walks down into the restaurant. Half the tables are taken, and the other half are sure to be filled with reservations. She walks us to the far right, and I see seven archways. She waits at the entrance to one, and I step in and see the table set for six in the middle and two round benches on each side. The benches with six back pillows. I sit at the far end of the bench and then look up at the hanging chandelier. The walls have candles hanging on them. Jeff sits next to me, and the blonde comes in and hands us the menus. Her smile brightens when I reach out and grab it from her. I nod my head, and she turns and walks away.

"Are you sick?" Jeff asks right away, and I look at him with my eyebrows pulled together. "She was coming on to you, and you didn't even say anything to her. Nothing. No smirk, no smile, no how you doing? Nothing."

I shrug, a little surprised at my own willpower, but don't even bother to answer him. Instead, I put my menu down and look over at him, but I stop when I see the blond lady again but, this time, with someone behind her. When she moves, I finally see it's Erin. She is standing there with her long hair loose. She is wearing another pencil skirt, but it's white, and her top is off her shoulders with long sleeves and a light orange color. The front of the shirt is tucked in. She looks at us and then looks at the blonde and smiles. I look at her shoes, and they are strappy and high as fuck. My mouth waters.

71

"Erin." I hear Jeff say to her, and she walks over.

"Good evening, gentlemen," she says, sitting on the bench in front of us and placing her beige Yves St-Laurent clutch on the table beside her. She sits right in front of me, but she hasn't looked at me once. I'm about to say something when I hear Ryan.

"Sorry we are late," he says, and I see that Sylvia is behind him. "My plane landed ten minutes later than we thought," he says, getting into the bench beside Erin. He turns and smiles at her. "Did you just get here?" She nods her head, and then Sylvia sits beside Ryan.

"Saturday night. Spago. My PR team. This should be fun," I finally say, grabbing the water glass to bring it to my lips. "Let the good times roll."

EIGHT

Erin

SITTING IN THE BACK of the town car on my way to the restaurant, I try to relax. I was fine this morning, well, just a touch. When I finally looked down at my phone last night, I saw he texted me, and I saw the picture and then I wondered if he was banging that girl or if he was already done. I turned off my phone and ignored the pull to respond, and then this morning, I wanted to answer him, but instead, I ignored it. Then he called right when I was on the treadmill, and well, he gets me all riled up and angry, so I told him I had a boyfriend.

I'm so nervous he is going to bring it up at dinner that I literally think I'm going to vomit. The hostess looks me up and down and then leads me back to the table, and it must be my lucky day because it's just Carter and Jeff. Luckily, Ryan and Sylvia get here right after, so there is no small talk.

"Saturday night. Spago. My PR team. This should be fun," Carter says, and I look at him. All of him—the smirk is out, the fucking dimple is on point, and his eyes are ready. "Let the good times roll."

Ryan looks at him and laughs. "I thought it would be good to touch base right before we started filming, so everyone is on the same page."

"I think this is a great idea, so we know where everyone stands," Jeff says. "I know that Carter and Erin spent the day working together yesterday."

"Erin," Ryan says to me, and I look over at him. "How do you feel it went?"

I start to think of my words, and then I look up at Carter. I think it's the worst thing to do because he just stares at me. "It went well. At least, I think it went great. I checked his Instagram, and he gained followers after he posted the photoshoot video. Now, I have no idea about last night. I haven't seen any pictures."

"That's because there aren't any," he says, and he is almost glaring at me. "I ordered Chinese and went to bed."

"So you say," Sylvia says, then looks at Ryan and then back to Carter. "The point of this meeting really is that you leave on Monday for Montana."

"And?" he says, not sure of the question.

"And last time you went to the 'country,' you had an orgy," Ryan says from beside me but stops talking when the waiter comes over to introduce himself and gives us the specials before walking away.

"Having friends over to enjoy the hot tub is not an

orgy," Carter says, shrugging.

"There were eight girls and one man," Ryan says, and I shake my head and roll my eyes. "I believe the picture had a tagline of Johnson's harem."

"It wasn't that bad," Jeff says, but his voice is anything but convincing.

"Not bad?" Sylvia says, grabbing her phone and placing it in the middle of the table. I casually look over at it and see it. Carter is in the middle of the bed, and the women are draped all over him. Every one of them is touching him while one is lying across his lap. You know that they are all naked.

"That was a long time ago," Jeff says, and I refrain from saying anything. Instead, I pick up my water.

"If you guys are so scared of the temptation and possibilities in Montana, then why don't you guys send Erin with me?" Carter says, and my head snaps to him.

"What?" I whisper, but Carter just continues talking.

"It's obviously a big job to keep me on the straight and narrow, so having Erin there for two weeks will help. We can go over all the tricks, and she can be in charge of my social media while I'm there, so it will also create buzz for the movie if she does the pictures from on set. You have to admit it's a brilliant plan."

I look over at Ryan and Sylvia. "Surely, you aren't entertaining this ridiculous idea?"

Sylvia looks at Ryan, and then Ryan turns to me. "That isn't a bad idea. Actually, it would be like hitting two birds with one stone. We can get the word out about the movie, and we can show that he's changed his ways and is serious about his professional life more than his partying ways."

"What's the matter?" Carter says, and I turn to look at him. "Afraid the distance would be too much with your boyfriend?" he says, and if I could kick him under the table with my heel, I would.

"Your boyfriend?" Sylvia says, shocked, looking at me. I turn to look at her, and both she and Ryan are looking at me.

Turning back and glaring at Carter, I say quietly, "It's a new thing."

"This is a great idea," Jeff says, and I'm baffled that everyone is agreeing to this crazy-ass plan.

"Hold on a second," I finally say loudly, and everyone looks at me. "This is crazy. I'm going to go to Montana with him and follow him around to make sure the lock remains engaged on his chastity belt?"

"Erin, it won't be like that. We aren't asking you to follow him around but to do marketing," Sylvia says. "We will also give you control of the company's social media account, and I think it's also a smart idea to create one with the movie title."

"That is a great idea," Ryan says. "It's never too early to get the buzz going." I shake my head, knowing I am not going to win this fight, and I'll be spending the next two weeks in Montana with him.

Carter claps his hands together, knowing that he won, but I'm wondering why he's so excited. Surely, me being there will be the major cock block that will prevent any activities on the down low. "I'm starving."

He picks up his menu, and I push to get out of the bench, grabbing my purse.

"Excuse me," I say to the table and walk away before I do something stupid like tell my boss to fuck off or get his own ass to Montana. I'm about to push the brown door to enter the bathroom when I hear my name being called, and I turn to see it's Ryan.

"Listen, I'm sorry we just blindsided you." He starts talking, and I have to move out of the way when someone comes out of the bathroom and gives Ryan the once-over and then leaves with a smile. I look at him with his black hair short on the sides and long on the top pushed back no doubt by his hands. His brown eyes look almost black, and his scruff has a salt and pepper look to it. He's wearing a black suit with a white shirt and no tie. His hands go to his hips. "We have invested a lot in this movie, and I need it to be perfect. And I need Carter to be angelic."

I inhale a deep breath and then look at him. "I get it but Montana for two weeks? What if I can't control him?"

"We will talk daily, and the minute you say the word or he crosses the line, I will pull you out," he says to me, and I look down and then up again. I'm about to say something when Sylvia joins us.

"Sorry to break this up"—she looks at Ryan and then me—"but the waiter is going to be back in two minutes."

"I'll be right there," I say, turning and going into the bathroom. I sit on the bench in the bathroom, the attendant in there waiting to offer me either hairspray or soap, and lean my head back and close my eyes for a moment. I make my way back to the table, sliding back onto the bench and putting the white linen napkin on my lap. The waiter comes back, and I can honestly say I have no idea what is discussed at dinner.

"So are you excited about Montana?" Carter asks me when everyone is eating, and Jeff, Sylvia, and Ryan are talking about politics.

"No," I say, not looking up at him as I eat my fish.

"That's too bad. It's beautiful there. It's called Big Sky Country for a reason. I think you'll love it there," he says, and I look up at him. He picks up his glass and brings it to his lips, trying to hide the smirk. "I'll show you around." I look down at my food without answering, and the rest of the meal drags by. When I can finally make my exit, I do.

"If you guys will excuse me," I say, getting up, "I have another engagement I have to get to."

Carter gets up, tossing his napkin on the table.

"I'll walk you out," he says. "I was leaving anyway." He shakes everyone's hand and then turns to walk with me out of the restaurant. "Did you drive here?"

"No," I say as I walk, and I feel his hand on my lower back. "I'm going to grab a cab." Walking out of the hotel, I see the valet.

"We need a car and driver," Carter says, and I stand here holding my purse in front of me. "I'll drop you off and then go home."

I don't stand next to him as we wait for the car. The flashes are going off, and they are all screaming his name for him to turn around to them, but he looks down at his phone instead. After the black town car pulls up and the valet opens the back door, I step into it while Carter walks around the car and gets in beside me. I give the driver my address, and he takes off.

"Why are you so angry?" he says, and I turn toward him, my back against the door.

"You just blindsided me in front of my boss by requesting I come with you to fucking Montana,"

I finally say.

"I just thought it would make everyone happy," he says. His body mimics my position except he stretches out one arm around the back of the seat. "Remember, this arrangement is *huge* for both of us."

"Isn't having me there going to be, um, me cock blocking you?" I ask him, and I don't wait for him to answer. "We are going to be living with each other for fourteen days, and the thought of walking in on you in one of your *compromising positions* when I'm there to do my fucking job isn't high on my list of must-see sights in Montana."

"It's a nice house," he says, not even answering the first part of my question or responding to my vitriol about me being there to do a job.

"Tell me something, Mr. Straight and Narrow, what's the longest you've gone without sex in days . . . or hours, whichever is the longest?" I fold my arms over my chest, not even sure I want to know or why I asked this question but needing to know what I'm truly up against.

He shakes his head. "I'll be fine celibate, no worries. And to answer your question, fifteen years is the longest, but the minute I lost my virginity, it was game on." That fucking smirk is back. He starts tapping the seat with his finger. "Besides, what are you going to tell the boyfriend?" I don't have to answer him because the car comes to a stop. "I'll pick you up Monday morning at nine. The plane takes off at ten. It's a three-hour flight." I grab the handle of the car door to open it, and his hand falls on my other hand that is still on the seat.

"I promise you that I'll be on my best behavior, and I won't let you regret it." I look down at his hand on mine, his whole hand covering my small one, and I just nod at him. The driver walks around to open the door for me, and I get out and walk to my condo without looking back. I feel his eyes on me; I feel him following me until I am in the safety of my apartment. I don't turn on the lights as I make my way into my bedroom. Undressing, I enter the bathroom and wash off the light makeup that I put on and then turn to get into bed. I don't bother with any pjs. I toss and turn most of the night, thinking. Finally giving up, I grab my robe and make my way to the kitchen where I make myself a cup of coffee and go to the couch, flipping the television on. I grab my phone to see the Google alerts going off about Carter, and I open my mouth when I see the first picture that comes up of me and him walking out and getting in the same car.

Is Carter Johnson getting tamed?

Reading the headline, I shake my head and then see

fifteen different pictures of us on Google. My phone rings in my hand. Looking down, I see it's my father, and when I check the time, it's just past eight.

"Good morning," he says when I finally answer. "Did you sleep okay?"

"No," I tell him. "I'm going to Montana. Fucking Montana."

"It's very pretty there. Big Sky Country and all," he says. "Are we still on for lunch?"

"Yeah, I know about Big Sky Country. Dad, I have to pack," I tell him.

"You have to eat also and relax a bit from the sound of it," he tells me. "I already told Christina you are coming, and she's been cooking since seven." He mentions his personal cook who has been with him for a decade.

"Fine, I'll swing by but not for long," I tell him and then hang up. "Two weeks." I shake my head. "Fourteen days." I sit on the couch still baffled.

Nine

Carter

"I CAN'T EVEN BELIEVE that you got them to agree to Erin accompanying you," Jeff says from the phone that I'm holding with my shoulder to my ear as I throw my things into my luggage.

"I have to pick Erin up in forty-five minutes. Should I bring her coffee? How does she take her coffee?" I stop packing and think about what I just said. Not once have I ever given a fuck about how a woman takes her coffee. Jesus, what is wrong with me?

"Just order it black and bring the stuff on the side," Jeff answers, and I have to sit on my bed. Am I dying?

"I'll call you tomorrow. Don't forget to cancel my other number," I tell him and toss my new phone on the bed. I was not going to fuck up this opportunity with temptation and invitations from women, so I went online and bought a brand-new phone. Cancelling my other one. I've given my number to one person so far, Jeff, for now. "What do I care what she takes in her coffee, and why do I even want to bring her coffee?" *Because you want her to like you.* I shake my head and rub my face with both my hands. I haven't had sex in two days. Wait, when was the last time I had sex? Thursday night so I start counting on my hands, Friday, Saturday, Sunday, Monday. Four days. I haven't gone four days since I was fifteen years old. Maybe going without sex will have a long-term impact on my damn brain.

I finish packing and bring my two bags to the door. Well, my big luggage and my backpack that I put my iPad and the script in. I walk into the garage and grab a baseball hat and then get into my Range Rover. I make my way to her house, stopping at Starbucks right before. When I pull up to her condo, she is downstairs waiting with her luggage next to her.

"Sorry, I'm late," I say, getting out and opening the trunk. "I stopped to get you coffee," I tell her as she rolls her luggage to me. I see that she is wearing tights and a white shirt with a long mustard-colored sweater, and she has a big black, gray, and beige scarf rolled around her neck, covering the top of her shirt. A black backpack is slung over her shoulder. I can't see her eyes with her black squared glasses hiding them, and maybe it's a good thing, so I can't see the death glare I'm sure she's giving me.

"Thank you," she says when I pick up her luggage and put it in the back next to mine. She opens the back door, putting her backpack there and then opens the front passenger door, but she doesn't get in. "How many coffees did you get?" she asks, looking down at the two carryout trays that hold eight coffees.

"I didn't know which one you drank, so I improvised," I tell her, smiling and getting in as she gets in and places her feet on the sides of the carryout containers. "I got regular latte, vanilla latte, Americano, white chocolate mocha, regular mocha, chai latte tea, green tea, and if you don't drink any of those, hot chocolate." She looks down and then she looks up at me, and the smile she gives me makes it worth the crazy amount of money I just paid for coffee. It makes everything worth it.

"What do you drink?" she asks me, looking down.

"Regular coffee," I say, laughing and pulling away from the curb to make my way over to the air field. "Why aren't you drinking?" I ask her when she sits back and looks outside.

"Because I'm going to wait until we get on the plane, and we can have coffee together," she says, and I just nod. I don't know why it feels good to have her not just take the coffee and drink it but also want to wait for me to enjoy it with her. I guess it's the normal thing that people do, but I'm not used to it. When we pull up to the airport, I drive straight to the plane. The white plane waits with the red carpet rolled out and the stairs down. When I pull up and shut off the car, I get out, and I see a guy running over to us.

"Good morning, sir," he says, going to the back hatch of my Range Rover and opening it to grab the luggage. After I open the back door and grab my backpack, I walk around the car to see that Erin is already out with her backpack over her shoulder, and she is holding a tray of coffee.

"I'll get the other one," I tell her, and she moves away from me, and then I lean in and grab the tray. "I left the keys in the car," I tell the guy who just finished loading our luggage in the plane. He is going to drop off my car, another service that money pays for. "Ready?" I ask her, walking up the five steps that lead into the private plane.

"Good morning, Mr. Johnson." The blond man stands there at the door in his blue suit with his hands folded in front of him. "Welcome aboard."

I nod at him and walk onto the plane. White cream leather lines the sides with two white leather seats on each side and a table in the middle. I place my tray on the table and look over to see that the man is now laughing with Erin. I grit my teeth. "You can put it down here," I say loud enough, and they stop talking. She walks to me, placing the tray on the table. I'm expecting her to look around and ooh and ahh over a private plane, but she doesn't. She takes off her sunglasses and puts them in her backpack, then sits down on one of the chairs. "After we take off, we can go sit on the couch," I tell her, motioning to the couch that is just behind the chairs. There are two chairs in front of the couch also.

"Is it just us?" she asks, looking around.

"We are getting ready for takeoff," the pilot says over the speaker, and I look over at the flight attendant who is shutting the door and bringing in the stairs.

I sit in front of her. "It's just us." I answer her question and then change the subject before she jumps off the plane. "So which one are you going to drink?" I ask her, and she leans back in her chair.

"Let's do a taste testing," she says and leans in, opening all the covers. "Maybe you will find one you like instead of just 'regular.'" She uses her fingers to do air quotes. The plane starts to move when she takes one out. "Okay, this is a regular latte," she says, reading the label on the side. She brings it to her mouth and takes a sip. "I mean, it's basic." She hands me the cup, and I bring it to my lips.

"It's coffee," I tell her, and she just shakes her head as I put it back into the holder. "So far, that's my favorite."

"We've only done one," she says, laughing, and I like the sound of it. It's comfortable. "This is the vanilla latte." She takes a sip and passes it to me.

"That's too much sugar," I say to her. She laughs again when I grimace, and the sound of her laughter does something to me. I bring my hand up to my head to feel if I'm warm; maybe I'm coming down with a fever. After tasting all eight drinks, I find some are downright nasty. "So, I'm going with number one followed by the green tea," I tell her, and she throws her head back and lets out a huge belly laugh.

"I'm going with the vanilla latte. No second," she says and then grabs the glass of water that the guy put in front of us right after we took off. He comes back and picks up all the coffee and then asks us if we are ready to eat. "Take a selfie for Instagram," she says, and I take my phone out of my pocket and snap a picture of myself. I show it to her, and she just nods. "Send it to me so I can put it on the movie Instagram page."

I send it to her, and her eyes look up at me once she hears a ping on her phone. "What number is this?"

I lean back in my chair and watch her face. "It's my new number. I canceled my other one."

She mimics my posture, leaning back in her chair. "Why?"

"Because if I'm going to do this, I'm going to do it right," I tell her honestly.

"You mean you don't want temptation?" She sees right through me.

"Either way, the bottom line is I have a new number, so just store it in your phone," I tell her, and she doesn't say anything because our food arrives.

He comes out with two trays, placing both in the middle of the table. Eggs, bacon, and sausage are on one, and pancakes and waffles are on the other. He leaves and comes back with empty plates for us and a basket of fresh bread. "Would you like coffee with that?" he asks, and I shake my head, grabbing a waffle.

"Can I have a mimosa?" Erin asks, and he looks at me, and I just shake my head again as he walks away. "You don't drink?"

I grab a roll that is still steaming. "No."

"Is it okay if I drink it?" she asks, her tone soft. "It's fine either way."

I pick up the spoon and scoop up some eggs. "When I turned eighteen, I basically almost hit rock bottom. I was getting shitfaced every single night." I take a bite of food and look at her, and she looks at me with a sadness in her eyes. Not pity but sadness. "Anyway, I blacked out more times than I cared, so when I went to Jeff, I went cold turkey, and now I don't drink. Not that I have a problem but because I choose not to."

She leans over, her hand grabbing my hand next to my plate. "That is a really mature thing to do," she says. "You should be proud."

I shake my head and move my hand away from hers. "Yeah, it's not that big of a deal. I just replaced one addiction with another. Women are my vice now." She sits up now. "And for the next sixty days, I'm obviously in sex rehab, and you are my counselor." She doesn't say anything; she just stares at me.

"Why do you do that?" she asks me and doesn't wait for me to answer. "You open up just a touch and then you turn into an asshole two seconds later?"

"I have no idea what you are talking about," I say, but I know exactly what she's talking about. I did it, knowing I did it. Opening up to people is not my strong suit. Besides, I've been burned in the past, so the less I say, the less people can use to hurt me. "I was having a conversation with you."

"No, you were opening up about a piece of you, and then you decided that 'wait, I was too normal, so let me pull out my asshole persona.'" She throws her hands in the air, and the guy comes back with her mimosa. "Actually, I'm sorry, I changed my mind. Can you get me a water please with a wedge of lemon?" She waits for him to walk away, and she grabs some food. When the guy walks back with water, she smiles at him. "Can I have some fruit please?"

"Most certainly. I'll cut some up now. Would you like some yogurt and granola with that?" He smiles at her.

"That sounds wonderful." She is being so fucking fake. "Carter, would you like some also?" I just glare at her and then she turns back to the guy and says. "That would be all." When she turns to me, her smile is gone and her eyes are glaring. "See, that's you. Nice one minute and then shitty the next."

"I'm not that bad," I say, then she glares even harder, and her eyes narrow to slits. "Fine, okay, I just don't open up to people as easily as you do."

"I'm not asking to write your memoir. I'm asking you to be real with me and not an asshole. What the hell are you afraid of?"

"Nothing," I say right away. "I didn't mean anything by it."

"Whatever," she tells me and stops talking when a plate of fresh berries is delivered with a bowl of yogurt and granola on the side.

"You just told me to fuck off," I tell her, grabbing a bite of the waffle, and her eyes coming to me.

"Excuse me?" she says.

"Saying whatever is basically saying fuck off," I tell her. "It's like when someone texts you and you put K instead of okay."

"Are we even talking about the same thing?" she asks me, eating some yogurt.

"We are saying whatever is as rude as when people

abbreviate a word in a text," I tell her, and she rolls her eyes. "That is also rude."

"What? Rolling my eyes?" She laughs, and whatever I was feeling or however the conversation was going, it just feels better with her laughter. I feel better. "My father used to joke that my eyes would get stuck inside the sockets if I rolled them back any farther."

I laugh at her, and right here, at this moment, I feel just a touch free, just a touch myself. No one is watching to take a picture or holding a notebook. It's just the two of us, and for the first time in a really, really long time, it feels good.

Ten

Erin

A FTER I CALLED HIM out, I saw his guard lower just a touch, and when I say a touch, I mean a sliver. But I kept the conversation light, and I never asked him any personal questions. When the plane finally touched down, I got up and picked up my backpack, saying goodbye to the flight attendant. I walked out of the plane and waited for Carter to follow me. A black Range Rover was waiting for us. The airport official took our bags and put them in the back of his SUV while we buckled up inside.

The address is already stored in the GPS, so when he starts the car, he follows the highlighted route. When we start driving, I look outside at all the huge mountains in the distance. I see a couple of them with white dusting. "Look, snow." I point at them as he makes his way around the huge lake.

"I told you it was beautiful here," he says as I take in the breathtaking mountains and green trees. He pulls up to a gate where he presses the code on a keypad. The gate opens, and we make our way up to the house. He drives through the winding forest, and then I see the house come into view. I think I gasp out loud because it's so pretty. It looks like six different houses all merged.

He pulls right up to the front door of the house under an awning. I get out and see about ten pine trees in the middle of the huge asphalt driveway. I grab my backpack and meet Carter in the back of the car, and he is rolling our luggage to the front door. The door has a keypad also, and he enters the code. When you walk in, there isn't anything much except a cast-iron bench that sits on the brown slate floors. The walls all around are brick, and a staircase is right in front of the door. "Go on up. I'll follow you," he says to me, and I walk up the steps holding on to the black cast-iron railing.

Once I get to the landing, I stare at the room with wooden beams on the ceiling. The whole back wall is huge square windows, and you can see the mountains in the distance. A huge rock fireplace in the middle of the room faces two huge red couches and two leather chairs. A brown wooden coffee table sits in the middle. "Is that a moose?" I ask of the black head hanging above the fireplace.

"I think it's a caribou," he says, putting down our luggage. He walks inside and places his bag on the kitchen counter that is on the left-hand side of where the wooden floor turns to slate. The L-shaped countertop has five stools. I see the counter has two different heights and then see the huge island in the middle. The back wall has the ten-burner stove and double ovens, the fridge right beside it, and facing the kitchen to the right is a dining room. The windows are in a half octagon. The round table has eight huge chairs, and the chandelier looks like it has two rows of candles burning, but they are lights. "The bedrooms must be through there," he says, gesturing toward the hallway. I turn to grab my bag and roll it down the hallway, coming to a rocked archway with stairs leading down. There is another rocked archway in front of the stairs that lead to the bedrooms.

Two wooden double doors are open on both sides. "Pick a room," I tell him. He walks into the right one, and I enter the left one. The ceilings are high, and in middle of the room is a king-size four-poster canopy bed. An old-fashioned black and gold fireplace sits on an elevated rock floor. Lantern lights hang on either side of the bed. I walk in and see that the bed faces the lake. Two huge windows and a glass door give an outside view. I walk to the door and step out onto the balcony, the glass railing preventing any barriers to the view. The sound of the running water fills the air. I walk to the railing and rest my hands on top of it and just look out. "Erin." I hear my name being shouted and walk back into the bedroom. "Let's take a tour of the house so we know what we have." We explore the house and are shocked to see it has a movie room with six huge leather couches that recline. We even have a wine cellar, a wooden dining room table with ten chairs is also in the middle of the cellar, and a game room with a pool table.

"This house is insane," I tell him as we walk back up another set of stairs that lead to the backyard and outside. When we walk outside along the slate tiles, we see a huge fire pit and two steps up to an outdoor living space. "It's so pretty," I tell him, turning to him, and he just looks out at the mountains. "This is going to be my coffee spot in the morning."

He shakes his head. "You know that it gets cold, right?" He points at the mountains with the snow. "I'm going to go in and run through the script."

I turn to him. "If you want to get it, I can help you." The breeze comes through, and I grab the sides of my sweater and wrap them around me. He smiles and shakes his head. "What?"

"You're cold," he says, shrugging his blue jacket off and putting it around my shoulders, just leaving him in a short-sleeved shirt. His musky smell now surrounds me.

"I'm not cold," I tell him, and he rolls his eyes. "Rolling your eyes is rude. Don't let them get stuck in your sockets," I say, shoving him with my hand.

"I'm going to grab a sweater because I'm freezing." He laughs when I gasp. "Kidding, but I am going to grab one and the script."

"I'll be right here," I tell him, going to the huge couch.

"We should go and sit over there," he says, pointing at a huge rock fireplace on the right side. I look over and see that two round couches are positioned in front of the fireplace.

"Okay," I tell him, walking away. "I'll be over there." I walk toward the fireplace where a stack of wood is on the side. Upon closer inspection, I find a couple of pieces already piled inside the fireplace, so I look around until I spot a box of matches beside the wood. Lighting one, I toss it inside. I grab a cast-iron pick, squat down in front, and make sure the fire continues to burn.

"You started the fire." I hear from behind me, turning and looking over my shoulder at him as he walks back down to me. He's removed his baseball hat, but his glasses are on now.

"I did," I tell him, getting up and putting back the pick and walking over to the couch with his jacket.

"I brought you some water," he says, holding out a water bottle. I sit on the couch, crossing my legs under me, and grab it.

"Thank you." I smile up at him and see he has the script folded under his arm. "So tell me, how is tomorrow going to work?"

"We have a call at six a.m., which means I usually have to be on set two hours earlier." I open my eyes wide. "Good times, right?"

"Until what time?"

"Until the director thinks it's all good. I haven't worked with Ivan before, but from what I heard, he doesn't like to dillydally. He wants shit done," Carter says, sitting on the couch next to me. "Besides, I have a trailer you can hang out in and get some work done in private." *Great*, I think to myself, *that sounds like a great plan*. He grabs his phone. "The car is picking us up tomorrow at four a.m."

I nod my head, and for the next three hours, we run through his lines. He gets into his head, and his whole demeanor changes. He paces in front of me, back and forth, saying his lines over and over again. When he finally collapses on the couch next to me on his back, looking up at the sky, I laugh. "Did you always want to be an actor?" I ask him, and he looks over at me. He took off his glasses when we started running lines.

"No," he says. "I wanted to be a cop or a fireman." I laugh, and he chuckles. "But then Mickey Mouse had other plans for me." His tone changes.

"Were your parents supportive?" I know right away it's the wrong question when he sits up. "I'm sorry. You don't have to answer that," I say softly and start to get up.

"No, it's okay," he says, and I look at him. He sits crouched over with his elbows on his knees and his hands together. "I was their walking-talking ATM." The words make me stop. "When I was fifteen, I begged them to take a year off. I wanted to go to real school with real friends and join the basketball team," he says and then tries to make a joke to take away from the way his voice changed. "I mean, not that I was any good, but you know." I want to ask him what happened, but I don't know if he will answer me. "I was told that school was for losers, and that everyone in that school would die to be me." He shrugs. "So I never brought it up again. My parents actually bought a house and gutted it to make it into a school. The basement was the gym, the kitchen the cafeteria, and there were lockers across the living room, and the bedrooms were classrooms."

"That is kind of cool," I tell him, trying to focus on the positive efforts his parents made to make him feel somewhat normal.

"I guess, if that made them feel better because they took off for about four months, leaving me to fend for myself," he says, and his eyes just stare at the fire. "I mean, at that point, I was kind of used to it. I think the producers of the show suspected it, but I always got myself to the set on time." He shakes his head. "So I guess as long as the money was coming in, and I was well kept, they let it slide." The burning in my stomach starts to build. "I think someone asked for my parents once or twice, and I made an excuse for them. Meanwhile, they were in fucking Fiji spending my money." Oh. My. Fucking. God. I have no idea what to say, so I don't say anything. Instead, I cross my legs and hold my chin in my hand.

Needing to change the subject, I ask, "What's your favorite meal?"

"I have no idea." He laughs, looking at me, stretching his legs out now. "Why, are you going to cook it for me?" He nudges me sideways.

"Well, not right now, but I'm just curious," I say, and he puts his arm around my shoulders and brings me closer to him. It's done playfully, but it's the first time he's touched me. It's the first time that he's let me in without lashing out afterward, so I push him away, laughing.

"I would have to say anything Italian is my favorite," he says, and his arm just hangs over my shoulders. "Probably chicken parm."

"Really?" I say, and he just nods his head. We sit on the couch and watch the fire with his arm around my shoulder. Neither of us moves, and we just enjoy the quietness in the distance.

The beeping sound makes me open my eyes, and it takes me a second to remember where I am. I'm sleeping on my side in a fetal position, and the bed is heavenly. The thick white comforter is the perfect amount of weight. The beeping is still going, and I turn to the side, looking at the bedside clock, and see it's 3:00 a.m.

The beeping continues, so I throw my covers over me and get up to follow the sound. Walking to Carter's room, I knock on the open door and see that the covers are thrown back, and the bed is empty. I look at the door where his bathroom is and see that it's also open. I walk to the bedside table and pick up his blaring phone. After pressing the snooze button, I leave his phone exactly where it was, then turn around and walk to the kitchen where I find him standing in the middle of it. The lights are dim, and he stands with his back to me. His gray sleep pants hang low on his hips. "Your alarm was going off," I say, walking into the kitchen. When he turns around, his hair is all over the place, and his eyes are soft with sleep.

"Shit. I thought I turned it off," he says, reaching his hands behind his neck, flexing his arms. "Sorry I woke you."

"It's okay. I set mine for three fifteen," I tell him, going to sit on a stool. He starts opening the cupboard to grab two coffee cups.

"I don't have vanilla," he says, pouring the coffee and then turning around to place it in front of me. I watch him walk to the fridge and get the cream and milk. When we came in last night, we were happy to see that they stocked the fridge, and he cooked for me again, nothing fancy but it was still nice to watch him do it.

"I think I'll survive," I tell him, and he comes to sit on the stool next to me.

"I'm not sure if you eat breakfast, but I'm sure they will have some sort of craft service on set. If not, we can send someone to get you something to eat."

"I can wait," I tell him, getting up off the stool. "I have to get ready." I grab my coffee and walk back to my room. I'm slipping on my black heels when there is a knock on the door. "Come in," I say from my walk-in closet.

"The car is here," he says, and I walk into the room to him. "What in the fuck are you wearing?" he asks me in a gruff tone.

I look down at what I'm wearing, seeing the high-waist gray pants with a sash at the waist. I paired it with a white long-sleeved silk shirt with a vee collar and the buttons stop halfway with the sleeves rolled at the wrist. "Is it not dressy enough?" I ask, not sure if I have time to change.

"We are going on a film set that is dusty and most likely dirty," he says with aggravation. "You are like a walking wet dream wearing that getup," he mumbles, and I don't know whether to be happy with the comment or not. "Don't forget a jacket. It's cold outside," he says, turning and walking out of the room. I run back to the closet and grab my brown cashmere jacket, then pick up my Louis and walk to the front door. "You look like you are one of those girls from the porn movies. Not that I would know about that or anything."

"What the hell is your problem?" I ask, irritated. "I'm not used to a film set, so how the heck should I know how to dress? I'm also still working, so why should I be dressed casually?"

"Whatever," he says, and he walks away.

"Fuck you, too," I say to myself and walk out of the house, closing the door behind me. He waits at the car with the back door open for me to get in.

I get into the car, and I don't say anything to him. We don't exchange any words for the entire trip, and I think to myself *only thirteen more days to go*.

ELEVEN

Carter

I TOSSED AND TURNED all night, having almost wet dreams thinking about her. I never, ever told anyone any stories about my parents except Jeff. She sat next to me, and she just listened, and when I looked in her eyes, they didn't have pity in them, and they didn't have sadness. In fact, it looked like she was angry.

I woke up at two thirty and stayed in the bed until ten to three, then got up and made coffee. Actually, I stayed in bed, squeezing my hard cock until he went down. Then when I heard her voice, my cock stirred, and I had to talk it down. I was on edge. I needed to get laid soon, or my cock was going to self-combust. I had to google that to make sure it wasn't actually a thing, and then when I went to get her, she walked out of her closet, and I swear the only thing I thought about was sinking my cock into her. She oozes sex appeal, and she is so oblivious to it that it's even fucking sexier.

Then she put her jacket on, and I swear to God, I thought I was going to come in my pants. I got in the car, and all I could do was think of her with her hair up and glasses on bent over. Fuck, I needed to fuck period. She said nothing to me on the whole ride to the set, and I have to admit it was better because had she said something or sassed me, I wouldn't have stopped myself from taking her. Even while the driver watched. Okay, I would have covered her so no one could see, but I still would have taken her. I would have kissed her until she couldn't take it anymore.

When the car comes to a stop, I let myself out and wait for her to get out, but she doesn't get out on my side. Nope, not Erin. She gets out on her own side and smiles at the driver holding the door open. When she looks at me, her smile falls and the glare returns. I figure she's probably thinking about ways to kill me. In my sleep. And bury my dead ass in the snow not to be found until spring. I shake my head. "Stop scowling or else you are going to need Botox," I tell her, and it isn't my finest moment.

"It's okay. I'll send you the bill," she says, and we walk onto the lot. They rented out a huge ass warehouse. Actually, it looks like there are five warehouses. I see the row of trailers on the side and head to find mine. I walk down the path, looking at the names on the door, and finally see mine. It's bigger than the others, which doesn't surprise me since I'm the star. I walk up the two little metal stairs and open the white tin door. I step into the main room, which is in the middle of the trailer. To one side is the bedroom and bathroom, and to the other side is a long white leather U-shaped couch around a wooden table. Throw pillows on the couch face the kitchenette with a sink and microwave. I put my phone on the table. "Welcome to your office," I tell her, and she comes in and puts her bag down. "I have to go to makeup. Do you want to come with me and see where the food is and all that?" She doesn't answer me, obviously still pissed, and just nods her head. I walk back out of the trailer and see that people are slowly beginning to arrive. We walk back to where we were dropped off toward the door into the warehouse. The sign on the door says set one, makeup & costume, Ivan's office, and then craft service.

I open the door and walk in, and the lights are all on. The warehouse has four separate sections in each corner. Some of the crew nod at me and then their horny eyes look over at Erin. I'm just about to give her an "I fucking told you so" look when I hear my name being called.

"Carter Johnson." I hear Ivan's thick Russian accent as he walks toward us with headphones around his neck and a shit ton of papers in his hand. He's wearing jeans and a beige sweater over a dress shirt with the collar sticking up.

"Ivan," I say. Walking to him, I extend my hand to him. He takes it and then brings me in for a side hug.

"Are you ready?" he asks me, and I just nod my head. This movie is not action packed like my last one was.

This is an emotional one about a man on the hunt for his missing daughter who was kidnapped by his ex-wife. I knew I wanted this part. It was time for the world to see that I could do more than jump out of planes. "Did you see the other stages?" he asks me, and I just shake my head.

"No, we just got here," I say and then turn my head to Erin. "This is Erin. She works for Hillcrest."

His smile grows even bigger. "Such a beauty," he says. "Why aren't you in the movies?" I'm about to groan and roll my eyes, but I don't. I watch her smile and put out her hand.

"It's a pleasure to meet you," she says all professional, ignoring the comment about how beautiful she is.

"I have to make sure stage five is set up," he says. "I'll see you on set at six," he says and walks away. I didn't even notice the quiet young girl by his side. I turn back and continue walking when I see the makeup corner. Four chairs in front of huge mirrors with lightbulbs all around them.

I see the same makeup girl who is on almost every movie set I'm on. She sits in her chair, her brown hair twisted up in a bun, while she eats a piece of fruit and scrolls on her phone. "Do you want me before I eat or after?" She looks up, and I see her brown eyes light up.

"There he is, Mr. Johnson." She waves at me and then looks at Erin. "Don't tell me you bit the bullet and got an assistant?" She moves her head to the side, smiling at Erin while I shake my head. "Holy shit, are you two dating?" She puts her head back and howls out a laugh.

"You owe me five thousand dollars."

"What?" I hear Erin beside me.

"I don't owe you shit," I tell her. "This is Erin. She works for Hillcrest and is in charge of making sure I stay a good boy." She then looks at me. "She bet me five thousand dollars that I would fall in love one of these days."

"It'll happen, and then I'll be rich," she says with her hands in the air. "I'm Mandy." She looks at Erin. "And I take it back. No way would someone that pretty date you." I roll my eyes at her. "You may be hot-to-trot, Mr. Johnson, but your belt is full of holes."

I shake my head. "I don't even know what that means." I pretend and then Erin leans in.

"She means your Johnson gets around," she whispers, and I look back at her. This time, I'm the one glaring.

"Whatever," I say. "I'm going to eat."

"I'll see you when you're done," she says and goes back to her phone.

"I like her," Erin says from beside me as we walk toward the craft service. I finally notice the hanging signs. They have put up walls, and there are about ten white plastic tables with chairs. Three tables are against the three walls. One table has cutlery, one has the drinks, and then there is a table with the food. I walk up and see a tray of sliced tomatoes, a tray of bagels, and another tray of cookies. A basket of chips. They do have a fruit bowl with apples, oranges, and bananas, and then a full bowl of berries.

"What do you want to eat?' I ask Erin over my

shoulder.

"To be honest, I'm really not hungry, but I will take another coffee," she says as she walks over to the drink station and then looks at me. "Do you want one also?" she asks me, and I nod my head, grabbing a chocolate chip cookie and eating it. "Here is your regular coffee," she says to me.

"I have to head to makeup," I tell her, and she just nods. "Are you going to keep me company or head back to the trailer?"

"I don't know," she says. Taking a sip of her coffee, she debates what she wants to do.

"I would prefer you stay with me," I tell her the truth, and she looks at me, tilting her head. "It's dark out there and a long walk back to my trailer, and I don't know if anyone is outside to watch."

"So it's not that you want me to stay and keep you company?" She laughs. "But you want me to stay in case I get slaughtered and then you feel bad."

I shrug. "Yeah, something like that." I wink at her, and she rolls her eyes. We walk back to Mandy, and I get in the chair. It's been two months since I've seen Mandy, so she fills me in on everything I've missed, and like usual, I just smile and nod. I add in a comment here and there, but in the end, she never asks me what I was doing. I just have to think it's because she's asked in the past and I've never told her.

"There," she says. "Nothing else is going to help this mug." She laughs, and I get up. We walk out and see that the sun is slowly coming up. We walk toward the trailer, and I see more and more people showing up. When we get back into the trailer, my wardrobe is there for the day.

"Jeans and a plaid shirt," Erin says. Shrugging off her jacket, she sits at the table and grabs her bag. I grab the clothes and start undressing in front of her. "Hey," she says loudly, "go change in the bathroom."

"What's the matter?" I hold up my hands. "Stop being such a prude." And I want to take the words back as soon as they come out because from the hurt look on her face, the comment clearly bothers her.

"If a prude means being respectful, then yeah, I'm a prude," she says, and if she wasn't stuck here, I think she would actually get up and leave. "I don't undress in front of you, so can you show me the same respect?"

"Yeah, well, no one really wants to see you naked, so I think we are safe with that." And again, I'm wondering how much shit can spew out of my mouth in the same breath. It would seem that was the straw that broke the camel's back. She gets up, and I'm about to go to her, but something stops me. She picks up her jacket and purse and then looks at me.

"You're right. No one probably wants to see me naked," she says while she puts her jacket back on, "but I, for one, am not interested in seeing you naked, so stop fucking assuming every double-X chromosome is hard-wired to want to see your dick." She grabs her bag and starts to walk out.

"Erin," I say, but she doesn't stop. She just continues to the door. "Come on."

"No," she says, turning around. "I'm not going to be your punching bag anymore. You want to lash out, then get one of your whores to do that to. Or do they not get the good side of Carter?" She opens the door and walks down the two steps, and I hear her heels click on the asphalt as she walks away. I put my stuff on and walk back out, grabbing my phone and texting Erin. I wait two seconds and finally look down and see she hasn't answered me back, so I call her and it goes straight to voice mail. I walk back to the craft table, and she isn't there. I walk over by Mandy and find her working on someone else. As I turn to walk away, I crash into the girl from before who was with Ivan.

"Sorry," she says, listening through her headset. "They are ready for you on the set, Mr. Johnson."

"Um, yeah, sure," I tell her.

"I'm Jennifer," she says. "I'm Ivan's assistant." I nod at her and turn to follow her. My eyes roam the room, but I don't see her anywhere. Stepping out the side door, I get into a golf cart while Jennifer gets in behind the wheel. She drives us right past stage two and three, stopping at stage four. "We are going to be here most of the day," she says, and I get out, going to the door, and send Erin another text.

Me: Can you please answer me?

I wait to see if the three bubbles come up, but they don't. When I walk into stage four, I see that the warehouse has two sections. One is a living room and the other is the kitchen. "We are filming in the living room first," Jennifer says, and I walk over to find Ivan sitting in the chair with his name on it, and next to him is the woman who has me all up in knots. The woman who is making me say shit I don't mean and driving me crazy. The woman who is going to be the death of me.

Twelve

Erin

WHEN HE CALLED ME a prude, it got me in the heart. Fine, I wasn't out there, and yeah, I didn't just have sex to have sex. And yes, people did call me a prude because I just couldn't wrap my head around the idea of casual sex. So hearing it from him hit a nerve, a nerve that had me blinking away the tears stinging my eyes. Then he made the cheap shot about no one wanting to see me naked. Fine, I didn't really have much to show. My hips were really not there, my booty was just starting to grow since I began doing squats, and yes, I only had a B cup.

I wasn't going to fight back. I wasn't going to say anything to him. Instead, I was going to get my jacket on and go back to the house. Except in my haste to get the fuck away from him, I realized I didn't even have the address to the house. I took my phone out of my pocket and saw that it was way too early to call anyone back at the office for the address, and that is when I bumped into Ivan.

"There you are," he says. "I just got a phone call from Ryan about the work you are going to do here."

"Yes," I say, not knowing how I'm going to break it to him that I'll be quitting this job. I was going to wave the white flag and admit defeat. When my phone buzzes and I see it's Carter trying to message me, I do what every other woman would do. I put him on "do not disturb." Take that.

"Come, we have to talk," he says and pulls me away. He takes me in the golf cart, and we make it to stage four, and I sit in the chair next to him. "This film is going to be his big break," he says of Carter. "I'm going to push him to be his best. I'm going to push him until there is nothing left in him, and then when he gets up to accept his award, it'll be mostly because of me." He laughs, and I laugh with him. "The boy hasn't had much luck in the past. Maybe it's his time to have better luck."

I'm about to ask him what he means by that when I hear the booming voice. "Where have you been?" I see Carter with his hands on his hips, and I take in his outfit. He looks so rugged and not like the Hollywood prince that he is.

"I was here catching up with Ivan." I smile at him like nothing happened, but he just glares at me.

"I've been calling and texting you," he says between his clenched teeth.

"Did you?" I pick up my phone. "Nope, not me. Perhaps it was someone else?"

He looks at me, but he doesn't have a chance to say anything because Ivan claps his hands. "Okay, children, it's time to work." He gets up and walks to the set where he talks to a couple of the crew.

"I called you," he says, coming to me, standing in front of my chair. "Twice." He holds up two fingers.

I lean back in the chair and shrug my shoulders. "No idea."

"You sent me straight to voice mail," he says, and I just smile.

"I have no idea what you're talking about. I didn't get a phone call or texts," I tell him, and he holds out his hand.

"Let me see your phone." I hold out the phone for him. He presses the middle button and then looks at me. "What's your code?"

"Try the word asshole," I say and then slap my hand to my head. "Fine, it's my birthday." I wait for him to ask me what it is.

"Can you put your code in?" he asks, and I do, and then he looks through the phone. He takes his phone out and calls my phone, and it's obviously sent straight to voice mail because he then presses his name. "You blocked me?"

"Did I?" I act shocked as I take the phone away. "No." I pretend to look at my phone "I have no idea what you're talking about."

"Erin," he says, his jaw tight.

"Carter!" Ivan yells. "Let's get the show on the road."

I look at him and smile. "Break a leg." He glares at

me, and I hold up my two hands. "Fingers crossed," I say, crossing my two fingers together.

He comes a touch closer, resting his hands on the armrests of the chair. "I'm going to table this discussion for later."

"I'm not talking to you because you're a horse's ass." I lean in closer to him, hissing out ass. "Actually, I take that back. I don't want to insult the horse."

"Carter!" Ivan yells, and he just looks at me and walks away. I watch him walk over to him as they stand in the middle of a fake living room with a staircase in the back. If I wasn't here seeing the entire surroundings, I would think it's actually a house. There is a guy waiting on the side with a long mic and a huge box hanging from his neck. "Okay, places everyone." Ivan walks back to his chair and sits in it. He puts on his headset, and someone wheels what looks like a television on it. "We can see them close up," he says, informing me. A woman goes up to the set where Carter is now sitting on the couch.

Jennifer steps in front of the scene, and says, "*Risking it All*, scene twenty."

I look around while people start to shout things.

"Picture's up," one person says, and someone else repeats it.

"Roll sound," another says, and I hear someone shout, "Rolling!"

"Sound speeds!" the guy at the end shouts.

"Camera speeds," comes from my left and then one from one right. "Slating and mark."

Then Ivan shouts, "Action," and I watch as the scene

plays out. The knock on the door and his co-star coming in who, in the film, is his brother as they go over the fact that his wife kidnapped his daughter, and he can't find her. It takes him five takes before Ivan has it just the way he wants it. "Cut and print." Ivan tosses his headset on his seat and goes to talk to the two men, and they go over a couple of things. The three of them discuss something I can't hear.

When they break, they each go their separate ways, but Carter comes right to me. "I'm off for about three hours. Do you want to get something to eat?" His voice is off and weird, and I just look at him.

"Yeah, that sounds good," I say, grabbing my bag and walking with him outside where he just gets into a random golf cart. The sun shines bright in the sky. "Is this anyone's?" I ask him, looking around to see if anyone is running after us as he leaves.

"No. It's for anyone's use. I park it with the others, and then someone else can take it," he tells me, pulling up to stage one. We walk in and go to the craft service room and see that the food has been changed. This time, hot plates filled with eggs, potatoes, sausage, bacon, waffles, and pancakes are on the table. You name it, it's there. He loads his plate, and I follow him, filling my plate. We walk out to his trailer, and I watch him go straight to the table. I put my plate in front of him and then shrug off my jacket.

"I need the address of the house." I walk to his little fridge, hoping that it is stocked, and I'm happy it is. I grab a water bottle for myself and one for him also, but

I put it in front of my plate.

"Why?" he asks between bites.

"So if I want to go back to the house, I have it," I tell him, grabbing the plastic fork and digging into the scrambled eggs.

"You were going to leave me here and go back to the house?" he asks, grabbing a water bottle and opening it.

"You mean after you were an asshole earlier? Yes, I was going back to the house."

"I'm sorry." The two words I don't think he's ever said he just uttered to me.

"Really?" I answer, surprised. "What exactly are you sorry for?"

He looks at me. "I'm sorry for calling you a prude."

"That wasn't even the point," I tell him, pointing at him with my fork. "The point was to respect my wishes and not undress in front of me. You might be okay with having your shlong all over the place, but not everyone wants to see it."

"Shlong?" He laughs. "You know that means I have a huge dick, right?"

I groan. "What the hell are you talking about?" I scoop up a forkful of eggs and eat.

"It's in the urban dictionary. It means not for regular size dicks but for dicks with substantial length and girth." He winks at me. "You are not wrong in either case."

"You have to be the most infuriating person I have ever met," I tell him, shaking my head.

"I needed this," he says softly, and I look up. "After

that scene in there, I needed this to take my mind off it."

"You can't do that," I tell him, dropping my fork. "You can't be an asshole one second and then be soft and gentle the next."

"I didn't mean to be an asshole. I guess I inherited that from my parents." He shrugs his shoulders. "And if it's worth anything"—he leans in—"I will be more than happy to see you naked." I shake my head, trying to hide my laughter. "Too much?"

"Too much." I agree with him. "You know, I don't know the story of your parents and what's become of them since, but I do know that at one point you need to stop blaming them and start making yourself unlike them."

He laughs. "You sound like my shrink."

"Not even trying to be. My parents, thank God, are great," I tell him. "They were never together. I mean, they dated but were not exclusive. My father could have said sorry, I'm out, but he didn't. He took it and ran with it. They co-parented me, and I never felt that I was missing anything."

"My parents spent every single last cent I ever made by the time I turned eighteen," he says, leaning back. "Everything. I had nothing to show for all my hard work." I try not to open my mouth in shock. "They were off living the lavish life, and they stuck me in a one-bedroom condo from when I was fourteen and then stuck me in my fake school house. They would show up when they knew people were asking questions." Oh my God. "They would swoop in and pretend they were the best parents in the world." He laughs bitterly. "There is this one picture of us on the red carpet. I was in a mini tux, and my mother actually showed up wearing a mink fur wrap. It was July in Hollywood." He rubs his face with his hands. "I need a nap." He gets up and walks to the bedroom. "There is only one bed, but if you want to nap, I can sleep out on the bench."

"No," I say to him. "I'm good. I'm going to get some work done." He nods his head and falls onto the bed but keeps the door open. He falls asleep on his back, and he didn't even kick off his shoes. I grab my computer, and instead of working, I end up on Google and go in search of the picture he was talking about. I find that one and so many more, and I want to jump into the computer and smack his parents. You can totally see the sadness in his eyes. I spend way too much time looking at his old pictures, and then I find one of him with a girl. He looks like he's eighteen or nineteen. I click the picture and then a whole bunch of them pop up. Looking into the room where he's sleeping, I suddenly feel guilty, like I'm snooping in his black book of sorts. I close the screen and open another and start really working because at the end of all this is the big prize. My career means more than this assignment, and I'm in this for the long game, not for what the next thirteen days will bring.

CHAPTER THIRTEEN

Carter

I FALL INTO BED, and I think of the story I just told her about my parents. I don't know what she does or how she does it, but I just want to tell her everything. She isn't going to sit there with googly eyes looking at me. No, she is going to sit there and tell me when I'm an asshole. And I have to admit, around her, I'm more of an asshole than I want to be. I stay in bed until someone knocks on the side of my trailer. "Thirty minutes to roll call."

I roll off the bed and stretch my arms, hitting the roof of the trailer. Walking out of the bedroom, I see that Erin is typing away on her laptop, and her fingers are going a mile a minute. "Are you going to come on set?" I ask her, opening the fridge and grabbing an orange juice.

"I am, actually," she says, turning to me. "I'm going to take a couple of pictures to get the movie Instagram page started and also one with you on the set."

"After this scene, I'm off for the rest of the day," I tell her, looking at the clock. It's almost noon, and I feel like it's already bedtime. I nod at her and then make my way to the makeup corner. Mandy is there waiting for me. "Make me beautiful."

"There are not enough hours in the day to make you beautiful"—she snickers—"but I can try." I close my eyes, waiting for her to put the gunk on my face.

"I'm going to take a picture of him just like that," Erin says. I open one eye, and she snaps a picture. "'If you think I'm sexy, come on and tell me so' is going to be the caption."

"Oh, Jesus," Mandy says. "She is going to break the internet."

"Not yet," Erin says, "but I'm going to do my best. Maybe if we can get a shirtless one. The ladies love that."

"Sweetheart, if you want me to take off my shirt, all you have to do is ask," I tell her with a wink.

"Please, I think I'm going to be sick," she says, holding her hand to her stomach.

"I like her," Mandy says. "She doesn't fall for your movie star looks or your corny pickup lines."

"That she does not," I say to Mandy and watch Erin in the mirror now as she types away on her phone.

"All done," Mandy says. "I'll see you tomorrow morning." I get up and walk to the door.

"Here we go." I get into a golf cart and wait for Erin to get in with me. "One scene and I get to go home and shower. I might even nap."

"You just took a two-hour nap," she says from beside me, and I look over.

"Yeah, but I didn't really sleep last night," I tell her, and she looks over at me. I pull up to the warehouse and get out. I hold the door open for her, and we come face-to-face with Jennifer.

"There you are, Mr. Johnson. I was just coming to get you," she says. I just nod at her, and she turns and hurries away.

Ivan's standing in the same living room set where I filmed this morning. We go over how he wants the scene, and I walk to get into the zone. I'm playing a father whose daughter was kidnapped, and just the thought makes my stomach turn. I never want to have kids, ever, but if I did, I would be the best person I could be for them. I wouldn't stop searching until my last breath. I try to get the scene in one take, but it takes fifteen, and by the end, I'm emotionally spent. I nod to Ivan when it's done and look around. Erin is standing on the side with her eyes on her phone. I walk to her, and she looks up, and I see that she has tears in her eyes.

"What's the matter?" I ask her, and she just shakes her head. "Are you hurt?" I grab her by her shoulders and almost shake her. "Did someone say something to you?"

"No," she says softly. "That scene was crazy good." I watch as she blinks away tears. Wrapping her in my arms, I just stand here with my chin on her head. After the scene, I was in my head. I didn't want to talk to anyone, and I struggled with how it was going to be, but this, with her in my arms and hugging me back, was exactly what I needed. I think the last time I really hugged someone was ten years ago, and we all know how that turned out.

"Are you good?" I whisper, and she nods her head so I let her go but keep my arm around her shoulders. "It's okay, sweetheart," I say as we walk toward the door. "Spoiler alert, he finds the daughter and they live happily ever after."

She pushes away from me. "You are the worst," she tells me. We hop in the first available golf cart and make our way toward my trailer. She gets her stuff, and I change out of my costume, leaving it on the bed. Opening the door, she is there with her phone in her hand. "Four million likes in two hours." Her face is beaming as she turns the phone around and shows me. "And four thousand comments." I walk out the door and wait for her.

"So do they think I'm sexy or not?" I ask her, walking to the waiting town car.

"Sorry." She smirks. "It's a no," she jokes, and now it's me who pushes her. She throws her head back and laughs. I open the car door for her, and she gets in. When we get to the house, I open the door, and she slowly walks up the steps, and then she stops. "What is all this?" she says, and I stop beside her. I look at the room that has so many flowers it smells like a flower shop. Numerous different bouquets fill the room.

"This is my way of saying I'm sorry, and because I

didn't know which flower you liked, I ordered one of everything," I tell her, and she walks to a bouquet of roses and leans down and smells it. Her face is glowing. "So I called the shop and ordered everything that I could or, better yet, anything they could get with such short notice." I look around, and there are roses in white, pink, purple, blue, red, yellow. Daisies, orchids, birds-of-paradise, and tulips. If it's a flower, it's in this room.

"This is incredible." She looks around, and it really is, but it is nothing like her smile. I would do it all over again to see her smile like that. I mean, I don't mean I'd be an asshole again, but I would do the whole flower thing again to see her smile like that.

"This has to be the nicest thing anyone has ever done for me." She walks over to me and gets on her tippy toes and for just one second, my heart stops. My breathing stops, everything stops. Her hands land on my waist as she leans in and kisses my cheek. A simple and innocent move that shifts my world.

"Anytime, sweetheart," I tell her, and then I turn and walk away to my bedroom, where I lock myself in the bathroom to take care of my raging hard-on. My cock hasn't gotten the memo that she's off-limits. Stepping in the shower with the hot water flowing all around me, I close my eyes and picture her lips on my neck, her hands on my cock, and then my hands in her hair, and I come whispering her name on my lips.

I debate on a nap, but I choose not to, or else I'll be fucked tonight. So I walk in search of Erin when I hear pots banging. "Yeah, Mom. You already told me. Sauce then cheese."

I walk into the kitchen, and she has changed out of her dressy pants into tight yoga pants with a crop top and has her long hair piled on her head. My cock stirs again. She is standing at the counter with chicken in front of her. "Mom, I have to go," she says when she finally looks up.

"What's going on?' I ask, looking at two pots on the stove. Walking over, I see one has just water in it while the other has a tomato sauce that is boiling away and splashing everywhere. I lower the temperature and stir it with the wooden spoon that is on the counter.

"I wanted to do something nice, so I thought I'd make you chicken parm, but I couldn't really find an easy recipe, so I called my mother," she says, "and she was going on and on about how to make it, and well, I'm going to wing it and hope for the best."

"You did all this for me?" I say in shock, looking at this woman who, for the past four days has taken the brunt of my asshole ways, is going out of her way and winging it to make me chicken parm.

"I did it for me, too, but mostly for you," she says and then cracks an egg in a bowl and then another. "If you want, you can search and see if you can find a recipe that is easy." I just stare at her as she whisks the eggs and then goes in search of bread crumbs. She finds them and empties the whole bag on the plate and then slices the chicken breast into smaller pieces. "Do you think I need to add salt and pepper before I bread them?" she asks me, and I'm still here staring at her. She has turned the kitchen into a disaster, to say the least, but she has done it for me. I'm still trying to wrap my head around it. "Carter."

"Yeah," I say, blinking at her.

"Salt and pepper. Should I put it on the chicken?" she asks me and uses the back of her hand to scratch her forehead. "I think what's the worst that can happen, right?"

"I'll google," I tell her and go back to get my phone in the room. I have to sit on the bed and get my heart beating regularly. I sit here, and I breathe in and out, and then I see her standing in the doorway.

"Are you okay?" she asks with worry on her face. "You don't have to eat it."

"No one has ever cooked for me," I tell her. "I mean, I think my mother did once upon a time, but then she found that it was easier to pop things into the microwave, and then she used to order my meals."

"Carter," she says softly, and I shake my head.

"No, it's fine," I say. "I just need a second to process it."

"Do you want me to stay, or do you want me to go?" she asks, and I look at her. This woman pushes my buttons but then brings out something that I didn't even know was possible. This woman who hands down is the most beautiful woman I've ever laid eyes on. This woman who tells me to fuck off and then calls me an asshole and forgives me more this week than she should have.

"If I told you to stay, you would, wouldn't you?" I

ask her the question.

"Well, yeah," she says, coming in and sitting on the bed next to me. "Isn't that what friends do?"

"I don't know. Never had any real friends," I tell her the truth. "I've only had Hollywood friends."

"I take it those aren't real friends?" she asks. I notice she has a bread crumb in her hair.

"Did you turn off the stove?" I ask her, and her eyes go wide. Jumping off the bed, she runs to the kitchen, and I grab my phone and follow her. Luckily, nothing is burned, and the water is boiling.

"Okay, let me see if we can pull up a recipe and do this," I tell her, and she turns around.

"No," she says loudly. "I want to do this, so go watch television. Or, I don't know, read your script for tomorrow. I've got this."

"Are you sure?" I ask her, and she nods.

"You can make room for us to eat since every surface is full of flowers," she says. I look around, and she isn't wrong. The table is so full, as is the living room table and the counter, so I don't know where to start. When I look back into the kitchen, she is frying the chicken. She looks over at me and smiles. "Watch out *Iron Chef*, I'm coming for you."

I laugh at her when she finally places the chicken in the oven, and she is stirring the pasta. "The pasta is going to be done before the chicken is ready," she says and groans. "It's going to be so bad."

"It isn't going to be bad," I tell her. "Just broil the chicken since it's already cooked. All you need is for the top to cook."

"Great idea, sous chef," she says and turns the knob. Ten minutes later, she is plating the pasta and chicken parm.

She brings the plate over to the table that I set while she was cooking. She puts a plate down for me and a smaller one for herself. She sits and looks over at me and laughs. "If it's not good, we can order something."

Cutting a piece of chicken, I put it in my mouth, and believe it or not, it's the best chicken parm I've ever eaten. "It's really good," I tell her, grabbing another piece.

"It isn't too bad," she says, and I look back at her and see sauce has splattered on her shirt, and it will probably be stained by the oil splashes, but I wouldn't change it. "The pasta could use some salt."

"Everything is perfect," I tell her, and I mean it. I eat everything on my plate and even go back in for seconds. "Do you cook for your boyfriend?" I ask her the nagging question that has been looming in the back of my head since Saturday.

She looks at me, grabbing her bottle of water. "I don't have a boyfriend," she says, blocking her mouth with the bottle. My head tilts at her, and she changes the subject. "How do you stay in shape?" she asks me.

I look at her. "Did you ever have a boyfriend, or were you just fucking with me?" I wait a second for her to answer and then continue. "I work out five times a week," I tell her, "but honestly, it's good genes. I guess I can thank my parents for one thing."

"You assumed I had a boyfriend, so I let you assume," she tells me, then again changes the subject. "Well, I definitely didn't inherit my mother's boobs," she says, laughing. "Actually, come to think of it, she is the opposite of me. She's tall and curvy where I'm just tall and tall."

I laugh and then look at her. "You know what they say when you assume something?" I ask her, and this conversation now has us tiptoeing around everything. "You make an ass out of you and me." She laughs, and then my voice goes soft. "You are the most beautiful woman I've ever met." I tell her the truth. "And I've met a shit ton. But you, you have this easiness to you that brings you so up there that you're untouchable." She doesn't say anything. She just stares at me. "Whether you're wearing sweats or fancy ass shit, you just walk in, and everyone stops to look at you." I put my knife down. "You're stunning, Erin," I say softly, and then I lean in and kiss her on the cheek, smelling the light citrus she has on. "Now, since you cooked, I will clean." I smile at her. "Apparently, it's a universal rule."

"Um," she says, pushing away from the table. "I think now is a good time to shower." She turns and walks away, and I sit at the table a little longer, thinking about what I told her. About how I wanted to rub my nose on her cheek and then trail soft kisses down to her lips. To see if her eyes sparkle when my lips met hers.

It's right then that I realize exactly how fucked I am . . . and that's not in the good way.

Fourteen

Erin

"I THINK ALL THIS marketing for the movie is going great," Sylvia says during our Skype call one week in. "I think we were even trending on Twitter, and *Entertainment Hollywood* is coming next week, I think Wednesday, to tour the set."

"That sounds great," I tell her as I sit in the trailer waiting for Carter to finish filming his scene. I've been awake since two thirty this morning, and it's almost four p.m. "The movie's Instagram page is up to twenty-five million."

"That is incredible," Sylvia says, and now she leans back in her chair. "And I have to say there have been no negative stories in the press, so you're obviously doing your job."

I nod my head. "It's really hard to do all the sinful stuff when you're on the set for fourteen hours a day. So my job has been a lot easier than I expected."

"Well, from what I saw, you have tomorrow off, so sleep in and get some rest," Sylvia says. "I'm here if you need me."

"Thank you so much." Disconnecting the call, I rub my hands over my face. I look around the trailer at the two vases of flowers on the table that I brought from home. When I walked into the house and saw all the flowers, I was in shock. Every single place I looked had flowers. And so many different colors. I knew then I had to up it and do something for him. Chicken parm was it, but holy shit, did I want to die.

"I'm done," Carter says, walking into the trailer. "The car is already here, so if you can hurry, I would be so thankful."

"I just have to grab my jacket," I say, getting up and putting my computer in the Louis and then walking out. "Tired?" I ask him, and he just nods.

For the past week, it's been routine for us to leave together in the morning. Breakfast together, lunch together, dinner together. Except yesterday when he wanted to eat in his bed, which I was totally okay with, but five minutes later, he came looking for me and said it was too quiet in his room. So he sat on my bed as I watched television. He ate his grilled chicken that we had delivered and then put it on the side table. He then closed his eyes, and I felt bad and didn't want to tell him to get up, so I went under the covers and shut off the light. He stayed on his side of the bed, and when his alarm rang, he sprang out of bed. He didn't mention falling asleep in my bed, and I didn't mention it either. I guess if neither of us mentions it, it means it didn't happen.

"I swear I'm so tired I'm going to sleep until noon tomorrow," he says, putting his head back on the seat. I grab my phone and snap a picture of him with the caption.

"My plans for the next twenty-four hours."

I post it and put my phone away. When we get to the house, I get out first, and he follows me. When we make our way up the stairs, he goes straight to his room and shuts the door. I do the same and take a shower. I put on my dark gray jeans and big gray long-sleeved cashmere sweater. I walk out, seeing that his door is still closed, so I walk to the kitchen. I'm a little shocked when I see him standing at the fridge wearing nothing but shorts. "I thought you were going to sleep?"

He looks over his shoulder at me. "I have to eat before I hibernate for the day," he says, grabbing some eggs and bacon. "I'm craving breakfast."

"Brupper," I tell him, going to the cupboard and grabbing the box of pancake mix.

"Brupper?" he asks mid-step to the counter.

"When you have breakfast for lunch, it's called brunch, so when you have breakfast for supper, it's called brupper," I tell him, grabbing a bowl and a measuring cup.

"Clever," he tells me, cracking eggs while he throws bacon in a baking dish and puts it in the oven. We work side by side as I make the pancakes and he scrambles the eggs and makes the toast. We sit next to each other at the counter. "The weather is going to be nice tomorrow. We should go for a hike."

"A hike? I thought you were going to hibernate?" I ask him, and he just shrugs. "Where?"

"Some of the local crew told me about Yellowstone River. We can hike up and see." He gets up and puts his plate in the dishwasher and starts to clean up the pans while I finish eating.

"Sure," I say even though I'm not sure I even have clothes for a hike. I get up and put my dish away, and he goes back into his room. I go to my room, grab my Kindle and phone, slip on my Converse, and walk outside to the fireplace. I've been stuck in a trailer for most of the week with my only fresh air when going from one stage to another. I walk outside and see the orange sun in the distance setting behind the mountains.

I start the fire, and when it's roaring, I get on the round chair in front of it, grabbing a throw blanket stored in one of the plastic chests to cover myself with. I sit with my back to the house and scroll on Instagram, seeing that the picture of Carter has gotten four million likes and two thousand comments, most from women wishing he would sleep in their bed. I roll my eyes and grab my Kindle. But instead, I stare at the flames of the fire. The heat slowly warms me, but the breeze makes me shiver now. "You are going to catch a cold sitting outside." I hear his voice and turn around to see him wearing sweatpants, a thick long-sleeved beige turtleneck, and a beanie that just hangs on the back of his head. He gets on the round chair with me, sitting next to me. "I was looking for you everywhere," he says softly, putting his arm around my shoulders and pulling me close to him. I don't move and just fall into his side. My heart starts to speed up a touch, but I don't move out of his embrace. He grabs the blanket from my lap and covers his own. Anyone coming to check on us would think we were an intimate couple.

"I thought you were going to sleep until noon tomorrow," I remind him. My eyes focus on the fire, listening to the crackle.

"I was going to, but then I got into bed, and I tossed and turned and then just got up, and I checked around for you," he says, and I look over at him as he watches the fire.

"I came out to get some air. I've been cooped up all week," I tell him, and he grabs my Kindle.

"What were you reading?" he asks, and I almost turn the same shade as the fire when he starts to read it aloud.

"Christian Grey." He laughs. "Didn't you watch the movie?"

I push away from him and reach out to grab my Kindle. "I did watch the movie, and I read the books," I admit. "I haven't read in a while."

The sound of his laughter fills the silent night. He grabs my shoulder again, pulling me to him. "It's okay to admit that it turns you on."

"Of course, you would turn this into sex," I tell him. "This must have been the longest week of your life."

"I've gone without sex before, Erin," he says, and

I turn my head and see him smiling at me. "Just not lately."

"Serious question . . . when was the last time you went this long?" I ask him, thinking it's an innocent question.

"When I found out that my only girlfriend was cheating on me," he says, and I stop breathing when he says the next part, "with my father."

"I'm so sorry," I say, looking up at him. "I didn't know."

"Yeah, it isn't something that someone would advertise," he says, his voice low but steady. "Can you imagine the headlines? Hollywood prince's girlfriend cheating on him with senior."

"That's horrible," I answer, and my heart breaks for him. I wonder if it's the girl with him in all his early pictures.

"No," he says, shaking his head. "That isn't the horrible part. The horrible part was that we were together for over two years, and my parents were paying her for info about me." I try to swallow, the back of my neck tingling, and I feel suddenly ill. "It was after I kicked them out and started running things on my own. Seems they still wanted to have a hand in the cookie jar. So one night while I was in this club, she came up to me, and well, we had a lot of things in common." His laugh is almost like a sneer. "Fast forward two years, and we are practically living together."

"You don't have to," I say to him, hoping he stops talking, but he doesn't.

"I came home three days early from shooting and went straight to her apartment. Let's just say I'm the one who got the surprise."

"Do you think your mother knew?" I ask, hoping to Christ she didn't, and that what little she did for her son, she somehow stuck up for him.

"I have no idea. I didn't stick around to ask questions. I went home, packed her shit, and had it delivered to her. I changed my number, my credit cards, and sold the house. Changed everything for the second time in my life, and I started over at the beginning."

"I can't even imagine," I tell him the truth.

"It is what it is." He shrugs, and I get it now, the no-strings sex and the different women. He doesn't trust anyone.

"I still can't imagine," I say. He doesn't answer me, and I don't bother saying another word. I sit here looking at the fire, imagining the heartbreak that he went through. My eyes get heavy, and I force them open, but then I tell myself I'll just rest for a minute. My head rests on his shoulder one minute, and then the next, I hear his heartbeat echo under me. I try to open my eyes, but I give myself just a minute longer. I feel myself being carried, and I slowly open my eyes to find my cheek against Carter's sweater. "I can walk," I tell him, my voice coming out in a whisper.

"It's okay," he says, his voice is soft also. "This is the most action I've had in a week. Let me have this moment."

"If you try to cop a feel, I'm going to kick you in

your junk," I mumble to him, and then I'm placed so softly on the bed I don't even feel it.

"Good night, Erin," he says softly right next to my ear, and I can smell him all over me. I open my eyes, and now I see why I smell him all around me. His arms are beside my body as he leans in just a touch, and if I moved my head a bit more my lips would touch his. My eyes watch as his eyes roam over my face. His face gets closer and closer, and I hold my breath. I stop breathing and close my eyes, waiting for it. And then just like that, he's gone. "See you tomorrow," he says softly, closing the door behind him. I hear him go back outside, and I go to the shades and look at him sitting down in front of the couch. His head hangs down as he probably thinks of what a mistake it would have been to actually kiss me. I watch him get up and put out the fire. I undress, slip into my pjs, and slide into bed the same time I hear his door close softly. I look over at my closed door when my phone beeps. I reach out and grab it, thinking it must be work, but I'm surprised it's Carter.

Carter: Thank you for tonight.

Four words and I should just leave it, but I don't. Instead, I answer back.

Me: Thank you for carrying me to bed.

I place the phone next to me, wondering if he will answer me when I hear a soft knock on the door. "Come in," I say. He opens the door and stands there in his shorts that hang way too low on his hips. His chest is bare as he walks into the room.

"I can't sleep now," he says, scratching his head. "Do

you want to watch a movie?" I should tell him no; I should tell him that I'm tired and I'm going to bed. I know I should tell him all that, but my mouth, however, doesn't.

"Sure," I say, and even I want to shake my head at myself. This is not good. None of this is good. I'm here to do a job. "Do you want to watch it in here?" *No, no, no, no,* the good part of my brain chants. That isn't going to help anything.

He grabs the remote and turns on the television as he climbs into bed with me. Grabbing the pillows, he props himself up, leaning against the headboard. "Is there anything you want to watch?"

"*The Notebook*," I say, trying to hide my smile while I lie down and put my head on the pillow, angling it to see the television.

He groans. "Not *The Notebook. Anything but *The Notebook*."

I try to hide my giggle. "*The Lake House.*"

"Oh my God, I'm going to die," he says, and I finally let go of the laugh I've been holding in. "Jesus, I thought you were being serious," he says, finally laughing and turning on all the movies. We settle on an action movie, and halfway in, I'm asleep. And when I finally roll over in the morning, the bed is empty, but I can see the indent of his head is still on the pillow.

Rolling to my side, I see it's almost ten o'clock, and I smell coffee. I go to the bathroom to wash my face and brush my teeth and then head to the kitchen. He is sitting at the counter with his phone in one hand and the coffee in the other. "Good morning, sleepyhead," he says. His bedhead is still sticking up, and I have the sudden urge to run my hands through it.

"Morning," I say and look over at the box sitting on the counter next to him. "What is that?" I ask, going to grab my own cup of coffee.

"This," he says, "is for you."

"Me?" I ask in shock, getting my milk out and then finally taking a sip of the coffee. "Who sent me this?" I ask, going around the counter and seeing the box with no name on it.

"I didn't know if you had anything for the hike, so I had them send you stuff," he says, and I take the top of the box off to see that he had black Billy boots sent to me with the name HUNTER across the front. A black down-filled vest sits on the bottom of it. "We should eat and then head out."

"Oh, I'm excited now. I don't think I've ever had Billy boots before," I tell him, and he gets up. Going to the fridge, he grabs some bread, and I see the shocked look on his face. "I grew up in Florida."

"Did it never rain in Florida?" he asks, laughing, and I just shrug.

"My mother doesn't do anything that would require rubber boots," I tell him. "She would definitely frown on going on a hike, but she would probably look amazing wearing Billy boots. She looks good in everything."

"Then I guess you get that from your mom," he says, and I just look at him as he changes the subject. "I'm making grilled cheese with bacon."

"Do you need my help?" I ask him, and he just shakes his head. I sit at the counter and watch him. I watch his back, and I swear I think it's even sexier than his abs. He butters the bread and takes the bacon we had from last night. He grabs some cheese but not the sliced cheddar. He grabs special cheese like Gruyère, emmental, and provolone. When he puts the plate in front of me, I cannot hold back my groan after I take a bite. "It's so good," I say, and he just nods.

"It's my specialty," he says, laughing and sitting next to me as he eats three for my one. "I'm going to get ready." Putting his plate in the dishwasher, he walks to his room. "Twenty minutes, Erin. No need for any froufrou!" he yells before he slams his door.

I get up, putting my own plate away and grabbing my box. "No froufrou, my ass," I say to myself, walking into my own room and seeing my bed and the indent from his head still on the pillow. "This is a bad idea," I tell myself out loud, but my mouth just smiles as I walk into the bathroom and totally start with the froufrou but just lightly.

Fifteen

Carter

WHEN I WOKE UP next to her for the second day in a row, I had a slight panic attack. Especially since I was spooning her. I got out of the bad so fast I'm surprised she didn't wake up. I looked over at her, and I had to stop and just take her in. Her long hair fanned across her pillow, and her lips were slightly parted. Getting home last night after that crazy scene I filmed, I was gutted and destroyed. It was another heavy scene. This one with me holding my missing daughter's pjs and crying into it. I just wanted to be alone, and then when I was finally alone, I wanted her there with me. Not just any-one. I wanted her, her smile, her eye roll, her sassy, just fucking her. That is what I wanted, and when I found her outside shivering, it was a no-brainer to grab her in my arms even though I knew I shouldn't have. I knew the risk I was taking by letting my guard down, but with her, it's just natural and comes easy. She doesn't want anything from me. In fact, she wants the opposite from me.

Now here I am, getting ready to take her hiking, and I'm so nervous I feel sick. I run my hands through my hair and grab my blue vest, shrugging it on over my thick knitted wool sweater. I had to wear a thermal shirt under it so it didn't itch. My green khakis make the look. I grab my glasses and beanie, then open my door and am surprised when I see her door already open. I walk into living room and spot her looking at her watch, and I take her in. Fuck, I wasn't lying before when I said she looked good in everything. I never thought Billy boots could be sexy, but fuck, if she would just wear those, it would be sexy as fuck.

Leaning against the couch with her head down, looking at her phone, she is wearing black leggings with her black Billy boots. A long thick gray long-sleeved hooded sweater, the black vest on, and a black baseball hat on her head holding her ponytail in the back. I clear my throat. "Twenty-four minutes." She smiles and then puts on her glasses. "Did you put on froufrou?" It takes everything in me not to claim her mouth and kiss the sass right out of her. Instead, I shake my head almost like I'm erasing the image from my head. But nothing I'm doing is making it go away.

If only she knew I jerked off for a good five minutes before I could even think of getting dressed. I smirk at her. "Okay, let's go." I walk to the fridge and grab two bottles of water and chuck them into the black backpack that was dropped off with the boots this morning. Getting into the truck, I plug in the address and make my way there. Pulling into the parking lot, I see only two other cars in the parking lot. "Ready?"

"As ready as I'll ever be," she says and then grabs some lip gloss from her pocket and puts it on. Now all I can think about is whether she tastes like strawberries or cherries. She gets out, and I follow suit, and we walk to a guy waiting at the entrance of the trail.

He is wearing all beige with a brown hat. "Welcome, welcome," he says in a booming voice.

"Hi, I'm Erin," she says with a smile on her face and her hand extended.

"I'm Jim." He smiles at her, grabbing her hand, then looks at me, extending his hand to me. "Right on time."

"Yes, sir," I tell him, and he just nods his head.

"We are going to start at the bottom and work our way up," he says, pointing with his finger. "Then work our way down."

"That looks high," she says quietly, leaning into me. I chuckle and grab her hand. She intertwines her fingers in mine, and we just walk. It's natural, and she doesn't make a big deal that we are holding hands. We start walking up the hill with Jim in front of us, the sound of water running to the right of us. I walk closer to the edge, and she stops, letting go of my hand. "No."

"Don't be scared with me," I tell her softly, looking at her. I want to walk to her and grab her face in my hands, but instead, I just hold my hand out to her. "I promise to keep you safe." She doesn't look sure but walks to me and fits her hand again in mine. We stand and see that the water is coming down in a stream. The mountains on the other side are full of trees. Mostly pine trees.

She releases my hand. "Go walk ahead so I can take a picture." I walk ahead of her and look back over my shoulder, giving her my smirk.

"Put the caption "ain't no mountain high enough,"" I joke, and she looks at me. "What? Too cheesy?" I take my phone out of my pocket and do a selfie of the mountain in the back. "I'm posting mine," I tell her, and she just shrugs and then takes another picture of the mountain. "Where are you posting that?"

She looks over and smiles. "I'm going to send it to my mom and then post it on my Instagram." I walk to her.

"Why haven't you accepted my follow request?" I ask her, and the wind blows her ponytail. When some hairs get stuck in her lip gloss, she gently pulls them out.

"Because my Instagram page is boring. It's just travel pictures," she tells me.

"And?" I ask her, cocking my hip. "Accept my follow request, Erin," I tell her, grabbing her hand and continuing our walk up the trail. We get to a higher spot, and the water sounds like it's raging. I walk to the edge and see that it goes down steep on both sides. It looks like a sand slope, but it's rock all the way down to the swift blue-green stream. We continue walking, just looking around as we get higher and higher and the waterfall gets louder and louder.

The chirping birds and the sound of rushing water

fill the air as we walk deep into the trees and then down some wooden stairs. She holds my hand tighter as we make our way down. The stairs become steep at one point and then the mist of water hits us. "Oh my God, we're going to die," she whispers. "I want to go back." She walks back up the hill.

"I promise you that it will be okay," I tell her, and she looks up at me. We walk across the rocks to where a fence keeps you in on one side. We finally come to the square enclosure that sits in the middle with a wooden bench on one side, and just past the pine trees is the most beautiful, peaceful sight I've ever seen. A waterfall cascading down between two rocky mountains.

"Oh, my." She holds my hands by the tips now as she walks to the edge of the railing. "This is so pretty," she says and takes out her phone and snaps a picture. Then she steps back. "Carter, get in there. I'm going to snap a couple of shots," she says, and then she takes them. I motion with my hand for her to come to me. She does, and I put my hand around her shoulder and grab my phone from my pocket.

"Smile," I tell her, taking a selfie of ourselves with the waterfall in the back. The sun is peeking just onto the water, making it even more breathtaking. "Jim," I call him, and he comes forward. "Will you take a picture of us?" I hand him my phone, and he steps back. "Big smile. This is going on my Instagram," I tell her, and she just shakes her head, wrapping her arms around my waist. It's a pose that I've had with a million other women, but with her touch on me, I get goose bumps.

"One more," I say as I lean my head closer to hers. "Take off your glasses." He snaps a couple more pictures, and then finally, I turn and sit down on the bench.

She comes over to me, putting her hand on my shoulder. "You did good." She smiles, and I want to lean up and cup her cheek in my hand and just kiss her. Doesn't even have to be a deep kiss. It doesn't have to be a kiss to last for hours; it just has to be a peck. Just her lips on mine, and I would die a happy man. But I don't do any of that. I chicken out and then get up, and instead, I hold her hand all the way to the bottom of the mountain, and then we make our way home.

"Today was so good," she says, leaning her head back against the seat. "I can't believe we were out hiking for six hours."

"It's my favorite thing to do," I tell her as I drive back to the house. "I usually go by myself. It's my solitude."

She looks over at me. "I didn't know. I wouldn't have come if I had known." Her voice goes soft, and again, she puts my needs in front of the fact that she loved what she just did.

"I wanted you there," I say, and she looks out the window, sitting back, and when we pull up to the house, it's dark outside, but the lights are lit up outside, and when she gets out of the car, I grab her hand and walk to the back of the house to enter. She walks up the steps and stops when she gets to the top of the stairs. The fireplace is already lit, and there is a chef in the kitchen. "I thought after all that walking outside, it would be great to come home and have dinner already done."

"You did this?" she asks, looking around. "I was just thinking that I would have to cook since you took me to the waterfall." She smiles. "But this is so much better."

"Well, I'm happy I can assist you," I tell her, and then she turns around.

"I'm going to shower. I'll be back." I watch her walk away, and then I walk to my own room, getting into the shower where, for the second time in one day, I take care of myself. Walking to the kitchen, I hear her laughter and then see she is sitting at the counter talking on the phone.

"I swear, Mom, I have Billy boots," she says and then laughs again. "The next time I come home, I'm buying you a pair, and we are going to go hiking," she says and then she looks up at me. "Okay, Mom, I have to go." She looks at me. "Love you, too." Disconnecting the phone, she puts it on the counter. "Hey."

I walk into the kitchen, looking for the chef. "Where is Riccardo?" I ask her, looking around for him.

"He finished what he had to do, and I told him he could go. I'll serve us." She gets up, going to the stove and grabbing the oven mitt to take the food out. "He made steak with a peppercorn sauce, some sweet potato mash, regular mash, and steamed asparagus."

"It smells amazing," I tell her, and my stomach makes a loud rumbling noise. "Where do you want to eat?"

"The dining room," she says, and I nod at her. "Do you want one or two pieces of steak? He left us six pieces."

"One for now," I tell her, grabbing everything I can

to set up the table. "If someone would have told me I would be staying in on a Saturday night, I would have asked if they were drunk," I tell her, "but I have to admit it's not that bad."

"I can't remember the last time I actually got super dressed up to go out." She picks up the plates that she just finished making.

"There is a red carpet event next Saturday," I tell her, thinking about it. "It's this whole fundraiser."

"How red carpet?" she asks me, and I look at her confused as she cuts into her steak. "Like red carpet Oscars or red carpet MTV awards?"

"I have to wear a tux, so I have no idea what category that falls into," I tell her and cut my own piece of steak.

"Do you hate it?" She continues to ask me questions.

"I don't hate it," I tell her honestly, "but I don't love it either."

"We did the red carpet for the Tyler Beckett movie, and I swear it was the longest day of my life."

"I was there," I inform her. "I did arrive a touch late."

"I know you were there," she says, shaking her head. "You arrived with Roxanne and left with that reporter."

I shrug my shoulders. "I have no idea."

"How do you not know who you slept with and who you didn't?" she asks me, and I just shrug.

"It's just sex," I tell her the truth. "Have you never had just sex?"

"No," she answers, chewing. "I've had sex with five people my whole life, and with all of them, we were in a relationship."

"Five people?" I ask in shock. "But you're super-hot."

She laughs. "Well, thank you, I guess."

"I bet you can have any guy you want." The thought of that makes me sick, and I drop my fork. It clangs on the plates, making her jump.

"Again, thank you, but I'm good," she says, getting up and bringing her plate to the sink. She puts away the leftovers while I start the dishwasher.

"I'm going to bed," I tell her. "All that fresh air has left me exhausted, plus we have a call time of six a.m."

She nods her head, and I walk away from her. I force myself not to text her or go to her room, and I thought staying celibate for this contract assignment would be the hardest thing I've ever had to do. It turns out, walking away from her has to be the hardest thing I've ever done in my life.

Sixteen

Erin

THE ALARM RINGING MAKES me roll over and grab my phone, stretching along the way. I turn off the alarm and go back under the covers with the phone, taking one more minute to just chill. A knock on the door makes me open my eyes again. "Come in," I say loudly, and the door handle turns, and the door opens. I see him bending down to pick up the coffee cup that he put on the floor.

"Morning," he says and comes into the room, handing me a coffee cup.

"Morning," I say, sitting up in bed and reaching out to take the cup from him. I bring it to my nose and inhale it. There is nothing like the smell of coffee in the morning. "You are up early." I take a sip of the coffee and watch him.

"I woke up at three and couldn't go back to sleep,"

he says. "So I went to the gym downstairs and did my workout." I shake my head, thinking about him all sweaty. "The car is going to be here in thirty minutes," he tells me, and I just nod. He walks out, closing the door behind him with a click.

I get out of the bed and walk to the bathroom, starting the shower. I quickly shower and then apply just a touch of mascara when I get out. I curl the bottom of my hair, grab the coffee, and walk into the closet. I take the white and black checkered skirt and pull it over my hips. Grabbing the long-sleeved red silk shirt, I slip it over my head and tuck it in. The bell-shaped cuffs make it look fancy. I slip on the black sky-high Louboutins that will have my feet burning by tonight, but I can never say no to putting them on my feet, regardless of the pain and suffering I'll endure. I'm such a shoe addict. Grabbing my bag and jacket, I walk out to tell him, "I'm ready."

He looks me up and down, wearing a scowl on his face, and he just turns and walks down the stairs. I follow him and notice that there isn't a car outside. "Where's Benny?" I ask of the driver who has been driving us to and from the set.

"I told him to take the weekend off," he says, getting in the car, and I follow him to get into the front. I don't say anything while he takes us to the set. He parks in the parking lot, and I grab my bag, leaving my jacket since it's not that cold out. I walk beside him, and he nods to the crew members while we walk to his trailer. He opens the door to his trailer and waits for me to walk in before stepping inside. "Seriously, I'm going to go online and order you some functioning jeans. What size are you? This isn't Hollywood. We are on a grimy movie set, and you act as if we are walking down Rodeo Drive on a shopping spree," he says, his voice gruff and angry. I look over at him when I set my purse down and take a seat.

"What the hell is your problem?" I ask him.

"Nothing. It's just that you come to a movie set dressed like that after I've told you already that it's not appropriate." He motions with his hands up and down.

"Like what?" I ask, looking down at my outfit. "I'm fully covered. The skirt even covers my knees. For Christ's sake, would you prefer more *Handmaid's Tale* and less handmaid?"

"It's not what it's covering," he says, leaning back against the counter and crossing his arms over his chest. "It's that it hugs everything."

"I don't even know what that means," I tell him, throwing up my hands.

"Of course, you don't because you're oblivious," he says, and now I shake my head.

"I'm in no mood for whatever this is," I tell him, waving back and forth between us while grabbing my purse. "You honestly woke up on the wrong side of the bed this morning." Walking past him and out of the trailer, I head to the craft service and sit at one of the plastic tables after I get another cup of coffee. I obviously need more caffeine. My nerves are on the edge of the freaking Grand Canyon. There is nothing wrong with my outfit, and now I'm a bit pissed that I have to work on the plastic table, but I grab my computer and fire it up to see what the world of social media has in store for us today. I go on his Instagram, and I gasp out in shock. He put up two pictures from yesterday. The one selfie he took with the stupid caption "ain't no mountain high enough" has two million likes and seven thousand comments. Then the other one he put on is the picture he took of us. I laugh at the caption, which is "I don't know who is prettier." I also see that there are three million likes and eight thousand comments, and I scroll through them to finally see that mostly everyone agrees he is the prettier one. No surprise there.

"All by yourself?" I hear a soft voice and look up at Jennifer. I smile at her and move my purse.

"Not for long, if you want to join me," I tell her, and she sits down with her tray of a bagel and juice. "How are you?"

"I'm tired, but I'm just taking it all in," she says, sitting down.

"Is this the first time for you to work on a movie set?" I ask, and she nods.

"I'm an intern," she says, and I smile and lean in.

"Me, too," I whisper, and a shocked look comes over her face.

She leans in also and whispers, "No way."

"Yes," I tell her. "I'm at the end of my internship."

She picks up her juice and brings it to her mouth. "But you just have that thing . . ." she starts to say, and I look at her. "That whole 'I know what I'm doing' vibe."

I laugh at her. "Then I have you fooled because I

have no idea what I'm doing," I tell her. "I was a month away from finishing my internship when they gave me the biggest opportunity that was clearly something I couldn't say no to."

"Really?" she says, taking a bite of her bagel. "I mean, that's good, right?"

"It's great. It's just the biggest job that I've ever had, and if I fail, I lose the chance to work in New York, which is a dream for me." I take a sip of my coffee. "If I can keep Carter's image intact for the next thirty days, then I might actually succeed."

"Oh, dear," she says, and I just look at her.

"Yeah, so far, so good. But I have to change or rebrand him, so to speak. So as long as he keeps it zipped up, we're all winning. He gets a brand-new image, and I get my dream job," I tell her. I don't know why it bothers me to say that, but it just does. It's been over a week since he's been in the paper with a girl, and people have already moved on to the next scandal.

"Well, I think you are winning," she says. Before I can tell her all the ways I'm failing and that we're barely one-quarter of the way through my sentence, I look up to see Ivan coming toward her. "Good morning, Ivan."

"Good morning, ladies," he says, smiling at us, then turns to Jennifer. "We are thirty minutes out. Can you get Carter?"

She nods and throws down her bagel, and I get up. "That's okay. I'm going back there now," I say even though I wasn't. She needs to eat. "I'll tell him."

"Are you sure?" Jennifer asks, and I just smile at her.

"Yes. You finish your breakfast, and I'll get him," I say, grabbing my bag. "Thanks for chatting with me," I tell her and then look at Ivan. "See you soon."

Walking out of the stage, I go to the trailer. Right before I'm about to turn the knob, I hear him groaning. But not just groaning . . . the moaning kind of groaning. I step back from the door, my heart hammering in my chest. The moaning continues and then finally, he roars softly, and my hand goes to my stomach. I stand here in shock, the sounds of my heart now echoing in my ears. I turn around and walk away with my head going a million directions at once. The images of yesterday replays—his smile, his smirk. I look everywhere, not sure where to go. Everyone seems to be moving on fast forward around me. I spot Jennifer, and she looks at me strange. "Are you okay?"

"Um, yeah," I say, not sure of my words, not sure of anything. The tears sting my eyes, and I blink them away furiously. "Sorry, I just got lightheaded there for a minute. I guess I need to eat something," I tell her and then walk away from her, going into the stage and looking for a bathroom. I follow the signs and finally walk inside the stall, and I close the door behind me. My bag slips out of my hands, falling to the floor with a clunk. I lean against the door and look up at the ceiling, the tears trying to be released, but I don't let it. I blink them away, and I count to ten but that doesn't work either, so I count to twenty. Finally, I shake my head and put my hands in front of my face.

"He's not worth your tears," I whisper to myself,

unsure if the tears are because he's having sex with some random woman or because he's sabotaging not only his career but mine, too. I pick up my bag and step out, going to the sink, and see my face in the mirror. My nose looks a little red, but my eyes are the same. I keep blinking while I wash my hands and then walk out of the bathroom and crash into him. Carter. I know it's him from his smell and his hands on my shoulders.

"There you are. Jennifer told me you weren't feeling well," he asks with worry in his voice, and I move my shoulder to get his hands off me.

I don't bother looking up at him. "I'm fine." I walk around him and walk away.

"No, you aren't," he says. I just continue walking, but he speeds up to my side. "You look pale like you are going to faint."

"I'm fine," I say and look everywhere but at him. "You are needed on the set," I tell him while I stand here looking at the exit sign over the door.

"Erin." He says my name, and I want to look at him and tell him to fuck off. But I don't have the chance to because Jennifer approaches us out of breath.

"Ivan is waiting on set for you," she says and then looks at both of us. "I have the cart over there."

"Why don't you go to the trailer and lie down?" he suggests, and then I snap my head around and look at him. I expected him to look guilty, to keep from looking me in the eye, but no, his face is the same. Like he wasn't just fucking someone in there.

"No, thank you," I tell him, then turn to Jennifer.

"We should get to the set." I walk ahead of her, and she follows me, looking over her shoulder to make sure that Carter is following her. I get into the back of the golf cart. Thankfully, my back is to Carter so I don't have to look at him. Jennifer drives us to the stage, and I wait for him to get off the cart before I get up, but he waits for me there.

He reaches out his hand to put it on my shoulder. "Are you sure you're okay?" I move out of his touch, his arm falling to his side.

"I'm fine." One word, brokenhearted. I quit, another two words that run through my mind. You're fired, the final two words that I know I'll hear from Sylvia. I sit in the chair and watch him act in the scene, but the only thing running through my head is who did he sleep with. I look around at the crew and wonder which one it was. I get up softly and quietly and walk out of the stage door. I grab a golf cart and make my way over to where the car is. I pick up my phone and try to get an Uber here, but it's almost as if I'm cursed because nothing shows up.

"What are you doing out here?" I turn to see Mandy walking into the parking lot, holding a cigarette in one hand and a coffee in the other.

"I'm trying to get an Uber," I tell her, and she laughs.

"Good luck," she says, lighting her cigarette and taking a long inhale. "I tried to get one for an hour yesterday."

"Shit, what about cabs?" I ask her, trying to pull up one when I see a town car come into the parking lot. He stops at the front door, and I see that it's someone who stars in the movie. I know I should know, but right now, I don't know anything.

Benny's behind the wheel, so I know that luck is on my side. "Benny," I say loudly, and he turns around and smiles.

"Thank you for your help," I tell Mandy and then walk to Benny.

"I know that you just finished, but I can't get a cab or an Uber," I tell him. I'm about to get on my knees and beg him to just take me away from here.

"Of course, Miss Erin." He opens the back door, and I get in, and for the first time today, I breathe a sigh of relief. "Back to the house?" he asks, and I want to say no. I want to tell him to take me to the airport.

"Yes. Please," I say and look out the window as he makes his way back to the house. My phone buzzes in my bag, but I don't even bother taking it out. It buzzes and then stops and then buzzes again. When we pull up in front of the house, I get out and thank Benny over and over again. I walk to the door and put in the code. Walking up the stairs and straight to my room, I sit on the unmade bed, kick off my shoes, and think about my next move. I get up and enter the closet and bring my luggage out and start to put the dirty clothes away. I'm halfway from the closet with my clothes in my hand when I hear the front door slam shut and his boots stomping up the stairs. I get ready for whatever is going to come, but I'm not ready for it. Nothing can make me ready for him.

His eyes find mine and then go to the bag on my bed and then to the clothes in my hand. He stops to catch his breath. His eyes look almost crazy and ravished, and then they turn to anger. "What the fuck are you doing?" he roars, and I just stand here looking at him, shaking my head.

Seventeen

Carter

"WHERE IS ERIN?" I ask Jennifer once I walk off the set. I searched for her when she walked out of her bedroom this morning, and when I saw her, I swear I about came in my pants. She was the reason I woke up at three a.m. with my cock so hard it only took me three pulls before I came.

"I have no idea," she says and walks away. I walk out of the stage and go to a golf cart. I get to the stage and see Mandy coming back in.

"Have you seen Erin?" I ask her, hoping to fuck someone has seen her. She looked so pale before I almost shut down today and took her home.

"Yeah, she just left," she says, bringing her coffee to her lips. "I think Benny took her home. She was looking for an Uber." I run past her and get into the car, peeling out of the lot. Jesus, she is all alone and sick. What if she faints, and no one is there? I try not to think of anything bad. But I can't help it. What if she's throwing up and needs someone to hold her hair back? I make it to the house in record time, leaving the keys in the car. Walking into the house, I slam the door behind me. When I get to her room, the fear of her being sick leaves me when I see her standing there with her luggage on the bed and her clothes in her hand.

"What the fuck are you doing?" I roar, the fear leaving my body as the fury comes in. I know I should go in softly, that I shouldn't just pounce, but I just had a heart attack, thinking of her sick and alone, and she's here packing her fucking bags. "What the fuck is going on?"

"I'm . . ." she says as she dumps her clothes in the luggage, and I have the need to jump over the bed and take them out. "I'm organizing my stuff," she says, but she doesn't make eye contact. In fact, she hasn't looked at me once today.

"Look at me." I stop moving in the middle of her room, and she stops with her back to me. "Turn around and look at me." I see her hand on her head and then she turns around, and I see her eyes for the first time. She looks like she has been crying or that she wants to cry. I walk to her and stop when she takes a step back. "What's wrong?"

"Nothing," she says, and I know she is lying. I can feel it, and I can see it.

"You're lying," I say to her, and she looks at me. "Tell me." It's almost a whisper.

She puts her hand in front of her, holding both hands together when she looks at me. "I heard you," she says, and I look at her, confused. "I heard you," she says, her voice going a touch louder, and I hear anger in it.

"Okay," I say, putting my hands on my hips. "You heard me."

"Yeah," she says, and her softness is gone and in its place is her sass. "I heard you."

"So you've said already," I say. "Heard me what?"

"Oh, cut the bullshit," she says, putting one hand on her hip that she cocks. "Don't make me spell it out for you."

I put my hands up. "You are going to have to because I have no fucking clue what you're talking about."

She rolls her eyes at me. "You don't have to lie or pretend."

"I swear on my life I have no fucking idea what you're talking about, so just spit it out."

"Fine!" she yells, and I see the pain in her eyes. "I heard you having sex in your trailer earlier," she says, and I take a step back like she slapped me across the face. She looks at me as I stare at her with my mouth hanging open. "Yeah, that's right. I heard you. So you can stop with the stupid act."

"You heard me having sex in my trailer," I say softly, my stomach sinking. "You heard me having sex in my trailer." I repeat the words to make sure that is what she said.

"Yes," she says. "I came to get you, and I heard you, okay?"

"What did you hear?" I ask, and now my knees feel weak. I look around and think to myself why aren't there any chairs around that I could sit on.

"I didn't hear anything. I heard you moan and groan," she says. "Does it even matter?"

"It matters to me because I wasn't in my trailer having sex with anyone," I tell her softly, and she looks at me. "I swear, I was in my trailer, but I wasn't with anyone."

"I heard you," she says, and I laugh, relief suddenly washing over me.

"You heard me masturbating," I tell her. "Jesus." I rub my face.

"What?" she whispers.

"You left the trailer, and all I could see in my head was your perfect ass walking away, and well," I tell her, looking down and then up again, "Erin, you have no fucking idea the power you have over the male species. No fucking idea."

"What?" she repeats now, not moving from where she is.

"You really don't see it," I tell her. Looking her up and down, I feel my cock suddenly wake again. "You ooze sex, Erin. You don't have to even try, it's just there. I mean, after the hike, I had to take a shower and jerk off to a picture of you bending over wearing fucking Billy boots."

She shakes her head, and I walk to her now. She doesn't move back. She stands there, and I put my hands on her hips. With her heels off, she is shorter than me, her head reaching me just above my lips. "I woke up this morning at three," I say in a whisper, and she looks up at me. My hands move on their own, and one cups her cheek. "Ever since we've met, you've been in my dreams." My thumb rubs her cheek back and forth. "Tell me that this isn't one sided." I hold my breath, waiting for her to answer. "Tell me that it's not just in my head." My other hand moves up to her cheek.

Her hands grab my wrists, and I think she is going to pull my hands from her face. "It's not just you," she says in a whisper, and I take the biggest leap of faith I've ever taken when I lean my head down and crush my lips to hers. She moans out and leans into me. Her hands leave my wrists and move down my arms to my shoulders.

My hands go to her hips again, and I pull her flush to me. When she feels my cock, she gasps, and I take that time to slide my tongue into her mouth. And it's like heaven, or like I've died and gone to heaven . . . but either way, I'm there, and she's right there with me. Her tongue slides with mine, going around in a circle round and round. My hands finally find the reason for my outburst this morning when they reach her ass. Her plump, perfect ass and I swear it feels so much better in both my hands. Her hands move from my shoulders to my hair, and the kiss that started off soft now gets more frantic. My hands go from her ass to her back up to her neck, and I bury my hands in her hair. Tugging her back a bit, I pull her lips from mine and bend to devour her neck. I kiss her softly at first and then stick my tongue out right before I suck in. She presses her pussy into me. My cock wants to come out and play, and her hands go to my shirt. She unbuttons the buttons and finally loses patience and just rips it apart. Seeing me with my shirt open down the middle, she leans in and kisses a pec softly, and I step away from her. My willpower is stronger than I ever thought possible. But the look of hurt across her face brings me to a standstill.

"What are you doing?" she asks, reaching out with both hands to grab my shirt and bring me back.

"If I don't stop right now, I'm going to throw you on that bed," I tell her the truth, looking at her and seeing her smirking, "and as much fun as that sounds, I don't want to rush you into it."

"You aren't rushing me into anything, Carter," she tells me, getting on her tippy toes now to kiss my neck the same way I kissed hers but biting me harder than I bit her.

"Erin," I groan when she nips my lower jaw. "You have no idea how little self-control I have right now."

"I really wish you wouldn't be cautious right now," she whispers, and I step away from her hands because if she touches me even a little, all bets will be off, and I don't want her to regret anything with us.

"I'm doing this more for you than for me," I tell her, and she looks at me, tilting her head sideways. "If I take you now, you will wake up with nothing but regret." She doesn't say anything; she just looks down and then her eyes come up. "You will regret that we just rushed into things," I say softly. "I don't want to be a regret." I shake my head. "Not with you."

She walks to me, and I'm mesmerized by her. "Carter." She puts her hand up to cup my cheek.

"Don't," I tell her. "If you touch me, it's all going to be over." I grab her hands in mine and hold them in front of us. "This is the first thing that I've had that isn't because of who I am." I swallow down. "It's the first thing that is just mine that no one knows about or has smeared across the headlines."

"That's because you haven't given them anything to talk about," she says, looking down at my hands holding her wrists. "This thing." Her voice trails off, then she smiles. "This is the last thing I thought would happen." She shakes her head. "Especially not with you." I roll my eyes. "But you're right, if we jumped into bed now, I would wake up with regret." I try not to let her words hurt me. "Not regret that it's you, but regret that we didn't talk about it." My mouth suddenly goes dry. "Our jobs would be in jeopardy; my reputation would be scrutinized."

"My contract would be null and void," I say. "They will throw it out."

"Exactly," she says.

"So how about this thing with us stays with us?" I tell her. "Everything between us is only ours."

She smiles. "Keep talking."

"This thing between us is stronger than both of us. But I won't put you in the position that will make you a target. So it's going to be a secret. This thing between us is ours and only ours until we both decide to share it."

"What if we never decide?" she asks.

"Then the press is going to think I've become a monk." I laugh, thinking of the possible headlines. She shakes my hands free from her wrists.

"So we can go slow," she says, putting her hands on my chest, and my heart speeds up, her body coming closer to mine. "We can take our time. We can just be us," she whispers. "Not the asshole you but the kind you. The one who got scared I was sick and alone, the one who wants to hold my hand and hike. The one who wants to come home and cook for me." She gets on her tippy toes. "The one who I'd love nothing more than to get naked with." She kisses the under part of my jaw, and my cock springs into action, thinking about her naked.

I grab her hands away from me and lean in to lightly kiss her lips. "I'm going to the bathroom again," I tell her. "I promise I won't be masturbating to memories and the feel of my hands on your gorgeous ass. I'm surprised I still have any skin left, but I have to walk away from you for a few minutes."

"I can help you with that big problem you have, you know," she purrs seductively, her hands moving down to my apparent bulge.

"No." I jump back as if her hands are on fire. "I *need* you to leave me alone." I turn and walk away but then turn back and go to her, grabbing her face in my hands. "But when I come back, I want you out of that skirt so we can make out on your bed." I kiss her softly, then turn to leave. "Give me five minutes." She shrugs, and I turn and run out of the room. "Could be less," I tell her, shutting the bathroom door behind me. I walk to the vanity and put my hands on it and hang my head. "Holy shit, I just made out with Erin," I say softly. "This is a really bad idea." I look at myself in the mirror. "What are you doing?" Then I finally answer myself. "I'm doing what I want for me. And hopefully for her." I stop looking at myself and go back to her room. Gone is the suitcase from the bed. "Erin?" I yell, and she comes around from her closet wearing gray pants and a loose long-sleeved black shirt with her hair tied up on top of her head.

"That was fast." She looks from my face and then down at my junk. "I mean, it's been three minutes. I guess it's all about what you do in that time?" She tries to hide her smile.

"I didn't do anything," I tell her, going straight to her and grabbing her the way I want to grab her. Picking her up, I now have her legs wrapped around my waist. I groan into her mouth when she wraps her arms around my neck, and my hand roams up her back and I feel her skin.

"What are you wearing?" I ask her while my hand roams her back, and I feel just skin, no bra no nothing.

"It's called a keyhole back," she says, trying to get to my lips. "Carter," she huffs out, but I'm still roaming with my hand.

"You aren't wearing a bra?" I'm shocked. I didn't think I could get hard that fast.

She smirks at me. "I'm just making sure if you want to hit second base, there is nothing stopping you."

"Oh my God, I love when you talk sports," I say, walking back to the bed. "Although I'm more of a hockey guy than a baseball guy." I turn to sit on the bed, and it's the wrong thing for me to do because she sits right on my cock, and I swear I feel the heat from her pussy.

"Good to know," she says, grinding down on my cock. "Just so you know, I don't give a shit as long as it ends with your mouth on my body." She pushes me down now and takes over the kiss. Her knees are on either side of my hips, and I feel her nipples through her shirt. Fuck. Her tongue comes into my mouth again, and my brain shuts off. Everything except her hands and the feel of her in my arms. She sits up now on me while I lie on my back. Her arms cross in front of her, and she peels her shirt over her head. "Skin on skin," she says, and it's almost like it happens in slow motion. I see her stomach first, slowly rolling to her ribs, and then her perfect fucking tits. And I'm not lying when I say they are perfect. Perfect, round, and perk. My hands fly up to cup her in my hands. And I was wrong before. It's not perfect; it's way past that. I watch her close her eyes when I roll her perfect pink nipples between my thumb and forefinger. She grinds down harder on me. "Carter," she says, and I sit up now, taking one into my mouth and slowly rolling it with my tongue. Her hips slowly move, and I watch her struggle.

"Do you want me to make you come?" I ask her, going to the other nipple, and she throws her head back. "Tell me." She puts her hands on my shoulders, and with me going from nipple to nipple, she comes over my covered cock.

"That's never happened," she says. "Like that fast," she whispers, trying to look down, no doubt in shyness.

"Eyes on me," I tell her, and she looks up and tries to cover herself. "It's me and you always. You never have to be shy about taking what you want or asking for it," I tell her, and she smiles shyly. "I mean, if I'm doing anything right, you won't have to ask for anything because I'll know all the things to do to make you come."

"I'm not a virgin," she says, "but I've never been that into it that I've dry humped someone."

"Well, score one for me," I say. Her stomach lets out a huge growl, and she collapses on my chest laughing. "I swear if you give me a cigarette, this will just complete the picture."

I kiss her shoulder as she laughs in my arms, and I've never been this content with not getting my happy ending. I kiss her neck, and again, her stomach rumbles. "How about you get dressed, and we can go eat something and then go make out near the fire?"

"That sounds like a really good plan," she tells me and slowly gets off me. She grabs her shirt, pulls it over her head, and then turns and I finally see what a keyhole is.

"Why don't you go, and I'll catch up with you," I tell her, and she looks at me worried. And I look down at my cock. "Don't touch me, or I swear it's going to go off."

She puts her hand to her mouth and comes to kiss me, and I just shake my head. I wait for her to leave the room before getting up and taking care of my cock, again.

Eighteen

Erin

"We have to get up," I say between kisses I don't want to stop giving or receiving. "We are only going to have twenty minutes to get ready," I say, tilting my head the other way to deepen the kiss.

We just spent the night together. Not naked together. Well, not all the way naked together. We still have our bottoms on. After making out hot and heavy on the outside couch, we came in and watched a movie in my bed. Well, the movie watched us in the end. My shirt came off, his shirt came off, and I can say that he is that hard everywhere. "I need to shower," he says, and I laugh, kissing his neck.

"I can help take care of that," I tell him, and he slides away from me, getting out of my bed wearing nothing but his white Calvin boxers. His cock is perfectly placed, showing that he really does pack below the belt.

"You keep those pretty little hands away from this"—he points at his cock—"until it's time," he says, walking out and not closing the door.

"We could shower together and save water," I say loudly and hear him groan and slam the door. Getting up, I jump into my own shower. I grab my black lace thong with matching bra and walk into my closet. I hear him knock on the door, and I laugh. "You've already seen me pretty much naked. No need to knock."

He comes in, and I hear him moaning from the back. "What are you wearing?" he asks me, and I turn around.

"Um, this is a bra." I point up. "And we call these panties," I joke with him, and he just stares at me. I grab my black skirt off the hanger and slide into it, then grab the black long-sleeved silk shirt with white polka dots. I slide it over my head and tie the sash at my neck into a bow and tuck in the shirt, zipping my skirt up.

"Your jeans are arriving today," he says to me, and I look over at him, sliding my foot into my black shoes I wore yesterday. "You literally look like one of those porn stars whose only role in the movie is to bend over their boss's desk," he says, coming to me and grabbing my hips in his hands. I look back up at him, and he kisses me softly, but it only takes two seconds to turn hungry.

"How long are we on set today?" I ask between kisses.

"It's a long one. I think until nine," he says, and I grab another pair of shoes to toss into my bag and then walk out with him. We walk side by side, but his hand slowly grabs mine, and we link our fingers together.

"Are you driving us there?" I ask him. and he just nods his head. "Obviously, this thing is between us . . ." I am not sure what I'm asking, but I don't want to be known as the intern to fall for his charm.

"So you're saying I can't walk up to you and kiss you in public?" he asks, walking down the steps to the front door.

"Yes, that's what I'm saying," I tell him, and I'm not sure I'm okay with it. "I mean, I'm still working, and it's not."

He turns around. "We decided to be private," he says. "I don't want everyone to be in our business." He kisses me. "But once we get in the trailer, all bets are off."

"Oh, dear," I say, walking out of the house and getting in the car. And I have to say he is on his best behavior all day. Well, until we get into the trailer, and then all bets are off. He's on me the minute he shuts the door and locks it, and we don't come up for air until a knock lets us know it's time. I stay in the trailer when he goes to shoot and prepare my game plan for when we get back home on Friday. He is filming the next two weeks in L.A.. I'm just about to send Sylvia a message when the phone rings, showing me it's her.

"Erin." Sylvia's voice booms out of the speakerphone. "We are in a meeting with everyone. Ryan is here also."

"Hey, everyone," I say, hearing my voice echo as everyone says hello.

"We were talking about your amazing progress." Ryan's voice comes in. "The buzz about the movie is trending on Twitter."

I give myself a high-five. "We would like for you to stick with him for the remainder of the filming. Those behind-the-scenes pictures are gold."

"Sure," I say. "I was going to reach out to Jessica Beckett, and see if she would do a special on him."

"She's not in the game anymore," Sylvia says.

"She's still one of the best," I tell them. "She may be out of the game, but if an article is coming with her name attached to it, people pay attention."

"I agree," Ryan says. "Her piece about her and Tyler is still the most read article online."

"If you can make it happen, that would be perfect. The Grammys also asked him to be present."

"Okay," I say, grabbing the calendar. "It's next Tuesday."

"Yeah, it is a last-minute add, but with the buzz lately, they want him there," Sylvia says.

"That's good," I say and wait for the rest.

"We signed you up to be his plus one." And there it is. "We are going to send you the company card for you to go shopping for a dress."

I want to groan internally because I don't think I can do the whole red carpet thing. "I can take some shots of him before he heads out, and he can send me some from the event."

"Erin, he's been out of the tabloids for almost ten days," Sylvia says. "Ten days. Do you know what that is for him?" I roll my eyes. "I'm not going to lie. I thought he'd only last two days, max three. The thing is, we want him in the tabs, just not because he's sleeping his way through Hollywood."

"He's actually been really perfect," I say and then roll my lips. *Shut up*, I tell myself. "He has been to the set and then back to the house."

"And that is exactly what we want," Ryan says. "He can't fuck this up."

"I'll try my best," I tell them. They chat for a couple more minutes, telling me about some things that they are doing. I take some notes and then disconnect. I take a deep breath and then the door opens, and he comes in and comes straight for the table.

"Hey." He slips in next to me, kissing me on my lips, and it feels like he's always done it. "What are you doing?"

"I just got off the phone with Sylvia. You are going to the Grammys on Tuesday," I tell him, and he looks at me.

"Jeff called me ten minutes ago to tell me the good news," he says sarcastically, getting up to get his bottle of water. "I'm going to call my girl for a dress."

I turn to look at him. "A dress?"

"Well, since you're coming with me, you have to have a dress, and well . . ." he says, trailing off.

"And well what?" I glare at him. "And I need to be all that standing next to you?" I shake my head and roll my eyes. "Thanks, but I have it covered."

"I didn't mean it like that," he says, sitting next to me and taking me in his arms on the side. "I just meant I don't want you to spend crazy money to buy a dress for one day. Besides, they usually give me stuff for free."

"Again," I tell him, wiping my gloss off his lips, "thanks, but I got it covered." He leans in and slowly kisses me. His tongue playing with mine. His kisses leave me breathless; they leave me wanting more, they leave me feeling something I have never felt before, and I'm not sure I'm ready for this. The knock on the door makes him pull away from my lips but not let go of me. "Carter, did you lock the door?"

"No," he says when the door opens, and I fly to the side, lying on the seat pretending to grab something.

"Got it," I say, getting up and seeing it's Jennifer.

"Sorry, but Ivan wants to reshoot the last scene," she says, looking at him and then me. "You look better today."

"Yeah, I feel better. Must have been something I ate," I tell her and look over at Carter and see that he has my gloss all over his face. My eyes go big, and he must sense it and covers his mouth.

"I'll be right there," he says, getting up and walking to the bathroom. Jennifer nods her head and walks out of the trailer. He comes out of the bathroom seconds later. "My bad."

I shake my head. "No more kissing at work." Now it's his turn to glare. "You can save all that for when we get home."

"Let's table this discussion for tonight," he says and turns to walk out of the trailer. "I should be done after this." I nod at him and blow him a kiss, smirking. I finish my notes and email Jessica. I then also call my connection at my favorite fashion house, telling them of my predicament. They say they have the perfect dress for me.

I'm putting my computer away when he returns, announcing he's done. Getting into the car and heading home, we're quiet, and I just look out at the darkness. "We left in the dark, and we come back in the dark."

"Yeah, well, tomorrow we have to be on set at noon, so that should be good," he tells me, putting the car in park and getting out. I unlock the door and step in, stopping in the doorway when I see rose petals everywhere.

"What's this?" I ask. We don't have to turn on the lights because on each step leading upstairs are three tall vases filled with candles to light the way. I look back at him, and he just smirks. I walk up the steps, and when I come to the landing, I stop at the trail of roses all the way to the bedroom lit up with different sized glass vases with floating candles. I walk to the bedroom, smiling and looking behind my shoulder at him. When I finally get to the bedroom, I see rose petals everywhere. There isn't a spot without them. The floor is covered in them, and candles are all over the room.

"I can't exactly take you out to a romantic dinner," he says, coming to me, "but I can bring the romance to you." My hand drops my purse, and I jump into his arms, wrapping my arms around his neck while his arms circle my waist.

"This is the most romantic thing I've ever seen," I whisper to him and lean back to see his face. I lean forward and kiss him, and I'm expecting for it to be a kiss, but just like before, it feels like the first time. It always feels like the first time. He walks me to the bed, his mouth still on mine when he throws me down on it, and I land with a laugh as rose petals fly everywhere.

"I really want to just get on you, but I kind of stink," he says, laughing. "I had this all planned out, but I didn't think that when we got hot, I would need a shower."

I throw my head back and burst out laughing. "You really have never done this before."

He shakes his head. "Never." I'm expecting him to stop there, but he doesn't. "Never needed to." I am about to roll my eyes. "Never wanted to."

"Nice save," I tell him.

"I need five minutes," he tells me, walking out of the room backward. "Maybe even three." He turns and rushes to his room.

"Carter!" I yell, and he turns to look at me. "Don't take care of yourself." He stares at me, the words sinking in.

"Ninety seconds," he says, and I rush off the bed and get ready myself. I run to the closet and go through my bra and panties and give up. I didn't bring anything really sexy. I strip out of the clothes and step into the shower. Showering in record time, I don't even think I rinsed off properly. I dry off, throwing the towel to the side. Peeking in the room, I see he isn't there yet, so I go over to the bed and slide under the covers. I try to position myself as sexy as possible, but my heart is hammering so hard. I even look down to see if you can see it coming out of my chest. I don't have time to think because he comes back into the room wearing black boxers. His hair is still wet, and I watch him walk to the side of the bed and slip in next to me. He reaches out for me, and I go to him. "Hi," he whispers, lying on the pillow next to me. His hand goes to my hip, and his eyes get big when he just feels skin. His hand roams up and down on my side, and he feels that I'm naked. He throws the cover off me, and here I am. All naked and all for him. "You aren't wearing anything."

"I figured it would be a waste of time." His eyes roam down my body and then roam back up to my face. "You seem to be overdressed, Mr. Johnson." I try to be as sexy as I can, and I don't know if it's working or not, but his body crushes mine as he takes my lips.

NINETEEN

Carter

I HAVE NEVER WANTED to impress a woman so much in my whole life. When my hands roamed up and down her side and felt nothing but skin, I about came in my boxers. I swung the covers off her, and holy shit, nothing could have prepared me for this. I've seen naked women before, but she looks like an angel. It's cheesy to say, but it's true. With the candles giving the whole room a glow and her long hair flowing around her. Her perfect tits, perky with hard nipples I want to lean down and take in my mouth, but I don't. My eyes roam down her flat stomach to the middle of her legs. With one leg cocked up, she blocks what I want to see the most. I push her lightly on her back, and I finally see her pussy. My finger goes out to rub the little landing patch, my eyes mesmerized as I watch my finger just rub over her. "Carter." She whispers my name, and I feel the earth stop. Like literally stop turning. It's almost as if it's this moment for the rest of my life.

"You are so beautiful," I tell her, and my heart jackhammers in my chest. I lean in and kiss her lips, breathing her in, taking her in. I never ever want to forget this moment right here.

She raises her hand to cup my face, softly, gently, and I turn my face to plant a kiss on her palm. "I don't know what I did to deserve you, but I'm not going to jinx it by asking anyone." I bend down to place my lips on hers, kissing her softly, then trail my nose down the side of her jaw. "You are too good to be true," I say, kissing her jaw. Trailing it with my tongue down to her neck, I place open-mouthed kisses all the way to the middle of her chest. I feel her heart pound under my lips. I move over to her nipple, taking one into my mouth, and her back arches as she moans. Her hands go to my head, and I swear she could come just by playing with her nipples. I lean over and go to the other one. My fingers pinch the nipple I just left right before I roll it. I bite one nipple at the same time as I pinch the other, and her back arches, and her legs close as if she's trying to get friction. I laugh silently, thinking that she's going to take off with one touch. I move over her, then kiss her lips, sliding my tongue into her mouth. Her tongue fights with me, the kiss needy, urgent, everything. Her hands go from my head to my chest. She lays her palms open on my chest and lifts to me when I try to break the kiss. She finally lets me go and falls back on the pillow. I move down, kissing her stomach, and her breath hitches, sucking it in. I kiss her hips then move down. I look up at her when I place my first kiss on her landing strip, and she gets up on her elbows to watch me. Her legs opening to let me in.

"Are you sure about this?" I ask her, knowing once I start, I don't think I can stop. She just nods, and I dip my head and kiss right above her clit. My tongue comes out and licks up once, and I swear I've never tasted anything sweeter in my life. I lick up again, and this time, her head falls back, and her hips arch up. My tongue comes out and twirls around her clit, and she moans. I lick again and then suck on her clit and kiss it. I continue licking up and down, ignoring her clit, and every time I go higher, her panting almost stops like she's waiting for it. I get down and spread her legs wider. Her arms give out, and she falls back on the pillow. I attack her pussy with a vengeance, the softness gone, and her hips move up and down as she tries to ride my face. I feel her fingers come down to her pussy, and she puts one finger on her clit and slowly make circles. I remove her finger.

"I don't share my toys," I tell her, and I rub two fingers up and down her wet slit and enter her slowly. Her pussy is so fucking tight my fingers feel like they are strangled. Her hands go to her tits. I bite her pink clit and then lick it with my tongue while my fingers fuck her. Her fingers roll her nipples.

"It's too much," she says breathlessly. "It feels like you are everywhere." Her head rolls to the side, and her eyes close.

"I want to see your eyes when you come," I tell her.

I know she's close. Her pussy is tighter and wetter, and her hips are frantic now. "Every time you come, your eyes are always on me," I say as my tongue flicks her clit. Her moans fill the room as my other hand opens her lips, and I see her swollen clit. I know she'll come with a couple more touches. I know this because she keeps chanting it.

"I'm going to come," she says once, then again. "Carter," she says, and I bite down on her clit. She lets go, coming all over my fingers and soaking me. I don't stop fucking her with my fingers until her hips slow their pace. Her eyes on me the whole time. They went from hot to soft, and I gave her that. Me.

"Baby," she says softly. My heart skips, and she sits up now. My fingers slip out of her, and she about drags me up so her mouth crashes on mine. Her tongue is all over me as she tastes herself on me. She gets on her knees, and I raise also.

"It's time," she says when she lets my lips go, and I'm in a haze of sorts. That is what her kisses do to me; that is what she does to me. I'm on my knees in the middle of the bed, and so is she. She kisses my neck and then slowly trails the kisses to my chest. I watch her; my cock harder than stone right now. She trails her tongue down my chest to my abs, and I move her hair away from her face. Her hands go to my hips. She sits back on her feet with her face directly in front of my cock. I hold my breath, not chancing a peep and stopping her. Her delicate fingers go into the top of the waistband, and she slowly peels it over my cock, and I spring free.

I watch her face in the yellow glow of the candle. She's the most beautiful woman I've ever met, inside and out. Her hand comes over my cock, and I watch it. She grabs it in her hand, and I watch as she tries to wrap her hand around it, but she doesn't close it. "I guess the rumors were true," she jokes with a glint in her eye, and I don't even have a chance to answer her because she leans in and licks the head of my cock. It's my turn to have my head fall back. I open my eyes slowly, taking her in on her hands and knees. My cock in her mouth and her hand working my shaft.

"Fuck," I hiss as she goes to the side of my cock and sucks in, then does the other side. She finally licks up the front, then takes my cock into her mouth. She takes as much as she can, then lets go again, licking the side all the way down to the root and then trails down to suck one of my balls in her mouth while her hand moves up and down my cock. She does the other ball, and then she comes back up and twirls her tongue around the tip of my cock, taking me deeper this time. I hiss when her hot mouth leaves me as she plays with me, licking me up and then taking me in her mouth. I watch her play with me. Giving her this, I let her lead, but when she gets on all fours with her ass in the air, I snap. One of my hands goes into her long hair, fisting it and pulling it back, and she just smiles up at me as she takes my cock into her mouth. My hips start to move, and she slowly takes a little bit more each time. I fuck her face slowly, trying to keep my pace, but then she wiggles her ass in the air and closes her eyes, and I know she's playing with herself.

"Are you playing with my pussy?" I ask her, speeding up a little bit more. Her eyes close, but I pull her hair a bit more, and she opens them, groaning. "You rubbing that little pink clit of mine?" I ask her, and her ass moves a touch more. My balls start to get tight, and I know I'm going to come, but I don't want this to end. I hold out as long as I can and then hiss, "I'm coming." I let her hair go so she can let go of my cock, but she doesn't. She just takes me faster, her hand moving faster, her mouth sucking harder, and I come in her mouth. Her eyes remain on mine as she comes for the second time tonight. When my cock slips out of her mouth, she gets up on her knees, and her pussy is glistening. My cock twitches the minute I see it.

"Come here," I tell her, and she comes to me on her knees. I grab the back of her neck and pull her to me. I'm not sure what else to say. There are so many things I want to say, but I don't know if I should. I don't know if it's too soon, so I do the safest thing. I kiss her, hoping that everything in my head is put out into that kiss.

With her hands on me, my heart starts to calm because her touching keeps me at peace. "I need to go wash up," she says, getting off the bed and walking to the bathroom. I watch her walk there, then get up and take off my boxers. "Do you think we need to blow out the candles?" she asks loudly.

"The guy said that they will burn out on their own, but if you want, I can go and make sure that they don't burn down the house," I tell her, and she comes back in wearing a T-shirt, and I groan. "Why are you dressed?"

I ask her, almost pouting.

"I'm going to help you blow out the candles," she tells me, then turns to walk backward. "I'd put the boxers back on if I was you. Never know when hot wax will fall on your penis or if you get too close to the flame . . . wouldn't want to risk getting burned." I stop in my tracks and look down, thinking it could possibly happen. I grab my boxers, slipping them on, and walk out. She is halfway done when I see her bend over in the shirt that's not enough to cover her ass, and I suddenly want to fall to my knees and bury my face in her again. My cock tells me this is a fantastic idea, but when she turns and sees me, she says, "No."

"I wasn't going to do anything," I say, putting my hands up in the air in surrender. "I was going to help you with the *blowing* duties."

"Lies," she says, standing up straight. "I need food," she says, coming to me and hugging me, getting on her tippy toes to whisper in my ear. "Then if you want, we can bring the can of whipped cream to bed with us."

I grab her around the waist, picking her up, and go to the fridge. Grabbing the whipped cream, I carry her back to the room. "This will fill you up," I tell her, throwing her on the bed, and it takes us about five minutes to be out of whipped cream. We both fight over the can as she tops my cock with it, and I finally get her to come by just sucking her snow-capped tits.

We lie breathless in the bed, our limbs intertwined. I look over from my side of the bed to see her head on her own pillow, her hair fanned out all around her. Her chest is rising and falling as she tries to get her breathing under control. "I never thought I'd be satisfied without having sex," I tell her, and she turns to look at me.

Her hand goes to her stomach, draping over it. "I'm guessing you haven't ever done this without having sex after?"

I turn to her now, my hand reaching out and bringing her closer to me. "I don't want our first time to be with fear that we will get caught. I don't want the first time that I finally have you to be with us looking over our shoulder to make sure no one saw us." Her arm now goes around me, coming closer to me, her leg now hitching over my hip. "So from now until the end of my contract, I'm going to learn every single part of your body," I tell her, kissing her neck. "I'm going to claim every single part of you." Her head falls back, giving me more access. "I'm going to know how to make you come every day." Her breath hitches. "With my tongue." I trace her neck with my tongue. "With my fingers." My hand slides between us, and with her leg over my hip giving me easy access, I slowly slip my finger in, and she moans. "I take it you agree to this?" I slowly move my thumb over her clit, and she moans louder. "I'll take that as a yes," I tell her, rolling her to her back and then making her come with my fingers and then my mouth.

TWENTY

Erin

"ARE YOU DONE PACKING?" Carter asks me from the doorway, and I just shake my head.

"All that is yours?" I point at two piles of clothes on the edge of the bed. After the night I came home to the house full of candles and roses, he's been sleeping in my room. He didn't even try to sleep in his. It was now our room, and his stuff was mixed with mine. The top of my vanity had his razor and deodorant, and it was natural. We spent the days shooting, and then we spent the nights just with each other. If it was him cooking or me cooking, we did it together. I was well acquainted with his body at his point. I could tell you about the little birthmark he had on his chest. My mouth was *very* familiar with his whole body, and my body craved his touch more and more.

"We leave right after the shooting, so I have to put

the bags in the car before we go," he tells me, and I don't know why I'm suddenly sad to go. I mean, I know why. Tonight when I go to bed it won't be in his arms, but instead, I'll be in my bed by myself. "We have that fundraiser tomorrow night," he reminds me, and I nod my head. I am not sure I can say anything without my voice shaking. "Did you get a dress for the Grammys?"

"I did," I tell him of the silver dress waiting for me at home along with the dress I'm wearing tomorrow night. I close the suitcase and zip it closed, and he grabs his clothes and brings them in his room to throw them in his own. I wheel my suitcase to the hallway. "I'm ready," I tell him, and he comes out, and I just sigh.

"Are those the jeans I bought?" he asks me of the jeans I'm wearing. It seems that me in skirts that were tight and constricted my legs being open were not okay. So I came home to a box full of jeans. I mean, about thirty pair of jeans. I do a turn in them, showing him that the jeans are so tight you see my full ass. "Are you wearing a sweater with those?" he asks, and I just shake my head. "Okay, so I need to order you sweaters." I grab his phone from him. "You can't walk around like that."

"What is wrong with these?" I ask him, and he puts his head back and groans.

"Baby, you see everything," he says, and I just shrug.

"I could have worn my skirt, but you didn't want me to," I tell him and walk in front of him. I take a last look around and then walk out with him following. I close the door behind him, and he makes his way to the truck and puts our things in the back.

"One scene today, right?" I ask him, getting in, and he just answers with a nod.

When we walk into the stage, everyone is in a bright mood, knowing that they will be bringing the set back home to L.A.. "Finally done with this town," Mandy says while she puts on his makeup. "It's barbaric here. No Uber, no cabs." She shakes her head. "I need pollution in my life."

"I love it here," Carter says. When Mandy stops working on his face, he opens one eye. "What?"

"No hustle and bustle," she says. "No clubs or bars." She continues, then leans in and whispers, "No pussy." He shakes his head. "I have to say you cost me a hundred bucks."

"Why's that?" he asks, and I look up from my phone to listen.

"You've been here for two weeks, and you haven't had sex with one person," she says. "Not one." And my stomach drops, just thinking about it.

"I'm a changed man," he says. "Reformed."

Mandy throws her head back and laughs. "A leopard doesn't change his spots," she says and continues to work on him.

"Maybe I'm done with the meaningless sex," he tells her. "Maybe I'm done with the bullshit of people only wanting to be with me because of who I am." Mandy looks at me, and I just shrug at her. "People can change," he says, and Mandy just drops the subject. I don't let it get to me, but somehow, it does. I follow him to stage three, and I do my posts on Facebook, Twitter, and of course, my favorite Instagram. This time, I snap a shot of the stage with the caption.

"Last shot in Montana. Big Sky Country . . . you were beautiful."

I then go and accept Carter's follow request. My heart's a little heavy knowing that things are going to change when we leave, but I don't dwell on it. I post a picture of Ivan and Carter looking at a shot on camera. We say goodbye to everyone and walk out right when the sun is high in the sky. "It's going to be a good day," he says, getting in the car. We make our way back to the airstrip. Once there, he hands the keys to the guy who loads our bags on the plane. He waits for me to walk in front of him. "I want those jeans when you're done with them," he tells me when I sit down in front of him with the table between us.

"Why?" I ask him, buckling my seat belt.

"So I can burn them," he says, glaring at me, and I just throw back my head and laugh.

"Nope, you bought them," I remind him and then stop when the girl comes over and smiles at us.

"Welcome aboard," she says and then her smile goes a little bit bigger when she looks at Carter. "My name is Keira, and I'll be here to assist you with *anything* you need." I roll my eyes when she emphasizes the word anything.

"I'll have a water, and she will have . . ." Carter says, looking at me. "She will have the same." He doesn't even look at her. She nods and walks away. "Do you have a cat?"

"What?" I ask him and feel the plane moving. I raise the shades beside me to see that we are going down the runway.

"Prepare for takeoff," the captain says into the speaker.

"So do you have a cat?" he asks me again.

"No," I answer him. "Why?"

"Do you have a dog?" he asks, and I sit back in the chair as the plane takes off.

"No," I tell him. "This is so weird."

"What about plants?" he asks me, and I just shake my head. "Perfect. No reason for you to go home tonight." I look at him. "Spend the weekend with me at the beach."

"Carter," I say and stop talking when Keira comes back with a silver tray and two glasses of water. "Thank you," he says to her, grabbing his water and drinking it.

"Lunch will be served in ten minutes," she says and turns away.

"I have all my stuff to wash and put away, plus I have to grab the dress for tomorrow," I tell him.

"I have a washer and a dryer." He smiles at me. "We can pick up your dress on the way to my house."

"I don't know," I answer honestly. "What if someone catches us? I mean, in Montana it was normal for us to go home together, but it's another story if I spend the weekend with you there. There's a lot riding on your celibacy, you know."

"You're worried the paps are going to catch us?" he asks me, and I'm annoyed that he knows me. "I'll drive the car into the garage, and no one will see us.

We can spend the time in bed." He winks at me, and I stop talking when Keira comes back and places a tray of food in the middle of the table. Then she places a plate in front of me and then totally leans over to place it in front of Carter. She turns her face so she is face-to-face with him, and I literally have to lean away as her ass is now in my face. I unclip my seat belt, which makes Carter's eyes go big. "I'm sorry, you are making me really uncomfortable." She looks shocked. "If you could please step away."

"I'm sorry, I didn't mean anything by it," she says and turns back to run to the back of the plane.

"Were you going to hit her?" he asks, leaning in.

"Are you insane? I was going to go to the bathroom and throw up," I answer him, and he laughs loudly. "That's funny?"

"You're jealous," he says, and I shake my head, ignoring him, but when he continues laughing, I just glare at him. "Come sit with me," he says softly. We grab the plates from the table and go eat on the couch. By the time we land, I think we've only seen Keira twice more. Getting into the car, he heads to my condo where he parks, then walks in with me. "This is nice," he says of the apartment, and I nod at him. "Go pack a bag." I walk into my bedroom, and he follows me, sitting on the bed while I grab some things for his house. I grab the two dresses hanging in the covered black bag and the matching shoes that go with them.

"If at any time it isn't safe, I want you to promise me you will bring me back home," I tell him from the closet.

"Baby, I promise you that no one will know," he tells me, and when I walk to him, he opens his legs, so I stand in the middle of them and his hands go to my ass. "I promise you."

"Fine, it's just it's both our asses on the line," I say, turning around and locking up my house once again.

"Are you almost done?" I hear him knock on the closed door. Spending the night in the house with him last night was amazing. We sat outside listening to the waves while we talked about everything. We then came inside and fell asleep in each other's arms, and I woke with his face between my legs. Of course, once fully awake, I returned the favor. "Erin." I look up while I tie the strap around my ankle.

I get up from the bed and take one last look at myself in the mirror. I snuck off to the guest room to get ready. My hair is loose, and I added some waves. My makeup is natural with just some black mascara. The light gold eyeshadow with a light bronze liner make my blue eyes pop. The light pink on my lips makes them just a touch more plump. I take a deep breath and smooth down the sleeveless gown. And what a gown it is. It has a rounded neck and rose gold sequins that goes to a burgundy ombre at the bottom. It fits me like a glove with the bottom going just a touch looser so it sashays as I walk.

I grab my little rose gold satin clutch and walk to the door. Opening it, I stand here looking at him. He is wearing a black on black tux, making his green blue eyes stand out even more. His hair is combed back, but what I really like the most is the scruff on his face. I smile, reaching out and touching it. "This is going to give me razor burn," I joke with him, but his eyes are bright and blue, and he doesn't say anything. "What's the matter?"

"You," he says softly. "You take my breath away each time." He comes close to me and puts his hand on my hip. He does that often to bring me closer to him. "I don't want to leave this house." He comes down, rubbing his nose on my cheek. "I don't want anything to touch what we have."

"Carter," I whisper, "we have to go."

"Will you be by my side the whole night?" he asks me. "I don't know how to explain it, but when you're there, I feel like everything is aligned. My heart beats normally, I can breathe, and I can smile, and it not hurt."

"I'll be right by your side the whole night," I tell him. "I promise." Holding out my hand, he grabs it and links our fingers together. We walk down the stairs, and I stop. "We should take a picture."

He grabs his phone and raises his hand, taking one of the both of us smiling at the camera. "Okay, now one for us," he says and puts his arm around my waist, bringing me to him. One of my hands go around his waist and the other one goes on his chest. Our smiles match, and you can tell from the picture that we are together. "That one is for me," he says as he looks at the picture. I watch him walk ahead of me and call his name. He turns and looks over his shoulder where he winks with his smirk on full display. "I want you to caption that with "his eye is always on the prize.""

I shake my head and let out a huge laugh. "Will do," I say, walking out, and I'm surprised that he has a driver waiting for us. "I thought you were driving us?"

"No, it's easier to have a driver so we can just walk out and leave," he says, getting into the car, and I try not to worry. "Baby, we are going to leave out the back once we do the obligatory amount of time. I already have everything planned."

"Do you?" I ask, surprised.

"I do." He comes over and kisses me, and I let him. My heartbeat races a touch, and I could kiss him forever. I slowly look away just in case he sees something in my eyes. I think I'm falling in love with him, but I'm just not sure he's with me. And the worst thing in the world has to be when you love someone and they don't feel the same way. Talk about awkward.

"Just so we stick to the story. I'm your PR rep," I tell him, and he shakes his head.

"Baby, no one is even going to know what that is," he says, and I shake my head.

"Also mention how great filming is going and how excited you are," I tell him. "And under no circumstances do you mention dating."

"I wasn't that bad before," he tells me. The car comes to a stop, and I roll my eyes. "Watch it, those will get stuck in the sockets." I burst out laughing, and he continues, "Okay, but I'm not that bad now."

"Just think about the questions before you answer," I tell him, and he leans in quickly and kisses me. "Lip gloss," I say to him right before he gets out of the car. It's a red carpet, so even though no fans are here, reporters are lined up behind a barricade. He walks the carpet, and the paps yell his name. He stands in front of the white backdrop with one hand in his pocket. Smiling and smirking, he plays the part of Carter Johnson.

"Carter, look here!" they all yell at different times. "Carter." I walk slowly behind him, trying to stay in the shadows and not get my picture taken. I keep my head down, but someone spots me. "Carter, is that your girlfriend?" My head snaps up, and I smile, shaking my head. He looks over at me and waits for me with his hand held out to me.

"I'm his PR rep," I tell them and go to stand next to him. "See those three reporters at the end? You have to stop and give them interviews," I tell him, and he just looks at me, and I can see the mischief in his eyes as he leans forward.

"I've changed my mind," he whispers, and I look at him confused. "Tonight when we get home," he whispers, almost so close, his head so close to my ear, it makes my heart beat faster and faster, "I'm finally taking what's mine." I try to swallow. "And that's you." He turns to smile at the cameras and then looks back at me. "Nod if you agree to this."

I stand here in the middle of the red carpet all dressed

up with cameras probably taking our pictures, and the only thing I can think of is him, of going home with him, so I just look at him and nod. He looks at me, his shoulders going back and his smirk coming out. He turns, and I watch him walk away. The whole time, I try to catch my breath, try to make it return to normal because after that exchange, I know I'm way past the point of no return.

Twenty-One

Carter

I WALK DOWN THE red carpet, trying to talk my cock down. The minute I told her that I would claim her tonight, my cock went on full alert. Luckily, my jacket covers it, and the sight of the girl reporter with her heavy fucking eyeshadow and fake eyelashes makes him go into hiding. "Hey, Carter," she says, and although she's interviewed me a shitload of times, I can't for the life of me remember her name.

"Hi, Ella." I hear Erin next to me, and I turn and look at her. When she opened the door and I saw her, it took everything in me not to cancel tonight. I wanted to drag her back to my bed and bury myself in her. "Carter will answer three questions." She looks at me, and then I look back at the reporter.

"Carter, the feedback about filming has been amazing," she says into the microphone she has in front of her mouth. "How did you prepare for this role?"

"There really wasn't much I could do," I answer her. "I just put myself into the shoes of every parent out there who is missing a child. I can't imagine," I say, and I can't. If someone took my child away from me, I wouldn't be able to sleep until I had them back in my arms.

"From the gossip in the magazines, you've been on the down low lately, solely focused on work," she says almost with a purr. "Are the rumors true? Did you find the special lady?"

"He isn't answering any personal questions tonight, Ella," Erin says. "Thanks for the questions." She pushes me to the next person.

"Come on, Erin, you know I had to ask," she says, and I see Erin in action.

"Oh, I know you had to ask," she says, "but you have to know that I wasn't going to let it slide. I gave you a shot at three questions." She shrugs. "Not my fault you didn't want to play by the rules." She smiles at her. "Have a great night."

"Bitch." I hear Ella mumble, but Erin looks unaffected by it. I walk to the next reporter who is a guy, and he sticks to a script. We finally make it through the last reporter and walk inside the event. I look around and see all the A list people around. I've been to a million of these, and I'm already ready to leave.

"Carter." I hear from the side and look over to see Beverly and Aaron, the ones throwing this event tonight. He walks to me, extending his hand to shake mine. "So happy you could make it."

"It's for a great cause," I say, looking around all these people here dishing out money to make themselves feel just a touch better. A waiter comes over with a silver tray filled with glasses of champagne. I look over to see where Erin is, and I spot her over at the bar. It's no surprise she's already caught someone's attention.

"If you two will excuse me, I see a couple of items I should bid on," I mention, referring to the silent auction. I walk up to the sheets and place stupid bids and then walk toward the bar, and I hear the man talking.

"Yeah, I thought so with a beautiful smile like yours I know I would never forget," he says, and again, Erin smiles politely.

"Are you done hitting on the woman?" I say louder than I want to, and the man turns around, shaking his head with a smile.

"Carter," he says my name and extends his hand to shake mine.

"Tom." I shake his hand, the hatred stewing in my stomach. Two years ago, we starred in a movie together. I thought it went well, but I obviously was the only one who thought that. During the press tour, he threw me under the bus over and over again, spewing shit out of his mouth. Something about me sleeping with his girlfriend pissing him off. I didn't even know he had a girlfriend. "Have you met my girl Erin?"

"His PR rep," she adds in and extends her own hand. "I work for Hillcrest."

"Nice to meet you, Erin." He shakes her hand, then

looks back at me. "Carter, it's always fun." We both watch him walk away.

"That guy is such an asshole," I say, watching him walk away. "You said you wouldn't leave my side."

"I went to get water," she tells me, holding up her crystal glass with a slice of lemon in it. "See."

"Are you ready to go?" I ask her, and she looks at me shocked.

"What are you talking about? We just got here," she points out, but I'm about done with all this stuffiness.

"I came," I say. "I walked the red carpet." I look around. "I did three interviews." I put my hands in my pockets. "I said hello to the guy throwing the event, so he knows I was here. I bid on five items." I look back at her. "Now I want to go home and see what my girl is wearing—or not wearing—under her dress."

She smirks at me, coming closer. "I can answer that now." With my eyes on hers, she leans in and whispers, "Nothing." Whatever control I had is gone. I grab the glass of water she has in her hands and place it on the bar, thanking the bartender.

"Either you walk out with me . . ." I decide to give her an option. I, myself, am good with either one. "And fast, or I carry you over my shoulder."

She doesn't have to answer; she just nods. "Lead the way," she says. We walk out of the event through the back door, and the car is waiting there just as I planned. I watch her ass when she gets in the car. I follow, and the guy closes the door behind me. I suddenly reach out and yank her into my lap

"Are you really wearing nothing under that dress?" I ask and thrust up as she turns in my lap. She grabs the dress, bringing it up to her knees so she can straddle me.

"There is nothing stopping you from being buried in me except this dress," she says, smiling. "Well, that and your pants and boxers." She leans in and kisses my lips, and it always feels like the first time. Every time I touch her, it feels like I've been touching her my whole life. We kiss all the way to the house. Her hips continue to rotate on my lap until the car comes to a stop. I look out the window and see that we have pulled up in front of my house.

When I hear the driver close his door, I pick her up and make sure she's covered before he opens the door. I step out first and hold out my hand for her, and she grabs it. We thank the driver and walk down the steps to the front door. We get in the house, and she stands in front of me, moving her hair to the side.

"Can you unzip me?" she asks me, and I grab the zipper, and the sound of it going down echoes in the room. I lean in and kiss her neck. She steps out of the dress and stands before me completely naked. Except for the sky-high satin heels. Her hair sways side to side opposite to her hips. She walks up my stairs and finally looks at me. "Are you coming, or do I start coming without you?"

I don't walk to her, I run to her, and by the time she reaches the top step, I am right behind her with my hands on her hips. I turn her around and back her into the wall, her hands on my chest as I bend and kiss her.

Nothing about this kiss is soft—it's want and it's need. My hands go to her tits as she arches her back toward me. Her hands push my jacket from my shoulders, and it slips off my arms, landing on the floor. I grab her and walk her to my room, our hands frantic for each other. She rips a couple of buttons off the shirt with her impatience, and right before we get to the room, I push her against the wall and fall to my knees in front of her. I throw one leg over my shoulder and bury my face in her pussy. She's already wet, and the minute my tongue licks her, she goes off. With one hand above her head and the other buried in my hair, she rides my face until she comes a second time. I drop her leg to the floor, and then I'm done.

Picking her up, I urge her to wrap her legs around me, and I walk her to the bed. I get on the bed with our lips never unlocking. Her hands roam down the front, and she unclips my belt and then the button. I let go of her and step off the bed. Kicking off my shoes, I slip out of my pants and finally my boxers. She gets on her elbows, watching me with her feet on the bed locked at the knee. I open the side drawer, taking out the box of condoms I put in there yesterday. This whole time we've been together, I made sure there were never condoms in the house to ensure I didn't rush things. My own personal safety net, if you will. But now the gloves are off.

I grab one and get on the bed with her. She opens her legs for me to settle between. I rip the corner of the wrapper and take the condom out, tossing the package behind me. I grab my cock in my hand and start to put the condom on me, but she sits up, moving the condom, and licks the precum off my cock. She moves her mouth down, and I let her do it until it's too much. I push her back and put the condom on in record time. I grab my cock, and my eyes find hers while I rub it through her slit and position myself at her entrance. Our eyes never leave each other as I slowly fill her with my cock. Her pussy grabs me like a vise, my pounding heart almost drowning out the sound of her heavy breathing. It's only then I realize I'm not breathing. I'm holding my breath and start breathing again when I'm completely in her. I look down to where we're joined. Her legs come up and lock around my hips.

Her hips move up, trying to get me to move, but I can't, not right now. I need to take a minute, just one minute to remember this. It's better than I have words to describe. The need to go slow with her, the need to be with her is an overwhelming sensation that I've never felt before. My hands go to the sides of her head, and I slowly lower my chest to hers.

"Carter." She whispers my name, my face right above hers. I slowly move my hips out and then in again. Our eyes locked, my lips almost touching her as she sticks out her tongue, and I suck it into my mouth. I move over her slowly, taking my time, our noses touching, our lips so close I can feel her soft breath over me. Our eyes never leave each other while I take her. This here with her, she has to know that it's everything. I tell her all this with my eyes. I watch hers looking into mine, hoping she sees. Her hand goes to my face, cupping my cheek.

"Carter." She repeats my name over and over again. I know she's close because her pussy just got tighter—it got wetter—and her legs wrap me even closer to her.

"Carter," she says again as our lips move against each other, but we aren't kissing. I want to see her eyes when she comes. I want to see everything. I want to give her everything.

"I'm coming," she says and softly closes her eyes.

"Eyes, baby," I tell her, and she opens them. She comes with my name on her lips, and it's the push I need to go over the edge because I follow her, not with a roar or with a grunt, but breathlessly. Her tongue slides into mine, and I move my head to the side to deepen the kiss. I slowly roll her on top of me, and the kiss doesn't stop until I slip out of her. She lays her head on my shoulder, my arms around her waist, and no words are spoken. I don't trust myself to say anything at this point, so I just hold her. Her heart beats on top of mine, and I kiss the top of her head. I just made love to a woman for the first time in my life. I didn't just have sex to have sex or because I was bored. I wanted her more than I wanted my next heartbeat. I wanted her more than I wanted to breathe. I want her in ten minutes, tomorrow, the next week . . . Fuck, I can't think of ever not wanting her.

I feel her fingers making little circles on my chest. "Are you okay?" she asks softly.

I pull back, and she looks up from my chest. "What is better than okay?" I ask her. "What is a better word than okay? Fantastic, that could be one," I say, and she laughs and then kisses my chest. "Phenomenal is another one."

"Okay, fine, I get it." She laughs. "I'm going to go get cleaned up." She sits up. I sit up with her to rid myself of the condom, and she gets off the bed and bends over to untie her shoes.

"Baby," I say from behind her, and she looks over at me. "I want you to remember this first time because the second isn't going to be as good—and by good, I mean gentle," I tell her as I get off the bed and head to the bathroom. I make it out right before she unclips her second shoe. The second time I take her, it's with her bent over my bed and her moaning my name as loud as she possibly can. And this time, when I come, it's with a roar.

Twenty-Two

Erin

AM I BEING LIFTED? I slowly open my eyes and see that my face is still on the pillow, but my hips are up. "Morning, baby." I feel kisses on my back and then feel him over me. "Did I wake you?"

I open one eye now and look over my shoulder, but I feel his fingers enter me before I see him. I groan as he fingers me a couple of times, getting me ready before he slides in me. I close my eyes, getting lost in the feel of him. We've had sex seven times since we got home last night, one after another. We would take a two-minute break, and then we would lunge for each other. We couldn't even fix ourselves some food before he placed me on the counter and fucked me. Gone was the soft, gentle man who took me the first time, but to be honest, I loved it both ways. I loved the characters he played . . . the sweet and caring Carter and the rough and passionate Carter rocked my world equally.

"Carter," I say, and my hips fall to the mattress when he pounds into me so hard I come. "Don't stop," I tell him, but I don't have to tell him as his arms on either side of me hold him up, and he pounds into me. I lift my head and see him over me. I kiss his chin, and he places one hand under my chin, pulling my head back and sliding his tongue into my mouth while he fucks me harder and harder.

"I'm going to come," I tell him, and he doesn't let up. Just like that, my stomach starts to get tight, my nipples ache, and my pussy convulses around his cock. He doesn't let me ride it alone. He pounds me faster, and I know he's coming also. His cock gets even bigger right before he comes, making the fit even tighter. It's glorious. He collapses to the side of me, his twitching cock still in me. "Morning." I close my eyes again, waiting for my breath to return to normal.

"It's almost noon," he says, and I open my eye to look at the clock on the side table.

"11:52. I haven't slept in this long since I was seventeen."

"Well, we did go to bed at around five a.m.," he tells me, slipping away from me and walking to the bathroom.

"And whose fault is that?" I ask loudly, hearing the toilet flush, and he comes back into the room naked.

"Don't even pretend that you had a problem with it," he says, grabbing a pair of shorts. "Let's go get some coffee and sit outside."

"I have a better idea," I tell him, my body still limp.

"Why don't you go make us coffee, and we can have it upstairs on the outside balcony?" I point at the balcony right outside his room.

He turns and comes back to the bed. "No!" I shout and put out my hand to him, and he stops midway to me. "If you get closer, the plans change. The plans always change."

He throws his head back and laughs. "Fine." He holds up his hands. "I'll get the coffee; you get your ass outside." I salute him with my hand and get up when he leaves the room. I go to the bathroom and clean up, washing my face. I grab one of his T-shirts and a pair of shorts. His T-shirt fits me like a dress, and his shorts are falling off me, but they smell like him, and I could literally bathe in his pheromones. I hold the clothes in my hand to stop them from falling off me. I open the door and hear the crashing of the ocean. Walking to the railing, I look over and see people already in the water. Beachgoers walk along the shore as the surfers catch the waves, the sun shining bright with not a cloud in the sky. "You listened." I hear Carter behind me and turn around to see that he is carrying a silver tray. I turn and walk over to help him when he puts the tray down on the glass table that is in front of an L-shaped couch.

"What did you do?" I ask him, looking at the bowl of berries that he brought up along with two coffees, some orange juice, and a couple of containers of yogurt.

"Well, I know you eat yogurt and berries for breakfast with granola, but I didn't have that," he says with smile, and I walk to him.

"You were paying attention?" I wrap my arms around him, and the shorts fall to floor. I laugh, but even with my arms up around him, I'm still fully covered.

The wind blowing lightly has some of my hair flying in my face, and he pushes it behind my ear, cupping my face. "When it's about you, all I do is watch." I lean up and kiss under his chin. "In a non-creepy stalker kind of way, of course."

"Of course," I answer. Laughing, I release him and step out of the shorts. I pick them up and take them with me to the couch, stopping to grab the cup of coffee he made for me.

I sit on the couch with my feet curled up under me and take my first sip. Carter comes over and sits by my knees slouched down and watching the water with his own coffee in his hand. "What do you want to do today?"

"I was thinking I could do some laundry and maybe get some sleep," I tell him, looking over at him.

"Let's go out for dinner," he says, sitting up and grabbing the bowl of berries and handing it to me. I grab a strawberry and bite down, savoring the sweetness as it hits my tongue. "I want to go out for dinner."

"I don't know," I answer honestly. "The press will be all over you. You have been really quiet for the past three weeks, so they are waiting for a Carter Johnson sighting. You and I both know they are waiting for something salacious to report on."

"So what? I won't do anything bad. I'm going to a restaurant to eat a meal with a woman, and I'm leaving with the same woman," he points out. "It's a business dinner."

"I don't know," I say softly, thinking of a million reasons why we shouldn't but knowing it'll just take one sound reason to convince me to go.

"I want to take you out on a date," he says. "I want to go out with you and sit at a table and eat. Maybe hold your hand in the car."

"It's just not that easy, Carter." I look at him, and he grabs his own strawberry.

"It is that easy," he argues. "I want to take you out on a date. What if we go to a quiet restaurant?"

I tilt my head, taking him in. "I just want to take you out," he says softly. "I want to go out to eat with you. I'm not saying that we go there and fuck on the table." I shake my head and roll my eyes. "It's one meal." He takes my coffee from my hand and places it on the table in front of him. "We don't even have to order an appetizer." He pulls me onto his lap, and I straddle him. "We can even order before we get there." He pushes the hair away from my shoulder on one side, then leans in and kisses my neck. "I just want to be out with you." He repeats the action on my other side. "Please."

"Fine," I tell him, giving in to him even though I know it might not be the best thing. But when he smiles, I know that it'll be worth it. "I do have to go home."

"Okay, let me take a shower, or we can shower together, and then we can go to your house," he says, and it's almost like he doesn't have a care in the world. I don't have time to answer him before he stands up with me holding on to him. My legs wrap around his waist and my arms wrap around his neck. The shower really doesn't go as planned. I mean, if you planned to stay in the water fucking until the water was so cold it felt like ice, then our plan succeeded. To go home, I put on his shorts and tie the waist in a knot on the side.

When we get into my apartment, I open all the windows to clear out the stale air from the past two weeks. Opening the drapes, I let the sun in. He goes to the couch and sits down, grabbing the remote and making himself at home.

"There is water in the fridge and nothing else really," I tell him and look at him kick off his boots and lie down on the couch, turning on the news. He lies there in his gray chinos that are just tight enough with a white T-shirt and black jacket. Grabbing his phone and going on Instagram, he then looks up at me. "You finally accepted my follow request."

I roll my eyes at him. "It's not that big of a deal," I tell him and then see him looking at his phone and smiling.

"Scenery pictures, my ass," he says. "This picture of you in the ocean with your back to the camera looks like you're topless," he says, trying to zoom in on the picture. "I think I'm going to report it."

"Don't you dare," I say and walk the rolling suitcase to my room. Opening it, I put a load in the washer, then undress and change into my own shorts and T-shirt. I walk out to the living room and see that he is sleeping, and the television is watching him. I walk back into my bedroom and look at the time; it's already five, and our reservations are at six thirty. I fix my hair in the bathroom, leaving it loose and in beachy waves, and leave my makeup light like every other day. I walk into my closet and grab my white jean capris. I grab my black strapless bra and then the black off the shoulder ruffled loose shirt with sleeves that flow to mid-arm. I grab my new black strappy Louboutins my father just sent me, zipping the back closed. I stand and then look in the mirror. Grabbing my black Chanel purse, I switch my stuff and when I look at the clock, I see it's time to go. I find him still sleeping, and I go back and forth with letting him sleep or waking him.

"I'm up," he mumbles and looks over at me, his blue eyes going dark. "Jesus."

I look down at my outfit. "Is it not enough?"

"How do you make a loose top and jeans the sexiest thing I've ever seen?" he asks, getting up and putting on his boots. "You ready?" He gets up and walks to me, and then bending to kiss me. "You look beautiful."

"Thank you." Smiling at him, I wipe my lip gloss off his lips. He grabs my hand, and we walk out together with our hands linked. He opens the passenger door and waits for me to get in, then steals another kiss. This one is a touch longer, neither one of us wanting to end it. He finally pulls away, closing the door and walking to his side.

"You ready?" he asks, starting the car and putting his sunglasses on.

"As ready as I'll ever be," I answer and look out the window while he makes his way to the restaurant. I don't know what I'm expecting, or maybe I'm just expecting to be slammed with the paparazzi, but it's nothing like that. We pull up to the restaurant, and no one is there. The valet opens the door for me while another valet attendant walks to the driver's side, holding the door open for Carter. I step onto the sidewalk and hold my purse in my hand, waiting for Carter. He comes to my side and puts his hand on my lower back, making me walk into the restaurant first. The hostess smiles at me, but then sees Carter and smiles even wider.

"Hey, we have a reservation for Johnson," Carter says, not even looking at her. His eyes roam the restaurant as she grabs two menus and asks us to follow her. She finds a table in the back and sets down the menus with a smile before slinking away.

"Have you been here before?" I ask him, grabbing the glass of water from the table and looking at him grabbing the menu.

"Yeah, a couple of times," he mumbles, and then the waiter appears to tell us the specials of the night.

"I'm going to use the bathroom," I tell him, getting up. I want to go over to kiss him, but I stop myself. "This whole thing in public is harder than I thought."

"Is it?" He smiles and grabs his own glass of water. "I guess following you into the bathroom to cop a feel and maybe an orgasm would be a red flag?"

I glare at him. "Don't you dare." I turn, leaving him to chuckle to himself. The bathroom has four stalls in it, and all of them are the same size. I'm sitting down when I hear the door open and the sound of two women coming in.

"Did you see Carter?" one of them asks, and I hold my breath. "Fuck, he is even hotter than I remember."

"I know," the second voice says, "and I have to say he gave the best head of my life." My heart sinks. I get up, flushing the toilet, and the women stop. I open the door and come out to see the

Hostess from before standing there touching up her makeup. She opens her mouth when she sees me. The other woman has to be a hostess also since they are dressed the same. I ignore them, going over and washing my hands, then leaving them in there. My heart is pounding when I finally get back to the table and see that Carter is on his phone. He looks up, and he must see it on my face that something is wrong. His eyes fill with worry.

"What happened?" he asks, leaning in, and when I grab the glass of water, my hands shake a touch. "Erin."

"Oh, nothing," I say, putting down my water glass. "Just overhearing a couple of the hostesses in the bathroom discuss your oral skills talent," I say, looking down at the menu now, not really reading.

"Erin," he says my name softly. "Look at me."

I shake my head. "Not right now, Carter," I tell him. I feel the table move, and he gets up.

"We are leaving," he says, and I look up now. "Let's go."

"No," I tell him. "I'm not going to leave because then they are going to know it got to me."

"This was a stupid idea," he says and returns to his

seat when he sees that I'm not getting up.

"No, it was a nice idea," I tell him. "Maybe next time, you should choose a place where you didn't fuck the hostesses." He doesn't answer because the waiter comes by and takes our order. When he walks away, I look back at Carter.

"I hate that our night is ruined because of this," he says, shaking his head. "All I wanted was to take you out."

"You have a past," I tell him, leaning in. "A very active past." Shaking my head. "It was bound to happen."

"I regret it," he says, and I watch him. "This moment, right here, makes me regret every single thing I did." He shakes his head. "I'm sorry."

"It is what it is," I tell him the truth. "It could be worse."

"Really?" he asks, his voice defeated. "How could it be worse than I feel right now?"

I try to think of something, a smile forming on my face. "I have no idea, but I'm sure someone with a phone will post a video of previous encounters."

He laughs. "Thank you," he says, and I look up at him. "For not letting this ruin the night. For giving me tonight." He stops talking. "And for coming home with me."

"Oh, I never said I was going home with you." I point at him.

"We will see." He smirks at me, and I know with him, I will do whatever he wants to do. I'm not even going to lie and say I fought him. The second we got into the car, he drove straight to his house. We didn't make it to the bed the first time, nor the second, but by the third, we were actually in a horizontal position on his bed, and it was fucking spectacular.

Twenty-Three

Carter

"AND CUT," IVAN SAYS, and I get up from the chair. We are in L.A. on the lot that Hillcrest owns to film for the next two weeks before we go back to Montana to finish it. "It was good." Ivan comes to me. "This take, you had more heart in it."

I nod at him. "It's starting to sink in that he may never see his daughter again," I tell him. This script is gold. It could have gone to a dozen other actors, but I fought for it, and now I am playing my dream role.

"Perfect. See you Wednesday," he says and walks away. "Don't forget the dinner we have with the crew Friday night. Yeah?"

I nod, grabbing my phone and checking my calendar. Tomorrow is the Grammys, so I have the day off, but I have to be on set Wednesday, Thursday, and Friday bright and early. I walk out to the trailer and open the door, finding Erin sitting at the table. We've been inseparable for the past two and a half weeks, and every night I slip into bed with her, I sleep better than I did the night before. After the restaurant, I thought she was going to call it quits. Fuck, I don't even want to think about it, but she didn't. She sat at the table with her head high and enjoyed the whole meal, never once giving those girls any inkling that it bothered her.

"Jessica, that would be amazing." I hear her talking on the phone when I walk in and grab a bottle of water. "Friday would work perfect. He can sit down with you at five." She looks over at me, and I nod. "I will see you then. Thank you." She looks at me. "I just got you an interview with Jessica Beckett."

"Cool," I tell her, not sure what to say.

"Cool?" she repeats. "Carter, it's better than cool. It's the best thing that you could ask for. She doesn't do interviews anymore. So the fact that she is for me is huge."

"You did good, baby," I say, walking to her and leaning down to kiss her with a smile. "You deserve a reward," I say, and my cock gets hard just thinking about her. I swear we have sex sometimes five times a day, and it's never enough. Not for me and not for her either. This morning, I was the one who was woken up with her sliding her mouth over me. I had one eye open when she rolled the condom on and then slowly slid down on me. It was slow until she started to come, and then it took off.

"Put that thing away," she says, pointing at my cock

that is now up and ready. "Sylvia and Ryan are due here any minute, and I'm nervous."

"Don't be nervous, baby," I whisper to her, and I'm about to lean in and kiss her when the door opens, and I see Ryan coming up the steps. I move away from her and cover my cock with both hands in front of me.

"Hey, there you guys are," he says and then looks over at Erin. "I just saw Ivan." He comes in and Sylvia follows. "I have to say I haven't seen him smile since he filmed *Russian Roulette*."

We both laugh at that comment only because it won him an Oscar. I walk over to Erin, and she moves over, so I slide in next to her, and Sylvia comes in and slides in right before Ryan takes a seat in front of me.

"Good news," Erin says. "Jessica is coming out on Friday to interview Carter."

"I can't believe she's going to do it," Sylvia says, and I look over at Erin with a smile, proud of her. "The buzz for this movie is through the roof, bigger than the buzz for *Adrenaline Run*, and that was insane."

"You did good," Ryan says to her. "Now to the reason we are here."

I look at them and then at Erin, who looks just as surprised as me. "As you know, the Grammys are tomorrow." I nod. "And I get that you would like to have a date, but . . ."

"I'm fine going solo," I tell him. I mean, I'm not going solo, I'm going with my woman, but he doesn't need to know that small detail.

"Really, and about the after party," he says, and I just

shake my head.

"Not an issue. I have an early call the next morning, so my plan was to walk the red carpet, interview with whoever Erin tells me to speak to, and then bounce as soon as the event is over."

Ryan looks over at me in shock and then at Erin who looks equally shocked by all the plans I made. That and I already set a plan into motion for when I take her back to my place.

"Sounds like you have everything worked out."

"I do," I say, and my phone buzzes. "I'm due on set in fifteen minutes."

"Perfect," Ryan says, getting up. "We will come with you." Leading the way to the stage with Ryan on one side of me and Erin on the other, I prepare for the scene, blocking everything and everyone out. When we finally finish the scene, I walk out and see only Erin there.

"Where is everyone?" I ask her, looking around.

"They left five minutes ago," she tells me as we walk to the trailer. "Is that the last scene for the day?"

"Yeah," I say, and we get our things and get into the car. I don't have to ask her if she is coming over. She usually does, and then we swing by her place in the morning for her clothes. She doesn't listen when I tell her to bring a bag, but soon, I'm just going to throw shit in a bag for her, and she can wear what I pack.

"I should sleep at home tonight," she says, and I just shake my head. "Carter, Ryan has the glam team coming to my house at one."

"Okay, I'll drop you off at noon then," I tell her.

"Problem solved."

"I haven't slept in my bed in over three weeks," she moans. "Three weeks."

"I am in the mood for Chinese, what about you?" I ask her, ignoring her comment. Hell, if it was up to me, she would be moved in.

"You can't ignore the topic every time it comes up," she points out, and I finally pull into the driveway. She gets out of the car, grabbing her purse. "You are very annoying when you get all barbaric."

"I sleep better when you're here," I tell her honestly. "And me sleeping better is showing on the screen."

"So I'm doing this for the good of the movie," she says, laughing as she walks to the front door and unlocks it. "You will stop at nothing."

I wrap my arms around her waist, pulling her to me. "Not when it comes to you and being in my bed." I kiss her neck and press my cock into her ass. "Are we eating before or after?"

"After," she says, moaning when my hands slide up and cup her tits. "Definitely after." She turns her head to the side, and I take her mouth, dragging her to the wall that is just to the side of the stairs. My hands go to her hips, and I try to pull up yet another tight skirt she wore today.

"Tomorrow, we are throwing out all the tight shit," I say between kissing her and ripping off her shirt. Her hands all over my body, frantically pulling the shirt over my head and going for my belt as my hand goes to my back pocket to get my condom. I slip the condom on while she shimmies the dress up over her hips. She moves her panties to the side, kicking up a leg over my hip and I thrust into her. I pick up her other leg while I pound into her. I've never not had this willpower before when she is in the room. It's all out the door, and the only thing I can think about is being with her, being next to her, being a part of her. When she rolls her hips and moans out my name, it's everything to me. We finish against the wall, and I slowly carry her upstairs, order some Chinese food, and then take her again in the shower.

"Just make sure everything is set up once I get home," I tell the man on the phone. I get out of the car and walk up the stairs to Erin's apartment. I dropped her off five hours ago, and I was going to stay, but she told me to go away and let her get ready without me. I went home and worked out and basically moped around my house until it was time to get ready. Now I'm wearing my black on black tux, and I'm already dying to get out of it. I knock on the door and wait for her, hearing her shoes click on the floor. She opens the door smiling, but I don't have time to look at her because she turns to walk away from the door.

"I just have to pack my purse," she says, and I see that the back is tied around the neck, but it's all open back. It's also tight with long sleeves, and it looks silver with some glints of black. When she finally comes back, I see the front, and I have to stop and just stare at her. The dress starts at her neck and comes down tight, cutting in on the sides all the way down to the floor. It's all silver, and her makeup is darker than she's ever worn it. The details of the dress look like flowers. You hear the slink when she walks. "You look nice," she says and leans up to kiss my lips lightly so I don't get lip gloss on me.

"I'm buying you a black garbage bag and a white belt," I tell her, and she shakes her head. Her hair is parted down the middle and tucked behind both ears. "Where is your bag?" I ask her, and she rolls her eyes.

"Right there"—she points at the small bag by the door—"and I packed enough clothes until Friday."

"Good," I say, holding the door open for her. "You're learning."

She walks to the stairs and picks up the dress to walk down the steps. I walk next to her, and we make it downstairs. "We should get a picture of you," she says, and I put the bag in the back of the car. "Turn my way," she says, and I look over my shoulder and give her the smirk.

"Now come and take one with me," I tell her, and she walks over to me. I snap a selfie of us, her head next to mine and both of us smiling. "That's a good one," I say to her as she gets in the car.

The line-up to get to the Grammys is insane. "We are car number twenty," the driver says from the front, and we move at a snail's pace. We finally get to the front, or near the front when I hear a roar take over the crowd. I look out and see that Kellie has arrived. Kellie is the artist up for the most awards tonight. We worked together on one film when she first started in movies. She actually just had her first baby, and it's the first time she's performing in years. So all eyes are on her tonight.

"Kellie just arrived." Erin looks up when the car stops. I get out and hold out my hand to her. "Come, I want you to meet Kellie." I tell her and we walk to Kellie, who is holding hands with a huge guy watching everyone. "I didn't think she could look more beautiful," I say to the side of her and watch the man next to her stand up full alert.

"Carter," Kellie says and walks to me, kissing my cheeks. "Look at you, all dressed up," she jokes, then looks behind me. "Where is your harem?" she jokes, and I burst out laughing.

"Erin." I turn to look for her and finally see her next to me. Her auburnhair is shining in the sun. "This is Kellie," I say, and Erin walks over to her smiling and holding out her hand.

"It's a pleasure to meet you," Erin says to her, and Kellie smiles, moving to the side.

"This is my husband, Brian." She reaches for his hand. "Brian, this is Carter, and his girlfriend Erin."

"Oh, no," Erin says. "I'm not his girlfriend." She shakes her head, and I turn and glare at her. "I'm PR for his brand."

"Oh, I'm sorry," Kellie says, and then looks at her husband, trying to hide a smile.

"No one even knows what that means," I say to her

and try to grab her hand, but she puts her clutch in it.

"It means I'm in charge of your image. We already went through this," she tells me quietly. "Now if you can please stop letting people think we are together."

"I'm not in charge of what people think," I say with a sly smile. I'm about to let the cat out of the bag because I'm done with the hiding and not being able to hold her hand when I want to. "Let's go take a picture so you can put it on my Instagram." I tell her this so she can stop the glaring, then I turn to Kellie. "See you in there, and good luck tonight." The sound of the bell lets us know that the show will be starting any minute.

"You can't do that," Erin says. "This is my job; this is your job," she tells me. "Please. It's not the time to tell everyone."

"We have to get inside, or they will close the doors." Putting my hand on her lower back, I see men look twice when she walks by them, and I want to put a tent around her. We walk down the red carpet. I stop and pose for pictures alone as Erin stands off to the side. I want to pull her on the carpet with me and pose with her. I want them to take pictures of us together.

I'm not able to give any interviews because it's so close to the doors closing. When we get inside, ushers lead us to our seats just as a loud, booming voice fills the room. "Showtime." The lights flick on and off, and then all of a sudden, the orchestra starts.

I lean into Erin and whisper in her ear, "You take my breath away."

She looks at me from under her lashes. "Nice try, Mr.

Johnson," she says, and I shake my head and watch the show. I don't know how long it is before they come to get me. I get up from the seat and wait for her to get up, but she doesn't. "I'll be here when you are finished."

I nod at her and walk to the back where I see a couple of people I know. I stop when someone calls my name and wave from afar. I walk to the table, and a man hands me the envelope. "Hey, there." I turn to see that Tyler Beckett is coming toward me, wearing almost the same tux as me.

"Look who it is," I say with a smile. "The legend himself."

He puts his head back and laughs. Tyler Beckett is the biggest box office name out there, and he just got married to an entertainment journalist. They hated each other, but thirty days together will change someone. Hell, I changed, and it's been less than a month. "There he is, the one who is looking to take my spot on the charts," he says, laughing.

I shake my head. "No way that can happen," I tell him, and then a producer comes out and tells us to take our place. I walk over and hear the emcee call both our names, and the girl signals us to walk out. The minute we walk out, the girls go wild, and I look over at him smirking while he just looks ahead at the teleprompter.

"What a night it's been," Tyler starts, and the girls up in the balcony go nuts.

"It's been one hell of a night, hasn't it?" And if I didn't think it could get any louder, well, the minute I talk, the girls go even more ballistic. Tyler looks at me and laughs.

"Looks like you have a fan club," he says, and I just nod. "Let's get to the last award of the night." Tyler introduces the nominees.

"And the winner is . . ." I say, opening the envelope and reading the name on the envelope, looking over at the person winning. "Kellie Kitch." Brian jumps out of his seat in excitement and looks at Kellie, who is sitting there stunned. She finally gets up and makes it up to the stage wearing a smile on her face.

She greets Tyler with a kiss on his cheek and does the same to me as I hand her the black and gold award. "Thank you," she says and walks to the microphone for her acceptance speech.

I wait for her to finish thanking everyone and then walk off the stage. The minute I'm able to dash away, I do and go grab Erin. She smiles at me, and we make our way to the car. She gets in first and then I follow her in. The minute we are in the car, and it's rolling, I grab her and kiss her, causing her to moan into my mouth. I put my hands on her face and feel her hands on mine. We kiss the rest of the ride home, and I let her go when the car comes to a stop. I watch her walk down the steps toward the front door. She opens the door and walks in, stopping once she gets to the living room, and I see why. The whole living room is gone, and in its place is a round table for two with romantic music playing. "What is all this?" She looks over at me and walks to the table. The only light is from the blazing fireplace.

"This," I say, putting her bag down, "is a do-over

from our first date."

She smiles at me, and then I play the song "You are the Reason." I walk to her holding out my hand. "Will you dance with me?" I ask her and she puts her purse down on the table.

She places her hand in mine, and I wrap my arm around her waist while she puts her arm around my shoulder. I bring her hand to my chest, pulling her closer to me, and I dance with her in the middle of my living room. The song tells her she is the reason I've changed, she is the reason I want to be a better man, and she is the reason I know what love is now. And one day, I'll work up the nerve to tell her all these things myself.

"CUT!" IVAN SHOUTS WHEN I walk into the stage with Jessica beside me.

"I can't even thank you enough for doing this," I tell her, and she just nods. It's been three days since the Grammys, and it's finally time for his interview with Jessica. For three days, I've thought of ways to tell him how I feel.

Every day, he puts a post on Instagram, a picture of him looking straight into the camera. But I know he was looking right at me since I took the pictures.

Does it get better than this? Only tomorrow can tell.

Three days of it being on the tip of my tongue, but something holds me back. Every time I think this is it, I am slowly brought back in, and I keep from saying it. When he danced with me the night of the Grammys, it was there. It was the perfect time, but I couldn't get over the lump in my throat.

"Scoring an interview with Carter is what everyone is dying for," she says, holding her purse in her hand. "Especially now that he's gone from all over the press to being a choir boy of sorts."

I nod, knowing she will ask the question everyone wants to know, but I also know that she will do it with respect and not twist things around. When the story broke that she and Tyler were dating, she did what everyone was dying to do. She told her own story, and to this day, it's the biggest celebrity story retweet. I walk to the stage and see that Carter is talking to Ivan, and he is pointing at something on the screen. They both agree on something, and then Carter turns and walks toward me. He smiles when he sees me and then sticks his hand out. "You must be Jessica Beckett."

"I am," she says, putting out her hand and shaking his hand. "It's a pleasure to meet you."

"You came highly recommended," he says, and then Jessica laughs. "And by that, I mean Erin said I have to do this."

I shake my head. "Okay, where do you want to do this?" I ask him, and he looks around.

"I think in my trailer," he says, and I nod, so we walk back to the trailer. Carter opens the door, and I let Jessica go in first, then I follow her. She walks over to the table and sits down, grabbing her phone out of her bag along with a yellow legal pad. I stand by the sink, and he walks over to the table and sits on the bench and then moves over so I can sit. "Jesus, I'm nervous," he says, rubbing his hands on his pants, and he takes the risk to put his hands on mine. I turn my hands over and squeeze his.

"Let's get this started," Jessica says and turns on her phone to tape the interview. She starts off slow, and it's easy until she gets to the one that I knew was coming.

"The past couple of years, you have built up the reputation as a playboy. A different girl every night, sometimes multiple girls a day," she starts, and my stomach starts to get sick. "But suddenly, you've gone off radar." I look down and then look over at Carter. "People want to know why the sudden change."

I wait for it, wait for him to compose his words, but he doesn't. "I don't know how I got that reputation," he says, and I laugh and so does he. "I mean, I know how I got it, but it wasn't something that I set out to do." He grabs a water bottle that is on the table and takes a sip. "I guess I'm chalking it up to the fact that I had to prepare for the biggest role of my career, and I didn't need any distractions." He puts his hands on the table now leaving mine. "The last time I went out was over three weeks ago, and when I knew I had to get my head in the game, I kept thinking that it was going to be hard, but it's been the opposite of that. It's shown me the kind of man I want to be, and it wasn't the one from before."

"So you like this Carter better than the other Carter?" she asks him.

"I love them both," he says, smirking. "But this Carter is more comfortable in his skin than he ever was before." She nods her head. "This Carter is a man I can be proud of, and that is everything."

"Good answer," I mumble, and he just smiles at me. Jessica doesn't ask any other rough questions, and when it's finally over, she puts her stuff away and then stands up.

"Carter, it was a pleasure," she says and then looks at me. "I will email you the final interview when it's ready."

I nod, and she walks out. "That wasn't so bad," he says. "I was more nervous during this interview than I was signing my first big contract."

"You did amazing, and you showed them who you really are," I tell him. "Now, go change so we can make an appearance at the party."

"You didn't even kiss me today," he says, and I walk to him, kissing him. "I missed you."

"Good news, we have the whole weekend off," I remind him. "Now go get dressed." He turns and walks to the bedroom, taking off his stage clothes and putting on jeans and a shirt. We walk out to the stage area and hear the music already playing, and people are mingling and simply enjoying themselves. We walk in, and I smile at the people I recognize. Jennifer waves hello, and I wave back and walk to the table, grabbing a bottle of water.

Carter grabs a water bottle and sees someone he recognizes, so he tells me he's going to be right back. I look around and then snap a picture, putting it up with the caption

"All work and no play make an unhappy crew. Enjoy

the weekend."

I put the phone in my purse and spot Carter walking toward me. "So how long do we have to stay here?" he asks in a low tone, but then we are joined by someone I've never really seen.

"Carter," she says, going to him and hugging him and kissing his cheek. "I was wondering if I was going to see you here tonight."

"Kasey," he says, smiling at her. "Nice to see you again. This is Erin, my PR girl."

Kasey looks at me and smiles. "I've been trying to get in touch with you all week," she says, putting her hand on his arm. "I was thinking we could catch up."

I look at Carter, who looks like a deer in headlights. "I can't," he says, and then continues, "I'm with someone."

I'm expecting her to take the hint and walk away, but she doesn't. Instead, she gets closer to him. "That's never stopped us before on multiple occasions." I swear, that bitch just licked his ear after she said that.

"If you'll excuse me, I have an appointment I'm running late for," I say and walk away. I walk out the door and into the night, and then hear my name being called.

"Erin, can you wait a minute, please," he says and reaches me, stopping me from walking. "Erin. Stop."

"I need a second please," I tell him, not sure a second is going to cut it.

"Come on, that isn't my fault," he says.

"I know it isn't your fault," I tell him. "I know that you have a past. I know that chances are it's going to be thrown in my face a little bit from time to time. But to actually experience it live, in person, in all of its in-your-face glory is something I just need time to digest."

"Let's go home," he says, and I shake my head.

"I think I'm going to spend the night at my home tonight," I tell him.

"You can't be serious," he says.

"Can I just have a minute to process everything? Can I just have that time to think?" I ask him, my heart pounding. "Just give me some space. You can fuck up both of our lives with one tabloid report with one unearthed sex video," I tell him, the anger running through me. "You have the power to destroy me in more ways than one." I watch his eyes narrow to slits. "You can still go on to continue to be the big time actor"—I shake my head—"but I will be the one to lose everything here, not you," I say, turning to walk away.

"So you are just going to walk away?" he shouts after me, and I just shake my head.

"Whatever," I say under my breath, and I flag down a cab and get in, giving him my address. I get home and walk up the stairs, not bothering to turn on the lights. I undress and crawl into bed, looking out into the darkness.

The night is horrible. I toss and turn, and finally, I toss the covers aside. I look at the clock and see that it's almost six a.m., so I grab my phone and see that he hasn't even attempted to call or text me. I get up and get dressed, stopping by Starbucks before heading to his house. I should have just calmed down before I spoke to him, I realize as I pull up to his house. I get out, grabbing the coffee, and make my way to the door. I wonder if he's sleeping or if his night was just as restless as mine. I walk in, and the house is eerily quiet.

I put my purse down and walk up the steps to his room, my heart pounding in my chest.

I walk to the doorway, and I stop, right there, and take in the room. The room we shared just yesterday morning. It's almost as if it's moving in slow motion. The naked blonde in the bed sits up, the sheet falling off her huge naked tits and her mouth opening when she sees me. My eyes move around the room, landing on the bedside table that holds an open condom wrapper and then to the entrance of his bathroom where I hear the shower turn off. My hands start to shake, and I think my knees are going to give out. I look around confused, my eyes going around the room again, taking everything in, not sure what is going on, and then he steps into the room. Fresh from the shower with a white towel wrapped around his waist. A white towel in his hands as he dries his hair. "Oh, you brought coffee," he says and walks over to me, grabbing the coffee tray from my hand.

"Cindy, this is Erin. She's my PR girl," he says to her, and I have to take my hand and hold the door to stop from falling. "This is Cindy. We met last night." I look at him, his eyes looking right through me. "Don't worry, though." He stands there. "We didn't get caught, so your job is still safe."

"What?" I whisper. I have to get out of here. I think

I'm going to be sick.

"No one took our pictures, so your dream job is still intact," he says with a snide tone. I look at him, taking one last look at him and the naked blonde lying in the bed I was lying in less than twenty-four hours ago when he made love to me. I turn and walk down the steps, looking around at all the places he made love to me. All the places that I almost told him I loved him. I get to the bottom of the steps, and the tears are now running down my face, making my vision blurry. I grab my bag, and my knees give out right as I'm about to walk out the door, but I hold out my hand, gripping the doorjamb.

I walk out, closing the door behind me, and a sob comes out of my mouth. I try to place my hand over my mouth but trip on the step. I can hardly see in front of me. Holding the railing, I take the steps as fast as I can. I grab my keys, and they fumble out of my hand right before I open my door. I bend to get them, falling on my knees and shaking my hand, landing palms out on the rocks. I get up and get in the car. The pain in my chest feels like little shards of glass going through me. I start the car, and reverse it, my heart pounding so hard I can't hear anything except the beating. I press the phone button and dial the one person I know I can go to. He answers on the second ring, his voice groggy.

"Daddy," I sob out, the tears flowing so fast I can't stop them. Rivers running down my face.

"Baby girl, what's the matter?" I hear the worry in his voice. "Where are you?"

"It hurts so much," I tell him, driving as fast as I can

get away from Carter. I drive until I can't see anymore, until my vision is so blurry I have no choice but to pull over to the side of the road, and my stomach turns. "I'm going to be sick." I open my car door and throw up on the side of the road.

"Where are you?" I hear him shut a door in the background, and I hear him turn on his car. "I'm coming to get you. Are you home?"

"Daddy," I sob out. "My heart. It hurts," I tell him, sobbing and trying to catch my breath so I can speak. "So much pain."

"ERIN!" he yells. "Share your location with me."

I grab my phone and share it with him and then toss the phone on the seat beside me. "It hurts so much," I tell him. I grab my hand, putting it to my chest, hoping to rub the pain away, except nothing I can do will dull the pain. Nothing he can say can kiss away the pain; nothing that anyone can say can make the pain go away. Nothing, it's empty. There is nothing left. Nothing of my heart, nothing of my soul. I sit here on the side of the road. I don't even know if it's five minutes or one hour. I know nothing but pain.

I see headlights coming at me and then stop on the side, and I know I'm finally safe. He opens my door and grabs me in his arms. "I can't breathe," I tell him, my breathing coming in pants now, the pants hurting my chest even more.

"You can breathe," my father says. "Just look at me." I look at him, and the breathing gets worse, the pants shorter, harder, more painful. "You are having a panic attack," he says, and I look at him. "Just look at me, baby girl, and inhale nice and slow." I focus on his eyes, his warm eyes, the love showing.

"He doesn't love me," I tell him, taking a huge deep breath. "He shattered what we had."

"Oh, baby," he says, holding me around my waist and walking to his car. "I'm here."

He puts me in the car and fastens the seat belt over me. I put my hand to my chest. "Hurts right here," I tell him of the pain that is so deep I feel it in my bones. I feel it straight down to my soul.

TWENTY-FIVE

Carter

I WATCHED HER GET in a cab and drive away. Looking at my watch, I was going to give her an hour and then go to her. Walking back into the party, I look around, and Jennifer comes up to me. "Is Erin okay?"

"Yeah, she's fine," I lied to her. "It's just been a long week."

"Don't I know it, but soon it will all pay off for her," Jennifer says, drinking her water bottle.

"What is going to pay off for her?" I ask her, my mouth suddenly going dry and my mind racing. This can't be happening to me again.

"Her big break," she says. "You know if you stay in line and don't fuck things up, she gets her dream job in New York." She shrugs her shoulders. "I mean, it's really a done deal at this point because you've been good for the past three weeks. Only one more week to go for her."

"Excuse me," I say, walking away from her. My hands are suddenly clammy, my throat dry, my heart beating so fast I think I'm going to have a heart attack. I get in my car, my mind going into overdrive. I think back to every conversation we had to see if she mentioned something, to see if she said something, anything that could make sense of this. Moving to fucking New York. Is this for real? My hand grips the steering wheel, and I head to her house, but then turn around when I'm almost there.

She is just like everyone else, I tell myself, yet my heart doesn't get on board, but I ignore the pull of reason. The night going by is a nightmare, the hours making it worse with all the memories that fill them. I sat at the window, looking out into the darkness, and set my plan in motion. When it was finally over, I thought I would feel better, I thought I would be vindicated, but instead, I was in more pain, more agony. More broken. Let her fucking go to New York after riding on my coattails, taking what she could from me just like all the others. I will burn this relationship down before I'll be hurt again.

I hear the door slam closed, and I have to stop myself from running after her. I look over at the blonde in my bed. "Get the fuck out," I tell her, walking back to the bathroom.

"Oh, come on," she says, getting on her knees, her big tits swaying. "You're paying me, might as well use me. I was naked all night long, and you haven't even touched me." She rolls her nipples, and I turn and walk out.

"When I get back, if you're not gone, I'm going to put you out on your ass," I tell her. "I paid you for the night, you did what I wanted you to do, now get out." I close the door of the bathroom and go to the toilet, and I sit down. My legs trembling, I close my eyes, and the only thing I can see is the pain in her eyes when I stepped into the room. A tear rolls down my cheek, and I don't wipe it away. I let it fall on the towel that I have wrapped around my waist. Another tear falls down, rolling faster than the last one. I pick up my hand to touch my cheek, but it shakes so much I have to put it back down.

She shouldn't be driving in that state. What if she needs me? I get up, my legs shaking again, and I hold the counter, grabbing the clothes I just took off when she walked in the house. I open the door and see that the blonde is gone, and the sheet she covered herself with all night lays on the floor. I walk down the stairs, grabbing my keys. I have to make sure she made it home okay. Walking to the garage, I get in my car and pull away from my house. The house that I shared with her and no one else. The house that was only mine is now ours. The road's almost deserted when I see her car on the side of the road, and my heart starts to beat even faster. I pull up behind her and get out of the car, almost running to her car. I see that she was sick beside her car, and the tears come now. I don't even bother to notice looking in the car to see if she's there, but it's empty. She isn't anywhere. I look around, yelling her name, wondering if she's sick somewhere on the side of the road. Did someone stop and kidnap her? Where the hell is she? I run down the road, my eyes going everywhere while I yell her name so loudly and so much my throat is raw. I run my hands through my hair, finally pulling it out. The pain is dull compared to the pain in my stomach. I run back to my car, picking up my phone and calling her. It goes straight to voice mail, her voice makes my heart beat normal, lets me breathe again. I hang up when I hear the beep and go up and down again and again. Nothing, not a trace of her except her car. I wonder if she walked to get help. Did her car break down? I call her again, and it goes to voice mail. I sit in the car not moving, waiting for her to come back. I'll be here when she comes back, but a tow truck shows up, and I get out of the car.

"Hey." I walk up to him, and he looks at me while he connects his truck to her car. "Is the lady who drives this car okay?"

"No clue, man," he says. "I was just told to pick it up." I nod at him and turn to walk back to my car. She must be fine if she managed to get a tow truck to pick up her car. I get back home and walk into the door, and I swear I can smell her. She's everywhere. I walk to the kitchen and start my coffee, ignoring the vanilla-flavored syrup I bought for her. I grab it and toss it in the garbage. I turn and walk to the liquor cabinet, grabbing a bottle of Jack Daniel's.

Outside, the weather mirrors how I feel. It's dark and gloomy and looks like a storm is coming. I walk down the steps to the beach, the wet sand sticking to my feet. Making my way to the shore, I sit down, watching the water. I twist open the bottle of Jack and bring it to my mouth, taking a huge gulp. The burn runs right down my throat. The water crashes onto the shore, and I feel like I've been beaten and run over by a truck. My whole body hurts. The rain comes, but I don't move. I sit here as the rain comes down, and the sand starts to whip me. I drink each time the burn goes away; I drink until the pain is almost numb. My eyes are on the amber-colored alcohol that is almost gone. My head spins, and I fall back onto the wet sand, looking up at the sky. The clouds rolling along having its own war. When the rain stops, only the darkness stays.

I finally get up and stumble back to my house, walking inside and going straight to my bedroom. The bed hits me right away with the lone sheet on the floor. I grab the bed and pull it out of the room, throwing it over the railing and hearing a thud, but then I see a glass vase fall to the floor, shattering everywhere. I jog down the stairs, picking the mattress up and dragging it outside, the sounds of crashing the whole time I pull it out of the house. I throw it down the steps to the beach. I stumble on the sand, walking back to the house where I pick up the sheets, then find some matches and lighter fluid. Grabbing another bottle of Jack, I balance everything in my hand as I walk to the beach. I sit down near the mattress, open the bottle, and take another long pull. I pick up the lighter fluid and spray it on the mattress until nothing is left in the can. I light a match, watching the orange flame, and toss it on the bed. There's a whooshing sound when it catches fire, and I fall back on my ass and watch it burn. The bottle of Jack never leaves my hand. The sky opens up, and the pouring rain soaks me.

"Holy shit, dude." I hear from behind me and try to focus, but the darkness of the night, plus the Jack makes it almost impossible. "What the fuck are you doing out here?"

I cock my head to the side. "Jeff?" I ask. "Is that you?"

"I tried calling you, but you didn't answer. Are you drinking?" He asks the question as he snatches the bottle out of my hand.

"Heyy," I slur out and try to grab the bottle back, but my arm falls like a noodle. "I neeed that."

"Your house looks ransacked," he says, trying to pick me up, "and you're soaking wet."

"She lied," I mumble the words. "She lied to me."

"Fuck," he says, trying to carry my dead weight body toward the house. He opens the gate, and we make it up the steps.

"I want to lie down right herrrre," I tell him, looking at the lounge chairs by the pool. He doesn't listen, though; he takes me inside and throws me on the couch. I turn to the side and look at the fireplace. I close my eyes, but the eyes that I see are the ones I'm running from. The pain in them cutting me straight to my core. But I don't have a choice. I keep closing them only because I can see her again, even if it's with the pain. I close my eyes one more time and whisper her name. She turns and looks at me, then walks away from me. I run to her, but the faster I run, the farther she gets. "Erin." Her name on my lips is the last thing that I say before falling into the dark abyss.

I spend the whole night chasing her in my dreams, but she remains just out of reach. I fall to my knees, begging her to come back, begging her to love me just as much as I love her, but she never comes to me. I can never catch her. I almost do; I reach out to touch her arm, and then my eyes flicker open. The bright sun shines in the windows, so I close my eyes to dull the pain in my head. The throbbing like jackhammers. I try to swallow, but my mouth feels like it's filled with sand. I moan, turning on my side.

"Good, you're awake." I hear and open my eyes. Jeff's standing there with a coffee in his hand, sitting on the table facing me. He puts his coffee down and picks up a glass of water and two pills. "Take this."

I sit up and have to stop moving because my stomach feels like it's going to explode, but nothing can describe the pain in my chest. "Thank you," I say, taking the pills and drinking no more than three sips of water. I hand him the glass, then put my head back on the couch, and close my eyes.

"I ordered you some greasy shit to help with the hangover," he tells me. "I have a cleanup crew coming in two hours. You can stay here, or you can come to my house." I open one eye and look at him.

"Cleanup crew?" I ask, confused, and he shakes his head.

"Look around." I turn slowly and take in the sight of my house. The vases on the floor are in pieces, the stools from the kitchen on the floor. The vase of roses that we got two days ago are scattered all through the house like it was dragged there. The side table by the stairs is knocked over, I think from the mattress. "Is any of it coming back to you?"

I rub my hands over my face. "I need a new bed," I tell him, and he nods his head. "I need to shower."

"Yeah, you do. You're covered in sand." I look down, seeing my shoes are still on, and the caked in wet sand is still on there. My clothes have little pieces of sand everywhere. "You going to tell me what happened?"

I take a deep breath, knowing that if I can tell anyone, it's Jeff. "I fell in love with her." I bring my hand to my chest when it starts to pound hard. "And then I found out she lied to me. She was going to take what I gave her, the notoriety of my career, and leave for New York. She was just using me, just like everyone else," I say the last sentence softly. "I'm going to shower." He doesn't stop me from walking to the stairs, the sound of the glass crunching under my running shoes. "I thought she was the one." I shake my head, and I could swear I hear her call my name. But I know it's my mind playing tricks on me.

Walking into the bedroom, I stand in the same spot where Erin stood when she came up the stairs yesterday. The pain across her face, her hand trembling, it's too much. The memories are too much, so I turn and walk to the guest bedroom. I walk to the bathroom, and there on the top of the sink is one of her shirts. I pick it up and bring it to my nose and smell her. I close my eyes and picture her in it when she hugs me. I'm numb, empty, broken, and I have no one to blame but myself.

Twenty-Six

Erin

"HONEY, YOU NEED TO eat something," my father says to me when he comes into the bedroom and sits on the bed. I'm lying here with my legs to my chest and staring out the window at the sunny day. "It's been two days."

I look at him. It's been two days since my life shattered, two days since I walked into that scene that plays over and over in my head on a loop. "I'm not hungry," I tell him the truth. Just the thought of eating makes my stomach feel queasy.

"If you don't eat something soon, your mother is getting on a fucking plane," he says, trying to make a joke, but I know she's one step away from it. When my father carried me to his car and then took me to his house, the first person he called was my mother. I heard his voice faintly through the closed door. He didn't leave my side, and when he did, it was for ten minutes, max fifteen. I finally sent him away yesterday, knowing he needed sleep.

"My stomach feels sick," I tell him.

"Why don't you come to the kitchen, and at least try having some soup?" he says, and I sit up. He gets up and holds out his hand to me. I grab it and walk down the grand staircase to his huge kitchen, sitting on the stool. "What type of soup do you want?"

"How many types are there?" I ask him and look over at the counter that must have about twenty takeout containers. "Is that all soup?"

"Yes," he tells me. "I didn't know which one you would want, so I ordered from five different restaurants."

"Just chicken is fine," I say, and I look out the window. "Is it hot outside?" I ask him, and he nods his head.

"There was a storm last night, but I think it broke," he says, pouring some soup in a bowl for me. He puts it in the microwave and then grabs me some water and crackers. He doesn't say anything else, and I know he has all the questions to ask me, and I have to tell him. The beep tells him that the soup is ready, so he grabs it and brings it to me and then grabs his own.

"Thanks, Daddy," I say, and a tear escapes and rolls down my cheek. "For everything."

"Baby girl." He hugs me from the side, kissing my head. "I would climb the tallest mountain on the coldest day naked for you."

I try to laugh but just a smile comes out. "That is some visual."

He grabs his spoon and starts to eat, and I do the same, blowing on it before bringing it to my lips. "What is going to happen?" I ask him while I eat my soup.

"Whatever you want to happen," he tells me.

"I don't think I can work with him anymore," I tell him, and he nods. His phone rings in his pocket. He takes it out and looks at me. "Go take the call, Dad."

He nods his head and steps out of the room. I get up and walk to the sink, putting my bowl in there, and then step outside, soaking in the heat of the sun. I walk past the infinity pool and lie down on the round couch he has outside. I close my eyes, thinking of him. I can almost hear him call my name, but it's all in my head.

My father comes outside and sits next to me. "How long will it hurt?" I ask him, and he looks at me. "The pain. How long will it last?"

"I don't know the answer to that, but I know that each day, it'll get a bit better. The pain will numb, and then one day, you are going to wake up, and it'll be gone," he tells me, looking out at the mountains all around him.

"The pain is more today than it was yesterday," I tell him. "I thought it would be lighter, but it's not."

"Because you haven't seen him," he tells me. "Even though he broke your heart, seeing him makes your heart know that he is right there." I nod, not asking him anything more. That night, I take a bath, a hot bath, and let the tears fall, thinking of him. Every single day plays in my head, every single time he smirked at me or smiled is there when I close my eyes. When I dream, it's of him calling my name and me turning but not going to him.

I walk away from the pain, but it just hurts even more.

When I walk into the kitchen the next day, my father is there with a coffee in his hand. "Good morning," he says with a smile, probably happy I got out of bed. "I have coffee."

I nod at him, taking a cup and helping myself. "I have to go get dressed," I tell him. "I'm supposed to meet everyone on set at ten," I tell him, looking at the clock and seeing it's almost eight.

"Honey, why don't you take an extra day off?" He tries to talk me into staying home.

"No." I shake my head. "I'm not going to let him know he broke me."

"Honey," he says, and I just shake my head. "Okay, we will play things your way."

I nod at him and walk up the stairs to my room. Opening the closet, I find the things my father has here for me just in case. I grab the pink dress, but I can't put it on, so instead, I grab the black pants and slip them on. I grab the black camisole and black jacket, and I slip on the black shoes he has there with the chunky heel. I go to the bathroom and tie my hair in a ponytail. I walk out of my room the same time that my father comes out of his own. "You look nice," he says, and I know he's lying. I had to put some makeup on under my eyes to cover the discoloration.

"Is it okay if I come back here tonight?" I ask him, and he stops walking.

"You never, ever need my permission. This is your home; all my homes are your homes." I nod at him.

"Now if it ever gets too much, I want you to step away. Do you understand me?"

"I do," I tell him and go to kiss his cheek. "Thank you, Dad."

He nods at me, and I walk out the door, going to my car, sending Sylvia a text that I will be on the set in thirty minutes. She answers back that she is already there. When I called her last night and told her everything, she didn't say a word. She only said she would take care of it, and that was it. I make my way to the set, my heart pounding in my chest and the tears burning my eyes. I let one slip by, thinking it'll be just one, but it isn't.

"You can't let him see that he broke you," I tell myself and blink away the stinging. "Tonight, you can cry rivers, but right now, you can't. Do not let him see you emotional." I pull in, and I force myself not to look for his car. I walk onto the set with my shoulders back, but my head hanging a touch. I step into trailer eight where Sylvia told me to meet her. I knock, and then I hear her shout at me to come in. I walk up the step, and I see her sitting at the table with her papers all in front of her. She takes off her glasses and looks at me. "You look nice."

"Well, at least I look nice," I tell her, going to the table and sitting on the couch. "Sylvia . . ."

"Don't," she says, shaking her head. "You don't have to say anything. You don't choose who you fall in love with. It just happens, and there was nothing you could have done differently."

"I think there are a couple of things I could have

done differently." I take a deep breath. "What time is the meeting?"

"Ryan will be here in thirty minutes, and we have the meeting in forty." I nod at her. "Let's start switching things over."

I nod at her, grabbing my notes and computer. We work side by side until there is a knock on the door, and Ryan comes in. "Morning," he says and then looks at us. "Are we ready?"

I nod my head at him. "As ready as she will ever be." I hear Sylvia say, and she leads the way out of the trailer. We walk over to stage three where there is a conference room set up. I look down while we walk there, not wanting to see him, not ready to see him. We stop right in front of the table, and I hear Jeff.

"Hey, guys," he says, and I look up to see Jeff and then right beside him, my eyes find him. I give myself a second before I look away. My father was right; it's not as painful as I thought it would be. It's worse. "Shall we get this meeting going?"

Sylvia walks to the table and sits at the far end with Ryan next to her and finally me. Sylvia took the seat in front of Carter. I don't know if they did it on purpose, so I can escape fastest or not, but I don't have time to think about it because Sylvia gets right to it.

"So there has been a change in plans," she starts, and I see Jeff look over at Carter who sits in his chair the whole time looking at Sylvia. He looks like he hasn't slept. "From now on, I will be the one working Carter's case," she says, and I am looking at Sylvia when I feel

Carter turn and look at me. "Erin set up everything already, and the transition should be smooth."

"No surprise there." His voice comes out, and it cuts me. What little piece of healing was done is now gone just from the sound of his voice. "She got what she needed from me."

Ryan now sits up straight. "If you will excuse us." He pushes back from the table, and I look up at him. "Carter, I need a minute."

"It's fine," I whisper to him, but he doesn't listen to me and just walks into the other room.

"Should I go with them?" Jeff asks, and Sylvia just shakes her head.

"I don't think that is necessary." She looks at me, then at Jeff. "Also, all communication between Carter and Erin will have to go through me. In fact, I don't think there is any need for him to contact her. If he needs anything, I will have all the answers."

Jeff nods at her and then pushes away from the table, walking past me and stopping. "They say you hurt the ones you love the most." I don't answer him. I just get up and walk away from the table, the whole time breathing slowly, so the tears don't escape. The more I walk away, the more my heart hurts, and it's knowing that I won't be with him that makes it beat faster in my chest. The pain shoots through me, but I don't stop moving. I grab my purse and make my way to my car and pull away from the stage, the pain deeper and deeper. I push it down. I push it all the way down, and instead of going to the office, I go back to my father's house.

Twenty-Seven

Carter

I'M NOT SURPRISED WHEN Jeff calls me on Sunday and tells me that we are summoned for a meeting. The weekend was a blur, and when the car picks me up on Monday morning, I look at the seven empty bottles of Jack on the counter. The only time it was easy to breathe was when I drank. Her face is clear in my head when I'm not drinking, making it hard to move, hard to think, hard to live. I get in the car, putting my glasses on. "Can we stop and get something to eat?" I tell him, laying my head back on the seat. He pulls up at Sonic, and I order the double egg and cheese, the grease soaking up some of the booze from my system. When I walk on set, I go straight to my trailer, but I don't know why I expect her to be there sitting at the table with a smile on her face.

It's even worse knowing that she is somewhere on the lot, and I can't see her. I sit in my trailer until I hear a knock on the door, and my heart speeds up just a touch, thinking, hoping, but then the door opens, and I see it's just Jeff. "You ready?" he asks me, taking off his glasses and tucking them into his suit pocket.

"As ready as I'll ever be," I say and walk out of the trailer, following him. My eyes roam everywhere to see if I can see her, to see if she is around here. We get to the table first, and I sit down at the far end, grabbing my phone and going through it. Nothing has been posted on Instagram since Friday night. I hear the noise of high heels coming closer, and my hands start to shake, my heart beating faster and faster. I look up for a second, and I see her. Her hair tied back in a ponytail, she's wearing all black, and her head is down. I don't stare more than that because I don't think I can take it. The pain is so much more than it was yesterday. "I need a drink," I say under my breath and then hear Jeff hiss.

"The last thing you need is a drink. You stink like the bottom of a fucking barrel." I look at him, and then he turns to say hello to everyone. I watch Sylvia sit in front of me, followed by Ryan, who looks like he's about to chew me a new asshole. He just glares at me, and then I look at Erin. Her eyes are sunken in, and she looks frail. She must have lost weight. I wonder if she's still sick from Saturday. I want to ask her, to make sure she is okay, but I don't. I sit in my chair and let the pain eat away at me.

"So there has been a change in plans," Sylvia starts off, and I feel Jeff look at me, then back at Sylvia. "From now on, I will be the one working Carter's case," she says. I turn to look at Erin. I didn't think she would actually come back and work with me, but I have to say a part of me was hoping she would. "Erin set up everything already, and the transition should be smooth."

"No surprise there," I say out loud, not listening to my brain telling me to shut the fuck up. No. Instead, I dig the knife deeper into her. "She got what she needed from me."

Ryan now sits up straight. "If you will excuse us." He pushes back from the table, and Erin looks up at him. "Carter, I need a minute."

I push away from the table and follow him to the room on the side. I walk into the room and take it in. It's supposed to be the house my kidnapped daughter is staying at, but instead, it's me who feels trapped inside these walls. The living room furniture is all set up. He slams the door closed, and I stand in the middle of the fake room. "We are going to get a couple of things straight." I know he isn't playing.

"Listen," I tell him, putting my hands in the back pockets of my jeans, "I know that she's your employee and all that, but . . ."

"My employee?" He shakes his head. "I'm not going to beat around the bush with you." I watch him. "You fucked up, Carter. So big you have no idea."

"I fucked up?" I ask, shocked. "Me?" I point at myself. "She used me."

"Carter, if you say another word about my daughter, so help me God, I'm going to put you through that fucking wall," he says with his teeth clenched together.

And I stare at him in shock.

"Daughter?" I ask, confused.

"Erin is my daughter," he says, "my only daughter. She didn't want people to think she got the job because of me, so we never told anyone until Saturday when I had to go and get her because she couldn't drive," he tells me, and he doesn't stop there either. "She couldn't drive because of the pain in her chest." He starts to come closer. "She couldn't breathe and ended up having a panic attack." His voice gets louder. "And you fucking did that to her."

"Ryan," I tell him softly. His words cut me, taking whatever little I had left, whatever pieces in me that weren't broken. I had no fucking idea he was her dad.

"If you so much as fuck with her or look at her, and I don't like it, I'll fucking destroy you," he says, and I know he isn't joking. "I told her that I wouldn't get involved, but when you sit at a table and spew the shit that you just did in front of me, all bets are off." He turns and walks away, stopping at the door with the handle in his hand.

"You had something precious in your hands. Something that no money in the world can buy, and you threw it away without so much as a second thought." He shakes his head. "You don't deserve her." He walks out and slams the door behind him.

"I know I don't," I say softly to the empty room. I walk back out and see that Erin is gone, but Sylvia and Jeff are waiting for me. "I have to get to makeup," I tell them and walk away to the makeup chair. Mandy takes one look at me and doesn't say anything. She just does her job, and I leave without saying anything. The day drags on. It drags on because I can't get my lines right, and each scene has to be redone a hundred times until I finally get it right. Ivan spends most of the day swearing in Russian every single time I fuck up.

I drive by her house on my way home, and I see that the lights are off in her house. I wonder if she's sleeping, but then I don't spot her car. I sit here, looking up at the window that I know is hers. Pulling away from her house, I go home to my empty house, grabbing a bottle of Jack and going to the guest room. I haven't been back in my room since she left. I kick off my shoes the same time I crack open the bottle of Jack and take four gulps before hissing out in pain from the burn. I lie on the bed, and I grab my phone, opening it up to the photos. I know I shouldn't, and I should just delete them, but I can't. Not yet. I look through them, starting at the very beginning when we were in Montana. Every single time I think of the memory that goes with the photo, I take another chug, the burning less and less. I drift off into the darkness with the phone on my chest and the empty bottle of Jack in my hand. The sound of it falling and shattering on the floor barely has me opening my eyes. I sleep through my alarm the next day, and I only wake when I feel my phone buzzing on my chest. I blink open and slur out, "Hello."

"Where in the fuck are you?" the woman asks me, and I cringe when I open my eyes and then close them just as quickly when the light is unbearable.

"I'm in bed," I tell them. "Who is this?"

"It's Sylvia," she hisses. "You were due on set an hour ago. I'm outside your door."

I lift my head, looking at the bedroom door but not seeing anyone. "I can't see you," I tell her.

"I'm outside," she says, and then I hear the banging. "Get up."

I sit up and groan, the headache that started off as a little throb has turned into full pounding. I climb out of the bed and get up, not realizing that I'm stepping on shards of glass in my bare feet. The sting makes me wince, and I look down, seeing the blood start to pour out. "Four-seven-one," I tell her the code, and soon, I hear the front door open. I sit back on the bed and hiss when I turn my foot over and see that it's sliced open. "I need help!" I shout, and I hear her running up the steps. "In here."

She walks in and sees the blood dripping off my foot and the glass all around me. "Fuck," she says and grabs her phone to call someone. "I need a doctor to come over to Carter's place." She looks at me while she listens to what the person on the other line says. "Yeah, get him over here right now. The set is on standby until he shows up." She hangs up the phone and leans on the doorjamb.

"Does it hurt?" She folds her arms over her chest.

"Stings a bit," I tell her the truth.

"Good," she says and then takes out her phone, and her fingers are flying across her phone. "We are probably going to have to postpone shooting for today."

Turning her wrist over to look at her phone, she says, "It's already late."

"Can you go get me some ibuprofen?" I ask her, and she just stares at me. "Please. Between the sting of the cut and the hangover, I don't know which is worse."

She turns and walks down the stairs, and I hear the cupboards slamming shut and then the water running. She comes back with two pills and a full glass of water. She watches me, or better yet, she glares at me until her phone rings. She answers it, walking out and then coming back in with the doctor. He comes in wearing a suit and holding a black bag. He places it on the bed.

"I'm Dr. Novack," he tells me, opening his bag and putting on latex gloves. He grabs a pillow and puts my foot up on it. "You need stitches," he confirms, "but first, I have to make sure all the glass shards are out." He looks over at Sylvia. "I'll need a towel." She nods and goes into the bathroom, coming back with a towel. He pours something over the cuts, and I lay my head back and hiss.

I close my eyes when he takes out a needle and numbs the area. By the time he leaves, I have twenty stitches in both feet. "He needs to stay off his feet for at least a week," he tells Sylvia. "I have to see him before then."

He takes off his gloves and tosses them in the trash near the bed. "A full week?" Sylvia asks. "What if he uses crutches or a wheelchair?"

"He needs the skin to heal correctly, or it'll be worse in the long run." She just nods at him, and he walks out.

"Jesus fuck," she says, taking out her phone and

calling someone. "He's out minimum a week," she tells the person. "I would make all the arrangements to film everyone else but him." She listens as the person talks. "Yeah, fine." She ends the call and looks up at the ceiling. "Why? Why me?"

"I don't have the answers for you," I tell her. "I've been asking myself that since I was eight," I tell her, closing my eyes and just letting the darkness take over.

TWENTY-EIGHT

Erin

"YOU DON'T HAVE TO go anywhere, honey," my father says to me when I tell him that it's time I go back to my own place. "This is your home, too."

"Dad, it's been two weeks," I tell him, cutting up the chicken that he just made for us. He's been home all week, and I know for a fact he's canceled three business trips. "Besides, you need to get back to work." I point my fork at him.

"I am working." He tries to hide his smile. It's been different at the office ever since they found out that I am his daughter, something that I didn't want anyone to know until I proved myself. He told Sylvia without me, but when he told Carter, I knew the cat would be out of the bag, so he announced and introduced me. Everyone was surprised, to say the least, but none have treated me differently.

"You canceled three trips east," I tell him. "You have to visit the set in New York, and you haven't."

"That's because I have everything under control from here." He tries to lie, but I know that the only reason he's been so successful is because he's the front man of his company, and everyone knows it. He doesn't just stay in his office. He goes to the sets, talks to the crew, feels everything out, and people can talk to him.

"Well, it doesn't matter," I tell him. "Tomorrow, I'm going home."

"But it's Saturday. Why don't you stay until Monday and then go home?" He tries to change my mind, but I know he needs to be in Atlanta on Sunday.

"I want to sleep in my bed and do my own laundry and just chill out," I tell him, and he frowns at me. "Dad."

"Fine." He puts his hands up, and I smile at him. "But I just don't want you to feel like you're alone."

I nod my head at him. "I know I'm never alone," I tell him the truth. If anything, they have been around me now more than ever. My mother FaceTimes me twice a day, and then my father is there for breakfast. He orders my lunch and then makes sure he's home to make me dinner. The pain is there; it's always there lingering. It's like a piece of my heart is missing, and I don't know how to fill it. I don't know if I will ever be able to fill it. I've been in love before; hell, we all have. I thought my boyfriend from high school was going to be the one I would marry and have kids with, but this is so different.

"I know how much you love him," my father says

softly, and it doesn't slip past me that he used the present tense of the word, "and I can honestly say that he feels the same way."

"Don't," I say loudly, dropping my fork onto the plate. My stomach feeling queasy again. "I don't want to hear it." My father told me about the conversation he had with him. Not so much a conversation but nonetheless, he said that regardless of what he did, he loves me.

"Erin," he says quietly, and I shake my head and get up, going to the sink.

"I don't want to hear it, Dad," I tell him. "I don't want you to sit there and dissect what he did or why he did it. He did it because that is who he is." I put my hand to my stomach when it feels like a wave just went through it. "I was the stupid one who fell for it."

"You weren't stupid for falling in love," he says, leaning back in his chair. "I fell in love with your mother when I was eighteen, and it was the best decision I ever made."

"You have to say that only because I was the outcome of that." I try to joke around.

"No, I don't have to say that." He gets up. "She was the love of my life," he says softly, "and no one after her ever measured up to her."

"Dad," I say his name softly, and he shakes his head.

"I love my life, I love that I have you, and I love that I have your mother. I wouldn't trade that for all the money in the world." He turns to me. "Now, do you want to go and watch a movie with me?"

I nod. "I'm going to go change, and then I'll meet

you in the movie room," he says, walking away, and I think about what he just said. I wonder if I will be like him and never get over Carter.

"Day by day," I tell myself, going into the movie room and starting the old-fashioned popcorn maker that sits in the corner of the room. There are ten huge brown recliners that sit in two rows in front of a projection screen.

He comes in ten minutes later wearing sweats and a T-shirt. "What are we going to watch?"

"Well, we have a couple to choose from," he says, going over to the DVDs that were delivered to him tonight. I follow him, and he flips through them, and I see the one of Carter's. He tries to hide it, but I stop him.

"Let's watch it," I tell him. I don't know why I'm doing this to myself, but maybe it's like ripping the Band-Aid right off.

"We can watch something else," he tells me, but I grab the DVD from him and walk over to the player. I put it in and meet my father by the second chair in the front. Sitting in it, I curl my feet under me. "If it gets too much . . ."

"Dad." I roll my eyes. "Just press play," I tell him, and he grabs the remote, pressing play and dimming the lights. The movie starts with the title of the film, and then his name flashes on the screen, and the wave in my stomach starts again. It's been a week since I've seen him in person. I do check his Instagram every day, telling myself it's just because of my job. His face fills the screen, and I stop and just look at him. His hair is pushed back, and you can see where his fingers ran through it, his eyes are crystal blue with the dark blue rim around the outer part. I watch him play his role to perfection. The movie isn't done, not even close to it, but for an hour, I'm under his spell and feeling every single emotion he is feeling for his daughter.

"Oh my God," I say when it comes to the end. "Dad."

"I know," he says. "I hate him for hurting you." I shake my head. "But I have to give it to him, he is really going to make a name for himself with this movie."

"I agree," I tell him, getting up and walking out of the room with him. He turns off the projection screen. "I'm going to hit the hay. I'm exhausted. These days, I swear it's a struggle to keep my eyes open after three o'clock." I kiss his cheek. "Luckily, I can't get fired."

He shakes his head. "Good night, sweetheart." I walk to my bedroom and get under the covers. Turning on my side, I stare at my phone and see no one has called me. I find myself checking my phone more often lately, my subconscious maybe hoping he'll call. Or he'll come by and explain why he did what he did. But nothing. I get nothing. I mean, is there really anything that he can say to explain why he did what he did? It's pretty self-explanatory that I wasn't enough for him. We weren't enough for him. I was just his safe place to use me, keep his job, and improve his image. I close my eyes and fall fast asleep within minutes, another thing that comes easily these days. In my dreams, there is no pain, and in my dreams, there are no mistakes. It's just me and him and his arms around me. I hear his voice, his laughter, and I feel him close to me. Then in the morning, I get to mourn him all over again.

I keep pretending I'm okay. I get in the car and make my way home and walk into the room. Again, I look around the quiet house and walk to open the curtains and the windows. I unpack the bag that I brought to my father's, and when I carry the things to my closet, I see his shirt. I stop in my tracks, afraid to get close to it. I drop the clothes in my hand and walk to the white shirt. The cotton feels so soft in my hands, and I do what everyone would do. I close my eyes and bring it to my nose and smell him. The tear escapes without warning, remembering when I wore this back home after he tore my shirt off. I take off my shirt and replace it with his, then walk to the bed and slide into it. I watch the outside, my eyes falling closed with the smell of him settling my heartbeat for the first time in over a week. It's all a daze; it's all just going through the motions.

I get up, go to work, come home to sleep, and then repeat five days a week. Sleeping is my escape from everything, but even with all the sleeping I'm getting, the dark circles are still around my eyes. I'm sitting in my office on a Friday afternoon when my phone rings from an unknown caller.

"Hello," I answer on the second ring.

"Hey, Erin, it's Jessica." I drop my pen that I was writing with. "Am I catching you at a bad time?"

"No," I answer her. "Not at all. How are you?"

"I'm good, a little sick, but hey, that's to be expected when you're knocked up." She laughs nervously.

"Oh my gosh, I had no idea," I tell her. "Not that I've been reading the tabloids lately."

She laughs. "We haven't announced it yet. But I was calling because I finally was able to finish the story." I take a deep breath. "I am just about to send it to you for your approval, and then I'm going to be publishing it."

"I'm actually not the one doing the PR for Carter anymore," I tell her, "but I can send it to Sylvia, and if she has anything she would like to change or add, she can get in touch with you."

"That sounds great," she says. "Whatever it is, just let me know."

"I will and congratulations again," I tell her, and we disconnect. I scroll on my phone list and dial Sylvia.

"Hey, Erin," she says, answering the phone on the third ring.

"Hey, Sylvia," I reply, "are you busy?"

"Not right now," she says. "We are waiting for the car to come and get us." I try not to think about who the we are.

"I just got a phone call from Jessica about the piece she wrote for Carter," I tell her. "I'm going to forward you the email, and you can check it out."

"Perfect. You can send it now. The plane takes off in an hour, so I can look it over on the plane." I check my email and forward the email to her. "I will be back in the office Monday morning."

"Perfect," I tell her. "Have a great weekend."

"Thank you, Erin. You, too," she says and disconnects. I do what I shouldn't. I open the document and read the article. It's baffling to me that it's already been three weeks since that day.

I open the calendar and write in a couple of items that I need to take care of next week. I schedule a meeting with Sylvia on Tuesday to go over the game plan to take care of the movie premiere in two months. I turn the pages and see the red circle around the date and then flip through the pages. My neck starts to burn, and my stomach flutters. I flip the pages again and count backward. This can't be happening. This can't be happening. I get up, grabbing my purse, and rush home, suddenly feeling sick.

When night comes, I don't sleep. I sit on the couch in the dark wearing his shirt. When morning comes, I slip on my clothes and get into my car.

The drive goes faster than I want it to go, my heart speeding up a bit and my hands holding the steering wheel so hard my knuckles turn white. When I pull up to the house, I get out and walk down the step, ringing the doorbell. I stand here holding my purse in front of me with both hands. My head's down as I count to twenty when I hear the lock click, and the door swing open. I thought I was ready for it. I was not.

TWENTY-NINE

Carter

"I CAN'T WAIT TO be home," Sylvia says from beside me, getting into the car. We are in Montana, where we have been for the whole week, and on our way home.

After the doctor ordered me to stay on bed rest, Jeff came over and brought a male nurse to help me around the house and do things for me since I couldn't be on my feet. Not only was this guy my shadow, but all the booze was taken out of my house like I was a child. Facing everything sober is worse than you think. Facing the pain in your chest day in and day out, thinking it's going to get better, but instead, it gets worse, so much worse, and at times, you think your heart's going to either come out of your chest or stop beating. I spent most of the time either on the couch or in bed, trying to shut off my mind. It replayed everything that I wanted to forget. My mind replayed everything that I missed and everything that I loved yet couldn't have.

I got back on set, and it was go time. They had filmed pretty much everything that they could without me, and now it was crunch time. Usually I would hate it, but it made me focus on anything but her. Every single time I saw Sylvia, I wanted to ask about her, but I didn't have the right to know anything.

Going back to Montana was not only the knife in my chest, but it was the knife being twisted. That was when the memories were the strongest. The pull toward the mountains, toward the house where I fell in love with her. I got in the car one night and drove there. Luckily, it was empty. I sat on the chair in the back without the fire lit and just let it go. Let myself have all the memories. I let myself look at the pictures, and I let my heart experience the pain I was feeling.

Every day, it felt like an elephant was sitting on my chest, and I was happy to go home, thinking that the elephant would stay there. I am sitting next to Sylvia when I hear her name, and my heart speeds up, faster and faster. I can't even concentrate. I close my eyes, hoping that somehow I will be able to hear her voice. If I listen close enough, will I be able to hear her?

"Perfect. You can send it now. The plane takes off in an hour, so I can look it over on the plane," Sylvia says and looks out the window, waiting for the car to come get us. "I will be back in the office Monday morning." I wait to hear what else she will say. "Thank you, Erin. You, too." She disconnects and then looks at her phone.

"We got the interview that Jessica did," she tells me.

"I guess Erin can't take care of it from New York," I tell her, turning to look out the window.

"She isn't in New York," she says, and I slowly turn my head. "She's in the L.A. office."

"I thought after she was done with me, she was taking the job in New York?" I say, my hands suddenly clammy. She shakes her head.

"No, she turned that job down," she says, and my mouth suddenly gets dry, my heart hammering in my chest. "She was never going to New York. I mean, at first that was her end goal, but halfway through your assignment, she emailed the team and said she wasn't interested in relocating."

"But I thought . . ." I start saying, and Sylvia looks over at me. "I thought she wanted the job in New York."

She shrugs her shoulders like her answer isn't the one that I've been waiting for. "No, she turned that option down when she got back from Montana."

It can't be is the only thing I think. It can't be; this can't be happening. "But . . ." I say, and I honestly can't focus on anything except the pounding echoing in my ears from my heart. "But she was going to take New York."

"I have no idea. It was never actually decided really," she says and then gets up when she sees the car pull up. I walk to the car, my body going through the motions, but my head spinning. But Jennifer told me that she was going to New York. She told me that.

What the fuck did I just do? What the fuck, what the fuck, *what the fuck*? I don't bother talking to anyone on the flight. I get on, go sit on the couch, and lay my head back. We land, and it's almost eleven p.m. I get in the car and instead of going home, my car goes toward her house to see if she's home. There aren't any lights on, so she's probably sleeping or out on a date. My stomach burns thinking that. I get home and walk upstairs to the guest bedroom and kick off my shoes, my feet still stinging. I lie in bed the whole night, looking up at the ceiling. The darkness outside fades into gray, then into light, and I get up, going downstairs.

I have to go see her; I have to explain. I just have to. There isn't a way around it anymore. I fucked up, and I did it in such a colossal way that I don't think anything will be good enough, but she has to know. I grab the coffee cup in my hand and bring it to my lips when I hear the doorbell. My eyes go to the clock on the stove, and I see it's a little after nine. Who could it be? I put down the cup and walk to the door, unlocking it and swinging it open, and there standing in the doorway is the only person who can make my heart beat normal. My first thought is how beautiful she is. Her hair blows in the wind while she holds her purse in front of her. "Erin." Her name on my lips makes everything okay. It's like my life was spinning, but now it's back on its axis.

"Hi," she says, her voice soft, and I look at her. She looks like she's lost weight and hasn't slept, and I did that to her. But my God, she's still fucking gorgeous. "I'm sorry. I should have called before I came, but I didn't even think."

"No," I say sharply. "Please come in." I move away, and I hope she comes in. If she doesn't, I wonder if I could just grab her and lock her in the house. Never let her leave so I can finally fucking breathe.

"I won't take up much of your time," she says, walking in and waiting for me to lead the way.

"You can take up as much of my time that you want," I tell her. All my time, all my time forever almost slips out, but I stop myself. "Is this okay?" I say, pointing at the couch, and she nods her head.

She sits down at the far end of the couch, and I see that her hands are shaking. I want to reach out and take her hand in mine and bring it to my mouth and kiss it. "Do you want something to drink?" I ask her nervously when she shakes her head.

"No, I'm fine," she says, then she looks down at her hands. "I just," she says, taking a deep breath. "I just . . ."

I reach out to grab her hand, and she moves it away before I can touch her. I put my hand back in my lap because she doesn't even want my hand on her. "I'm just going to say what I came here to say, and then I have to go," she says, and I see that she is blinking away tears. She is so strong. "I would ask that you please not interrupt me, or I might chicken out, and I really can't."

"Say whatever you need to say," I tell her. "And then I ask that you listen to what I have to say."

"I'm pregnant." She says the two words that stop everything that I was thinking. It just stops everything. "I know this is a shock to you, and I am still in shock myself." I don't say anything; I can't say anything because my tongue is numb. "I found out last night. I just lost track of the dates with everything that I had going on," she says, the last part trailing off softly. "I haven't told anyone. I wanted you to know before I told my parents." I look at her, my eyes blinking as I try to think of the words. "I know this isn't anything that you wanted, or we planned, but it's here, and I have to deal with it."

The shock to my system is more than I can digest right now, but my heart takes over where my brain is in freefall. "Erin, you don't have to deal with anything. You are having our baby," I tell her, and my heart is full of love, a love that I didn't even think I was capable of.

"Anyway, the reason I'm here is just to tell you that I don't expect anything from you. I don't expect you to be involved or for you to even care," she says, and now a lone tear escapes, and she wipes it away with the back of her thumb. "I won't tell anyone you're the father, and you can be as involved as you want to be or not at all."

"What?" I say to her, and she gets up now.

"I know it's a shock, and it's really not something you want to hear." She nods at me, and I sit here looking at her. "I have to go," she says, and she walks out of my house, and I'm still sitting here on the couch.

"I'm going to be a father," I say out loud with a huge smile on my face. "I'm going to be a father." Shit, I think, getting up and running out the door to chase her, but she isn't there. I run back inside and up the steps two at a time, ignoring the sting on the bottom of my feet as I rush to get dressed.

I grab my keys and rush out of my house and go to her. I run up the steps and ring the bell, and after one second, I knock. I don't hear anything, but then I look out into the parking lot to make sure her car is there. I turn again and knock when I hear the lock click. She opens her door just a touch, and I see that her face is so white, and her lips are even whiter. "Are you sick?"

"Yeah," she says softly. "It's like my body just realized I'm pregnant and now the morning sickness starts," she says. "What are you doing here?"

"You didn't even give me a chance to talk," I tell her, and she nods. But then her eyes go wide, and she turns to run away, leaving the door open. I follow her, but the bathroom door is closed and locked. "Erin," I say softly, and then I hear her getting sick. I grab my phone and google what I can do for morning sickness. I turn and go to her kitchen and try to find crackers, but there isn't much. I walk back to the bathroom and hear her getting sick again. "I'm going to be right back," I tell her, and I don't know if she is grunting to tell me she heard me or to get sick again. I rush out of the apartment and go to the closest store, pulling up Google. I grab a cart and rush through the aisles, throwing things in the cart. I check out and carry the bags to the car, then go back over to Erin's. I knock on the door, and she opens it, and the color is returning to her face but it's still white. "I've got some things," I say, holding up the bags in my hands, and she walks away from the door and goes to the couch.

"What did you get?" she asks.

"I got a whole bunch of things to help. Saltines, ginger ale, ginger tea, ginger root. Also, I got some prenatal vitamins for you," I tell her, grabbing the box of crackers and walking up to her. "This should help." I sit on the table in front of her.

"Thank you, but you shouldn't have done that. Someone probably snapped pictures of you buying prenatal vitamins, Carter," she whispers. "What are you doing here?" She looks up and shivers, and I pull my jacket off and slip it over her shoulders.

"You didn't even give me a chance to speak before you ran out," I tell her, and she looks down at the pack of crackers in her hands. "We need to talk."

"There really isn't much to say," she says to me. "I'm pregnant."

"We are pregnant," I tell her.

"Pretty sure I'm the one carrying the baby," she tells me. Opening the crackers, she grabs one and puts it in her mouth. I reach out to push her hair away, but she moves out of the way to make sure I don't touch her.

"We need to talk," I tell her.

"There really isn't much to talk about. The result is still the same," she says, folding her legs under her. "I'm pregnant."

"How far along are you?" I ask her. I want to know everything. "Do you feel the baby moving?"

"I have no idea. Maybe like a month," she answers and then throws the crackers down and runs to the bathroom. This time, I take off with her, and I reach out and hold her hair back.

I squat next to her and rub her back. "Can you go away?" she croaks.

"No," I say. "Never again." She looks at me and shakes her head and slowly gets up, walking to the sink and leaning down to take a couple of sips of water and rinse out her mouth.

I walk out with her and grab a can of ginger ale, bringing it to her. "I never slept with her." I say the five words that I've been repeating in my head since she walked out of my house. Her eyes look at me with tears, but I don't stop. "It was all a lie."

"What?" she asks, getting up now and walking away from me.

"I fucked up because I believed something that wasn't true," I tell her. "Honestly, that is what it comes down to." She looks at me, shaking her head.

"You broke my heart on purpose." She holds her chest, and I want to kick my own ass.

"It was a misunderstanding," I tell her. "Jennifer told me that you were taking a job in New York at that party." Looking at her, I say, "It was a misunderstanding."

"It was a misunderstanding? You had a naked fucking woman in your bed and a condom wrapper on the table by the bed," she points out, a sob escaping from her. "Why?"

"'Cause I'm a fucking insecure asshole who thought you were using him because he's an actor in Hollywood," I tell her, getting up and running my hands through my hair. "So I paid her to come home with me. I'm not proud of my actions.""Not proud of your actions? Are you kidding me?" she says, throwing up her hand and walking to the door. "Get out."

"Erin, we need to talk about us," I tell her, walking to her.

"There is no us." She shakes her head. "The only thing we need to talk about is the baby."

"This isn't over," I tell her, walking out of the door.

"It was over the minute you decided to do what you did," she says, slamming the door, turning the lock with a click.

"It's not over!" I yell at the door, waiting for her to say something. When she doesn't, I turn and go away but only for the time being.

Thirty

Erin

I SLAM THE DOOR behind him when he walks out. He lied to me. Everything that I went through, everything that I felt was because he thought I was using him. I shake my head and walk to the kitchen, opening the white plastic bags that he dumped there and taking out the stuff. He got everything from ginger root to ginger tea to ginger snaps. I shake my head and walk over to the couch, sitting down and closing my eyes. My hands go to my stomach, and I say, "I love you." Getting up, I walk to my bedroom and lie down on the bed, closing my eyes and slowly falling asleep.

I wake to a soft knock on the door, and I get up, the motion making me a little sick. I breathe in just a touch, and the knocking continues. I get up and see it's almost dark outside, the sun setting. I unlock the door and open it, and I'm stunned. He is standing there with flowers and a stuffed animal under one arm and both his hands holding plastic bags.

"I brought some more things." He walks in, and I watch him walking over to the kitchen, dumping the bags on the counter. "You look better," he tells me, and I walk over. "I didn't know what you were feeling like, so I stopped and got you a bunch of things. I have some soup, and then I have some pasta mild on the sauce so the acid doesn't give you heartburn," he says, taking out the containers. "I got you some chicken soup with rice. They said online that bland carb food helps."

"Carter," I say.

"I also got popsicles and Jell-O," he tells me. "What do you feel like eating?"

I shrug. "Chicken soup," I tell him, and he pours some in the bowl and puts it in the microwave. I walk over to the dining room table and sit down. "Thank you," I tell him when he puts the bowl down in front of me. He goes over to the bags and warms up his own food and comes back to the table. I stir the soup with my spoon and watch him sit in front of me. "This is a little overwhelming."

"I know," he says, cutting into his food that looks like chicken parm. "It's surreal."

"I took seven tests," I tell him, and he looks at me. "I wanted to be a hundred percent sure."

"Were they all positive?" he asks me and smiles when I nod my head.

"I am going to tell my father tomorrow," I tell him. "I'll FaceTime my mother at the same time."

"I'll come with you," he tells me, and I drop my spoon.

"Listen, this is all happening too fast," I tell him. "One day, I wake up and go about my day, and by the end of the day, I'm pregnant, and all of a sudden, I'm going to be a mom."

"Erin," he says, putting his fork down. "There are certain things in life you are never sure of, at least for me. But there is one thing I'm a hundred percent sure of. I love our child with everything that I am. I never thought I would be a dad, never thought I would deserve to be a dad." I look at him. "Maybe I don't deserve it, but it's here, and I'm so in love I can't believe it. I wanted to tell every person I saw today." He smiles. "Every single person. I don't deserve you to be kind to me, I don't deserve anything that you are giving me, but thank you for giving me the chance to be a father." He looks down and then looks back up with a smile plastered on his face. "I'm going to be a dad."

"So I guess this means you want to be fully involved?" I ask him.

"Every single step of the way," he tells me. "Doctor visits, Lamaze classes, crib buying. You name it, I want to be there."

"Okay," I say. As much as he hurt me, I would never take this away from him or our child. "When it comes to the baby, you will be there every step of the way."

"That means breaking the news to your father," he tells me. "Besides, there are some things that need to be said, and it's better if it's said with the family."

I push the soup away. "Are you not hungry?" he asks me, and I just shrug.

"Is there anymore of that?" I point at his dish. He pushes his dish in front of me and grabs my soup. "No, I'm not taking your food."

"You aren't, but my child is," he says, pointing at the dish. "Eat." I roll my eyes at him and eat the rest of his food. "Be careful how far back you roll those eyes. I've heard they can get stuck there." He cleans up and then looks over at me with that smirk on his face. "I'm going to go so you can rest, but I'll be here tomorrow at nine, and we can have breakfast before we head over to your father's."

I nod my head at him, and he looks at me. "Can you call me if you need anything?"

"I'll be fine," I tell him, and he just nods and walks out. Stopping at the door, he turns to say something, but he must change his mind because he just turns back and walks out the door.

"He's a funny guy, your father," I tell my stomach, turning and getting ready for bed. The next day, I wake, and the minute I open my eyes, I have to rush to the bathroom. By the time nine a.m. rolls around, I'm lying on the couch trying to eat ginger snaps but failing miserably. I pick up my phone and call Carter, who answers on the second ring. "Change of plans. I'm going to go to my dad's later."

"Why?" he asks, and I take a sip of water.

"Because I literally can't move off the couch," I tell him and then hear a knock. "Are you here?"

"I am. Open the door," he says, and I roll off the couch and walk to the door slowly, breathing in through my nose and out through my mouth. "How long have you been sick?"

"No clue," I tell him and walk back over to the couch, not even caring that I'm wearing my pjs and no bra.

He walks to the bathroom and comes back with a wet cloth. "Did you know that they don't call it morning sickness anymore?" He puts the rag on the back of my neck. "It's called nausea and vomiting from pregnancy." I look at him sideways. "I spent the night reading up on morning sickness." He sits down by my feet. "Also, if you are six weeks pregnant, our baby is the size of a pea and the shape of the letter C and little buds have formed that will be the arms and legs. Is there anything else you want to know because I'm pretty sure I learned everything around four a.m. this morning?"

"I can't deal with you when you're like this," I tell him and just lay my head on the back of the couch, closing my eyes. I drift off to sleep, and when I wake up, he's sitting at the end of the couch reading the book *What to Expect When You're Expecting*. A cover has been draped over me. "What time is it?"

"A little after eleven," he tells me. "Do you want something?"

"No," I tell him and slowly get up and go to the bathroom. I get dressed and get ready to go to my father's. I walk out of the bedroom and see him sitting on the couch. "I think we should go."

"Lead the way," he says, putting the book down on

the table. I walk out, and after arguing with him about taking two cars instead of one, he wins, and we make our way over to my father's. When he opens the door and sees us, his smile disappears, and in its place a frown comes over him.

"Hey, Daddy," I say, coming in. "Sorry to just drop in, but I need to talk to you and Mom," I tell him, and he just looks over at Carter who nods at him. "We need to do this fast," I tell him as the nausea returns in full force. We walk to the living room, and I take my phone out to FaceTime my mother. "Hey, Mom, it's me."

"Oh, hi, sweetie," she says, and I see she is sitting on the couch. "I'm here with Dad," I say, turning the phone, and she smiles and waves at my father who just scowls. "And Carter." I turn the phone, and now my mother scowls also. I place the phone down on the table and sit down, and I make sure she can see us all. "There is no easy way to say this," I start, and my father just shakes his head.

"You are not marrying him!" he shouts, and Carter now shakes his head.

"I'm not marrying him," I say and then look over at Carter who glares at my father. "But we are having a baby." I just say it, and my father shoots out from his chair. Carter springs up also, and I spring up, standing in the middle of them, the fast motion making me queasy. "Can you both calm down?"

"How can you do this?" He looks over at Carter.

"I am not going to apologize for having a child," Carter says.

"What about her finding you in bed with a whore?" my father shouts, and Carter just looks at me.

"I never slept with her!" Carter shouts. "Never even touched her."

"Lies!" my father shouts. "You are a liar."

"I'm a lot of things, but a liar isn't one of them," he says softly, and then I hear my mother suddenly sobbing, and we all look over at her.

"My baby is having a baby," she says and then looks at my father. "Our baby is having a baby."

"I know, sweetheart." His tone changes, and he grabs my phone and leaves the room.

"Well, that went well," I say to Carter who is just standing there.

"I never, ever touched her. Not even a hair on her head." His voice is husky. "After she left, I burned the bed on the beach." My mouth opens in shock. "You have to know. And as much as I want to forget that moment, you have to know," he says and then looks up and starts to say something, but my father returns, and you can see that he had tears in his eyes.

"I'm sending a plane for your mother. She wants to be here for the doctor's appointment," my father says, and I shake my head.

"I'm going with Carter," I tell him. "It's just us for the first one." My father stares at me. "I love you, but you know that it's the right thing to happen. No matter what he did to me." I look down, and the tear comes, and I wipe it away. "It's still his right to be there if he wants to."

"I want to," he says, coming to me and putting his hand on my back. "I want to be there as much as she'll let me."

"You better not fuck this up," my father tells him. "This isn't a game."

"You don't have to tell me," he says, and then he looks at me. "I will not fuck this up."

I nod at him, and when we leave my father's, I sigh in relief. "I'm happy that is over," I tell him, and he opens the car door for me. He doesn't say anything, and right now, I'm so tired I can't even think. When he gets in the car, he looks at me. "What?" I ask him.

"You're beautiful," he tells me, and I don't answer him. I just look out the window and stop myself from overthinking it. I'm the mother of his child; that is the only thing I am to him right now. It's really the only thing I have left to give him.

THIRTY-ONE

Carter

"ARE YOU NERVOUS?" I ask her, looking over at her. It's been ten days since she told me she's pregnant with my child. Ten days since I realized I loved her even more than I did before. Ten days since I've started to breathe again.

"A little," she says, and she flips through the pages of the magazine. I've been with her every single day. I am trying not to get her so annoyed she tells me not to come back or stops seeing me.

Every morning, I take off from the set and drive over to her house with a ginger tea to help with her morning sickness. Then I rush back, and we go through things. I set up to have food delivered to her work and also snacks during the day. The minute I'm done on set, I call her and show up with dinner. Every night when I get home, I sit in bed wishing she was with me and that I could hold her in my arms. So far, she hasn't pushed me away and told me not to come back, so I'm going back.

"Erin Crest." The nurse calls her name, and she gets up, and I follow her into the examine room. An examine table sits in the middle of the room. "You can change into this." She hands her a hospital gown. "But first, I need a urine sample." She hands her a plastic cup. "I will be in shortly." She nods at us and then turns to walk out of the room. Erin goes into the bathroom and comes back with the gown on and holding the back closed.

After a knock on the door, the nurse comes back in. "You can sit on the table," she tells Erin. She walks to the little stool and then steps up to sit in the middle of the table, leaving her feet hanging. "I'm going to ask you a couple of questions. When was your last menstrual cycle?"

"Eight weeks ago," Erin answers, and I just wait at the side as she asks all sorts of questions. She grabs the urine sample, going over to the counter and dipping something inside. She waits three minutes and writes down something.

"You are officially pregnant," she says and then smiles at us. "The doctor will be right in," she says, walking out and then after another knock on the door, the doctor comes in.

"Hello there," he says, smiling to Erin. "I'm Dr. Graves." He turns to look at me. "Nice to meet you." I shake his hand, and he comes over and grabs the chart, reading it. "Okay, let's get you checked out," he says and walks over to the stool in the middle of the room and asks her to lie back. He raises the stirrup and tells her to put her feet in them.

"Carter." She calls my name, and I walk over to her. "Stay on this side." She points behind her head, and I don't understand it until I see the doctor put on gloves, then grab what looks like a long beige stick. He grabs a condom and puts it on this thing and then squeezes some lube on it.

"What are you doing with that?" I ask him, ready to grab Erin and run out. Nothing I read online about pregnancy mentioned something that looks like a gigantic fucking condom-wearing dildo with lube on it going anywhere near Erin's vagina.

"She is still early in her pregnancy, so it's easier to use a vaginal ultrasound than a regular one," he says and then turns off the lights. He moves the gown up and pulls the machine to him and puts it in Erin.

"Does that hurt?" I whisper to her, and she shakes her head. I see the worry in her face. I push back the hair on her head and lean down to kiss her forehead. "I'm right here," I tell her. I hold her hand, and she lets me. She hasn't gotten close to me in ten days. Each time, she shies away from my touch, making sure if I do touch her, it lasts three second before moving away.

"You are going to feel some pressure," the doctor says, and then he looks at the gray and white screen. "All the black is fluid." And then I look at the screen, amazed; he uses his finger to circle the big black circle in the middle of the screen. "This is your uterus, and in the middle is the amniotic fluid," he says, and then slowly, a white thing comes into focus. "And in the middle of that is your baby." I watch the screen. "You look to be about eight weeks," he says and then points at what is the head and then the body.

"See this flicker?" He points at the small white thing blinking on the screen. "That is your baby's heartbeat. I'm going to take some measurements." He does something that makes a blue mark appear. "You are just a little over eight weeks," he says, and then the baby makes a sudden movement and flips over. He presses something, and it sounds like static, and then the sound of swooshing fills the room. "And that sound is your baby's heartbeat," he says, and I can't even stop the tears from rolling down my face as I watch my baby move again.

I look down at Erin, who is watching the screen as tears roll down her face. She turns and looks at me. "Our baby," she says to me, and I just nod and lean in to gently kiss her lips.

"Our baby," I say, smiling now, my chest feeling so full.

"It's one hundred and seventy-nine beats a minute," Dr. Graves says.

"Is that normal?" I ask, concerned.

"Yes, that is where you want it to be. It's supposed to be between a hundred and sixty to a hundred and eighty," he says. "We have four limbs, two arms, two legs." I rub Erin's head while he continues taking measurements, the sound of the baby's heartbeat still filling the room. I grab my phone and take a video of the baby moving. He takes the stick out of her and then cleans the condom off and wipes it down. "So everything looks good. Do you have any questions?"

Erin shakes her head, but I ask him about twenty-five questions, and he just laughs at the end. "Someone did their research," he says. "I will see you again in a month." He nods at us and walks out.

"I'm going to go change," she says, getting up and walking back into the bathroom. When she comes back out, we go back to her place, and I park the car. She took the day off. I follow her up the stairs and into her house. Walking to the middle of the living room, I turn to her.

"I know that you will never forgive me," I start saying, and she stops moving and looks at me. "I know that I have no one else to blame for that by myself. And I know that one day our child is going to ask why we aren't together, and I'm going to take complete blame for it," I say, my heart pounding thinking about how horrible that day will be. "It's going to suck."

"Carter," she says softly, wringing her hands. "We don't have to tell them anything."

"No," I tell her. "I want them to know that he or she was created with love." I watch her with tears now running over. "That I love their mother with everything that I have, and I will never stop loving her."

"Carter," she says again, and I hold up my hand.

"You don't have to say anything." I shake my head. "You owe me nothing, and I owe you everything." I take a deep breath. "All the good in me is because of you. That you showed me what it was like to love someone without any strings attached. You showed me that, Erin, so thank you." I need to walk out of the room. "I'm going to go. Call me if you need anything," I tell her and walk out the door. I walk to my car and get in, driving back home. I watch the video over and over again. I watch it until all I can do is hear the heart beating through the tears in my eyes.

I'm sitting in bed watching some infomercial when my phone rings, and I see it's Erin. I jump up and answer it right away. "Erin?"

All I hear is sobbing and heavy breathing. "I think there is something wrong with the baby," she says, and I'm running around the house, putting on clothes and rushing out the door. "I woke up, and there was blood," she says, and my heart sinks as she quietly cries.

"Baby, you need to breathe," I tell her, getting into the car. "I'm on my way right now."

"I'm scared, Carter," she says softly between her sobs, and I race over there. I don't even turn the car off when I get to her house and run up the stairs. The door is open, and she is lying on the couch crying.

"Come on, baby," I say, taking her in my arms. She wraps her arms around my neck and cries into my neck. I put her in the car and drive there with my hand in her lap. When we get to the hospital, I park the car right in front of the emergency doors, leaving the keys in and running around to get Erin. She gets out of the car, and we walk inside. The halls are quiet in the night.

The nurse looks up when we come to the desk. "I'm eight weeks pregnant, and I'm bleeding," Erin tells the nurse, and she gets up, coming around the desk. The nurse takes us to a room and asks Erin to undress and get into bed.

We don't say anything when she undresses and gets in the bed. I sit on the bed next to her. "Baby," I whisper, grabbing her hand, "it's going to be okay."

"You don't know that," she tells me.

"I don't, but I know that you're the strongest woman I know," I tell her. The nurse comes back into the room, wheeling equipment with her. I stand beside Erin, holding her hand. Bringing her close to me, I kiss her head, and she looks up at me. "I'm right here."

"Okay," the nurse says, grabbing a white bottle and squeezing some blue gel on Erin's stomach. "This is going to be cold. I don't know if I will be able to see like this. If not we will get the other machine." She grabs a piece of equipment and puts it down on her stomach moving the gel around. She turns on the machine, and the baby is there. "Everything looks okay," she says, and then we hear the swooshing sound fill the room. We look at each other, both sighing in relief. "Everything looks okay, but I'm going to have the doctor come in," she says, turning the machine off and taking a towel and wiping Erin's stomach. I sit on the bed next to her, pushing her hair behind her ear, and she holds her belly in her hand.

The doctor comes in and checks her, telling us that everything is okay, and that bleeding isn't uncommon, but he would like to keep her overnight for observation. I stand by her side, making her know that I'm here for whatever support she needs. When she finally falls asleep, I get up and walk out the door, bringing out my phone. I scan until I find the name I need.

"Hello." Ryan answers at the end of the first ring.

"Hey, it's me," I tell him and take a deep breath. "We are at Cedar."

"What happened?" I hear the worry in his voice, and I hear rustling in the background. "I'll be there in twenty." He disconnects the phone, and I walk in and sit on the chair beside her bed, watching her chest rise and fall. Twenty minutes later, the door opens softly, and I see that it's Ryan. He comes into the room, and I look to see if Erin is awake, but she is sleeping. "Is she okay?"

I nod my head. "Yeah, she's good." My eyes don't leave hers. "She was bleeding," I say, ignoring the lump in my throat.

"Did she miscarry?" he asks, coming to sit in the chair next to me.

"No," I tell him. "The doctor said it's not uncommon to bleed." The tears now escape, and I look over at him. "I thought my heart would stop," I tell him, sitting forward. "When she called me and was crying, I swear, Ryan, my heart only started again when I saw her."

"Carter, do you love her just because she is having your child?" he asks me, and I just shake my head.

"I would give my life for her," I tell him. "Even if she wasn't having my child."

"Then I suggest you do something about it before it's too late." I look at him. "Because you don't want to just go through the motions for the rest of your life. I did that, and I don't recommend it." He looks at me. "Don't let her slip through your fingers."

"I don't know how to get her back." I tell him the truth.

"Tell her." He grabs her hand and kisses it.

"I don't know if she will ever forgive me," I tell him. "I don't deserve what she can give me."

"You don't," he says, "but she does. She deserves a man who will love her with everything that he has. Who can make her smile, who can hold her hand, and wipe her tears away."

"I want to be that man," I tell him, watching her. "I want to be there with her every day, all day."

"Don't let it get away from you," he says to me. "Don't let your fear get in the way." I nod my head and sit with him until she wakes up. She opens her eyes, and we both move forward to her.

"Hey, honey," Ryan says to her, and she looks at him and then at me.

"How are you feeling?" I ask, and she just puts her hand on her stomach.

"Scared," she says softly, and I just nod. "Do you think they could do another ultrasound?" she asks me.

"I'll get the doctor," I tell her, knowing that I will pay for a private machine if it will make her sleep better. I walk out and see the nurse. "Sorry, Erin is up, and we were hoping we could see the doctor."

"I'll send him right in," she says, and I walk back to the room and take a deep breath before I open the door. The bed is empty, so I look at Ryan.

"She's in the bathroom," he says, and then I nod at him and wait for her to come out of the bathroom.

"No blood," she says hopeful. "Not even spotting." She gets back into the bed, and the doctor comes in. When we ask for another ultrasound, he nods and gets the machine again. I stand beside the bed, holding Erin's hand in mine as we look at the screen. When he places the gel on her and the swishing sound fills the room, my heart is so proud. Ryan leans over and kisses Erin. "Is everything okay?" Erin asks, and the doctor nods.

"Everything is looking good," he says. "I would like you to follow up with your OB."

"Can I have a picture?" Ryan asks the doctor, who nods and prints out two. He hands one to Ryan and one to Erin. She sits in the bed, holding the picture of our child in one hand and holding my hand in the other.

"You are free to go," he tells us, and Ryan gets up.

"Do you want me to drive you home?" he asks Erin, and I look at her as she looks at me.

"Can you drive me home?" she asks me, and I smile. Ryan kisses her goodbye and tells her he'll check in with her later today, and then she gets up and goes to change. She leaves the picture on the bed, and I sit down and take a picture with my phone. She walks into the room dressed. "I'm ready when you are," she says. We turn and walk out of the hospital. I drop her off at home and then place a phone call to put my first plan into action.

THIRTY-TWO

Erin

I PICK UP THE phone when I see it's Carter. "Hello?"

"Hey there," he says. "I was wondering if you would come out with me."

"Where?" I ask, sitting up. It's been two days since the whole hospital scene and the day I woke up with blood soaking through my underwear. So far, it's been smooth sailing. I mean, minus the morning sickness, which is turning into the all-day sickness. I have crackers stacked everywhere and munch on them all day.

"I want you to see something," he says. "It's a surprise."

I close my eyes. As much as I fight being nice to him, my heart just can't let him go. Now the fact that I am carrying his child is just so much more. "Sure. I just got home."

"I can pick you up in thirty, and we can stop for food

after," he tells me. I walk to my closet and change out of my work clothes and put on yoga pants. I'll need to get some new clothes very soon because the ones I have now are starting to feel a little snug. The knock on the door comes just as I've tied my running shoes. I walk to the door with my purse and open the door. He smiles when he sees me. "You're ready."

"I am," I tell him, and I walk out of the house and follow him down to his car. "Are you going to tell me where we are going?"

"Not yet," he says, starting the car. "It's a surprise. Do you want me to stop and get you something?"

"No, I'm good for now," I tell him and look out the window as he makes his way to the hills. We pull up to a black gate, and he presses a number on the key pad. We drive into the driveway, stopping in front of a white house.

"What is this?" I say, getting out and seeing that when you walk to the door, you have two garages on each side.

"This," he says, opening the door, "is my new house."

I look at him shocked and step into the foyer. The house is freaking huge. I step into the living room, looking up at the upstairs landing. "Are you moving?" I ask him, my heart beating.

"Come upstairs," he tells me and walks to a circular staircase. I follow him up, and he brings me to an empty room. "This is going to be the baby's room."

"What?" I ask, looking around the room with beige carpet.

"Two days ago, I thought for the second time in my life that my heart would stop," he tells me, and I watch him. "The first time was when I lost you."

"Carter," I say his name softly, not sure I want to hear this, but knowing that I can't not listen.

"When I lost you, it felt like an elephant was crushing my chest. I used to drink to black out all of our memories." He takes a huge breath. "I didn't think I would ever find a reason to go on." He smiles at me. "Then you came to me and told me that you were pregnant. Erin, I never in my life felt that my heart could be so full." I wipe away the tear rolling down to my chin. "When you called me, and we had that scare, I swear to God I thought my life was ending. The whole way over, I begged God to take me and spare you and the baby." I look at him and see the anguish in his eyes.

"Your father asked me if I loved you just because you are having my baby." I don't want to hear the answer, but he gives it to me anyway. "The answer is no." He walks closer to me. "I love you because you complete me. I love you because with you, I know everything is going to be okay. I love you because no matter what life throws at me, as long as I get to spend my days and nights with you, nothing could go wrong." He walks to me, and my tears just run down my face. "I told him I don't deserve you." He wipes my tear away with his thumb. "I don't deserve another chance, but I'm here begging you to give me one."

"I don't know," I tell him the truth. "I don't know if I can do that. I don't think my heart could take it if you broke me again."

"If you give me this chance, I will spend the rest of my life proving that I love you." His other hand comes up. "I want this house to be ours, and I want this to be the baby's room. I want to fill the rooms with our children. I want to come home at night and see you holding our children. I want to turn out the lights at night and hold you in my arms. I just want you."

"You broke me," I tell him. "You broke me, and you did it without a second thought." I put my hands on his wrists.

"And for that, I will spend the rest of my life regretting that," he says.

"I don't know," I tell him honestly. "I don't know if I can."

He nods his head at me. "Please," he begs me. "Just give me a chance." He puts his forehead against mine. "Let me show you."

I close my eyes taking in his words. "When do you want to move into this house?" I ask him, my chest pounding.

"I bought it this morning, so now would be a good idea," he tells me, and I smile.

"You bought this house, not knowing if I would say yes?" I ask, a bit shocked.

He shrugs. "I would have given it to you and the baby if you didn't want me back." My mouth opens in shock. "But I also bought this house knowing I wouldn't give up until you were here," he tells me.

"I've missed you," I tell him quietly.

"Not as much as I've missed you," he tells me, and he kisses my lips softly. The minute his lips touch mine, I feel a flutter in my stomach. He pulls me to his chest, and I finally hug him. When he wraps his arms around me, I feel safe.

"Can I see the rest of the house?" I ask him, and he smiles. Taking my hand in his, he shows me the house.

"All the furniture is optional," he tells me. "We can keep it, or you can get stuff you like."

"But do you like it?" I ask him, and he brings our hands to his mouth.

"I don't care." He looks around a guest bedroom. "As long as I have you and our baby under the same roof, that is all that I need." I try to hide my smile, but I can't. I see only half the house before I need to sit down, and he has to get me some crackers.

"The sickness should be easing up once you get past the first trimester," he tells me and gets up to get me some water. "After that, it should be okay." I look at him. "I read it in the books."

"Books, plural? I only saw you reading *What to Expect When You're Expecting*," I ask him.

"*What To Expect When You're Expecting, On Becoming Baby Wise, You: Having A Baby, We're Pregnant The First Time Dads Pregnancy Handbook*." He smiles. "And my favorite *The Sh!t No One Tells You About Pregnancy: A Guide to Surviving Pregnancy, Childbirth, and Beyond* ."

"You read all those?" I ask, shocked because I really haven't gotten any books.

"I didn't read every one all at once. Well, most are week by week, and it's like a surprise present to read it each week. Like Christmas for forty weeks, if that makes sense," he tells me. "We can read it together if you want." I nod my head. "I will have to get you yours because I make notes in mine."

"Notes? What kind of notes?" I ask him, baffled by this whole conversation.

"Nothing really," he says. "Just what you were feeling, what foods you ate that didn't give you sickness, how sick you were."

"You wrote down all of that?" And he nods. "You are seriously crazy."

"It's for the baby," he tells me. "So he or she can read it and see how much you did for them."

"I'm pretty sure me carrying the child and giving birth will let them know how much I did for them," I tell him. "But now that the nausea has passed for the moment, I'm starving."

He gets up, and I follow him with the glass putting it down in the sink of the huge white kitchen. "What do you want to eat?" he asks me, walking out of the house and opening the car door for me.

I look down, shy now. "Chicken parm," I say, and he just smiles.

"That's my baby," he says. His chest puffs out, and I roll my eyes at him. He takes me to an Italian restaurant. We walk in holding hands, and I have the best chicken parm I've had in my life, and I pray that it stays down. When we walk out, there is paparazzi there, and he holds my hand the hold time. They call his name and ask him who I am, but he doesn't say anything. He makes sure I get into the car, closing and locking my door, and then unlocks the door once he climbs in it. Social media and the tabloids are going to have a field day in five, four, three, two, one.

We make our way over to my house, and he comes in with me. I walk to the couch, and when he goes to the kitchen, he seems at home. I just realize that he's been here every single day since I found out I was pregnant. He puts the water on to make me a ginger tea, and everything that he has done is starting to come out. He makes me tea every night before he leaves. He prepares my coffee for the next day, so it's ready when I get up. I'm watching him when I hear his phone ring, and he looks at me. "It's your father." I sit up when he answers the phone on speaker. "Hey."

"Did you just buy the house I showed you this morning?" he asks angrily.

"I did," he says, coming to me, carrying the hot tea.

"Motherfucker," He curses, and I hide my smile with my tea. "You know I was buying that for my daughter, right?"

"Yeah, except I wanted to buy it for my woman and my daughter or son," he tells him.

"Your woman?" he says. "Did you tell her that she's your woman yet, or is your head still in your ass?" I finally let my laugh out.

"I'm here, Dad," I tell him, and his voice gets soft when he says my name.

"How are you feeling, baby?" he asks, and I hear the television in the background.

"I'm doing good, Dad," I tell him. "Now, are we going to talk about you buying me a mansion?"

"It was for my grandchild," he tells me. "So you can't say no."

"I can say no," I tell him. "Just like I said no to you today when you tried to fire me and get me to work from home."

"It was a suggestion," he says.

"That's a great suggestion. You should think about it." I glare at Carter. "I have to go back to Montana this weekend. She should come with me and relax."

"I'll tell Sylvia," he says. "Honey, I have to go. See you Monday."

"I can't even with you both right now," I tell him, taking a sip of the tea. "Just like that, you think I'm going to go to Montana with you, and my father agrees with you. I'm doomed."

"Yes," he says, leaning forward. "You most certainly are. Will you come with me?"

"I don't know," I tell him.

"I don't want to be without you," he tells me softly. "If you need me or anything happens, I want to be there.""You know you can't use the baby as your bargaining chip to get me to agree to do things," I tell him, leaning forward to put my tea on the table.

"What do you say?" he asks me. "Want to go to Montana with me for the weekend? We just have a couple of scenes left to film, so it should take us one day, but we can stay there for the weekend. Maybe go on another hike, just not as far if you aren't feeling up to it."

"I would love that," I tell him, and he just smiles. He gets up and gives me a soft kiss goodbye. I get up, watching him get into the truck. I place my hand on my stomach. "What do you think, little one? Should I give your father another chance?" I ask, feeling the flutter again in my stomach. "I think so, too," I say, turning and walking to bed.

THIRTY-THREE

Carter

"AND THAT'S A WRAP, folks!" Ivan shouts, causing the whole staff to clap. I hold my hands up and clap over my head and then walk out of the stage and make a beeline to the house. I rented the same house we stayed at before, and I'm going to make her dinner tonight. I walk into the house and up the stairs, expecting her to be on the couch, but she isn't there. I walk to her bedroom and see her sleeping in the middle of the bed, holding her stomach. I smile, going into my bedroom. It's killing me not to hold her in my arms, but I'm not going to push it in case she decides she doesn't want me there.I walk to my room, grabbing the three pregnancy books that I am reading along with the journal I started when she told me she was pregnant. I get into bed beside her and try not to wake her. Sitting against the headboard, I start with the first book. Then I take my journal out and start writing.

We are still in Montana. Mommy is pretty tired all the time. She spends her days working, and at night, she is asleep almost as soon as she finishes dinner. She sleeps with her hand on her stomach, but I don't know if she knows she does this or not. I wonder if you can feel her hand and know how much love flows between you and her.I'm going to cook for her tonight. Fingers crossed that you let her keep the food down.We love you little one.Dad

I look over at her and see that her eyes are open, and she is looking at me. "Hey, did I wake you?"

"No," she says, not moving. "What are you doing?"

"I'm writing in my journal," I say while I watch her.

"Do you do that often?" she asks me, and I nod.

"Every day, I write something in it." I shrug. "When he or she is old enough, they might want to read it. If not, it'll be just for me. It's sort of something I wish my parents had done for me, ya know?"

"What do you want?" she asks me, and I look at her with furrowed eyebrows. "Do you prefer a girl or a boy?"

"I don't care. The main thing is that he or she is healthy." I smile at her. "What about you?"

"I already love him or her so much, I don't care." She smiles, and her hand remains on her belly. "Will you read me something?"

"From my journal?" I ask her, and she just nods. "Any day in particular?" She shakes her head, and I open it to the first page, figuring the beginning is where we always need to return.

Dear Little One,I found out today I'm going to be your dad. There are no words that I can say to justify how happy I am that you chose me. That you chose us. I sit here in the guest bedroom of my house, and all I can think of is all the things I want to tell you. All the things I want to do with you. All the ways I'm going to show you how much I love you. Your mom is . . . she, she is just amazing. I never thought I would love someone the way I love her and you. She came into my life, and she just made it so much better. Made absolutely everything better. I messed up big time, Little One, so big I don't think she will ever forgive me, but no matter what, I'm going to love her forever. I don't think I know how to not love her.I can't wait to meet you, Little One.Dad

I look down and see her with a tear running down her face. "Will you read me another one?" Her voice is soft. I turn the page to the next entry.

Dear Little One,I met you today for the first time. Well, I saw you for the first time. I also heard your heartbeat, and my heart filled with so much pride and excitement that I thought my own heart would burst out of my chest. I was so proud to be your dad. I held your mom's hand and looked down, hoping she knew how much I loved her, how much I love you.I saw your two little nubs that will one day soon be hands and feet. You were spinning around and around. Don't tell anyone else, but you are the best-looking kid in the world. I can't wait to meet you, Little One.Dad P.S. If you can, try to go easy on your mom. You are giving her a bad case of morning sickness, and I worry when I'm not there to make sure she is okay.

"One more?" she asks, and I turn to the page when she called me when she was bleeding. The scariest day of my life so far.

Dear Little One, We had a big scare tonight, so big I didn't know what to do. I prayed for the first time in a long time, prayed that you would be okay, prayed and even tried to sacrifice myself for you and your mom. I would give anything to make sure you are never hurt. I sat there watching your mom be the bravest person in the world, and the only thing I could think about was you and your mom. The only thing I could think of was making sure that every single day you know that you are loved. I need you to be okay, Little One. I need you to fight to be okay, and I need you to know that I love you and your mom so much. I spoke with your grandpa Ryan tonight. He's a good guy, but don't listen to what he has to say about me. He told me that I need to fight for your mom. I need to fight for you and for her and for us. I need to show her how much I love her. I'm going to do it. Until my last breath, she is going to know that I love you both with everything I have. Be good, Little One. Dad

I look down at her, waiting for her to tell me she wants to hear one more journal entry, but instead, she just sits there, staring at me with a look I can't make out on her gorgeous face.

"I knew that, no matter what, you would be a good dad," she tells me, sitting up. "I know that now. No matter how you were raised or what your own parents did to you, you'd never make those same mistakes. You are amazing, Carter."

"I am going to try," I tell her. "I don't think I'm going to be perfect, but I'm going to be the best I can be," I tell her, putting my journal on the side. "I want to be the soccer dad, the football dad. I want to be there for the first crawl and first step. I want to teach them how to ride a two-wheel bike and how to swim. I want to be there every single step of the way not missing a thing." She smiles at me. "I love you," I tell her again. "I know I tell you that all the time, but I just don't want you to ever doubt it. I want us to be a family, and I want to wake up with you every morning. I want to go to bed with my hand on your stomach, so our baby knows I'm there." She wipes away a tear. "I want to put up the crib with you, and I want to hold your hand at night and in the morning. I want you to depend on me. I want it all, Erin." I'm putting all my cards on the table, so I will never have to be thinking I should have. "I want it all, and I want it with you." She comes to me and throws her leg over to sit on my lap. My hands go to her hips, and she leans her head forward. Her hair falls to the front, and I take both hands, tucking it into the back over her shoulder. "You are so beautiful," I tell her, and she puts her hands on my face.

"I love you," she tells me, her eyes lighting up. "I love how you put us first. I love how you love our child and didn't even bat an eye when you found out. I love that you haven't pushed or asked me for anything more than I was willing to give, and that you've given me that time to get there."

"Are you there, baby?" I ask her, hoping to Christ that I get to have her forever. "There is no going back," I tell her. "It's forever. I will not let us fail at this."

"My parents love me," she starts to say. "I knew that growing up, and I never doubted that. Not once did I ever feel I wasn't loved. But I missed my dad. I missed not being able to make him pancakes on Father's Day or get him to go to the store with me so he could help me buy a gift for my mother." Her fingers play with the scruff on my face. "This isn't happening like I thought it would," she tells me. "I thought I would be married when I became a mom, but I wouldn't change our journey for anything in the world."

"Marry me?" I ask her, and she gasps. "This is definitely not the way I wanted to ask you." I smile at her. "But it is only a matter of time." My heart pounds in my chest. "Marry me and be my wife." She puts her hands on my chest, and I know she can feel my heart pounding. "This isn't how I wanted to do it. I wanted to do it with roses, and candles, and for it to be romantic."

"Oh my God, you're serious?" she says out loud, and I move her from my lap. "Carter," she says my name, but I walk to the bedroom and grab the bag where the red Cartier ring box is. I grab it and then go back to the room.

"Can you stand up, at least?" I laugh nervously, and she gets off the bed and comes over to me. She is wearing yoga pants, but she is wearing my thick sweater over it. Her hair is loose. I'm wearing jeans; there are no roses, no candles, and no string quartet to serenade her. It's just me and her where I first fell in love with her.

I get down on one knee, and she gasps again, her hand going to her mouth. "I bought this ring when you told me that you were pregnant. Not because you were pregnant but because I knew I couldn't live without you." I open the ring box, and she silently cries. The blue ten-carat square diamond reminded me of her eyes. "Erin, I love you," I say. Suddenly, my words are gone. Everything is gone as I look at her. "Don't cry. Please don't cry." I look down at the ring. "I want you to be my wife, to be the mother of my children, to be my rock. But most importantly, I want to be your husband. I want to be the father to your children, and I want to be your rock. I want to hold you through the good times, and I want to hold you through the bad times." I look up at her, now the tears are flowing down my face also. "Don't let me live another day without you."

"Yes," she whispers and laughs while she cries.

"Oh my God. You said yes," I say, almost shocked. I get up and hold her face in mine and kiss her. Finally, we share a real kiss. Her arms wrap around my neck, and I wrap my arms around her. I let her go and then get down on my knees again. This time, I lift her shirt to expose her little stomach. "She said yes," I whisper to our child and kiss her stomach. "The ring," I say to myself and get up and grab her hand. "This means forever," I tell her, slipping the ring on her finger, and she looks down at her hand.

"You went a little overboard," she says, and I shake my head.

"Not even a bit," I tell her. "Do you think we can get married next week?"

"What?" she asks. "Highly doubtful."

"Challenge accepted," I say, and I hug her, bringing her to me. That night, when I close my eyes, it's with her naked in my arms. My hand on her belly, and her hand on mine.

Thirty-Four

Erin

"OH, BABY." MY MOTHER puts on my veil. "I honestly didn't think we could pull it off," she says, and I look in the mirror, "in one week."

"I can't even believe it." My stomach flutters. I put my hand on my little belly and think about when I said yes. The next day, he was out of bed at the crack of dawn and on the phone with my father. Nothing could stop those two together. My father had my mother on a plane that afternoon, and for the past week, we planned the wedding. I didn't even think we would have a big wedding, but when Ryan Crest and Carter Johnson send out invitations, people move. With everything going on, I can't believe the press hasn't gotten a hold of the plans. All week, Sylvia has been putting up pictures of Carter from Montana, so everyone still thinks he's there. I also didn't think I would be able to get a wedding dress, but boy, was I wrong. Dad had the best seamstress come to the house the day after we got back, and just like that, she sketched what was my wedding dress. I wanted it to be lace with long sleeves and backless. I wanted it tight all the way down because who knew if I would ever get this skinny again. I wanted the back to kick off with a train. Well, it was so much better than I thought it would be. It fit me like a glove, and although I had a little bit of a belly, you could hardly see it. I turn to the left and see that the veil has crystals all over it, making it glitter in the light.

"Are you feeling okay?" my mother asks me, and I just nod. "Good." I look at her, and she is in her own beautiful gown. Hers is a champagne-colored chiffon dress that flows around her with a beaded belt. Her hair is curled just like mine. "You look beautiful." I smile at her and then hear a knock on the door. "I swear if that is your man again," she says, shaking her head. Carter is not a fan of traditions especially when it means he isn't sleeping with me or waking up with me. He's come by at least ten times today just to check in and make sure I was okay. The last time, my mother said if he came back, she would take me away. He left with a huge belly laugh and shouted through the door that he would find me no matter where they hid me.

"Hey, princess." I hear from behind me and see my father walk in. He is in his tux, and he looks so handsome. He comes to me, and I see the tears in his eyes. "You are the most beautiful bride I have ever seen." Then he turns to my mother. "We did good." She nods, and he puts his hand around her waist and brings her close to him. "Are you ready?" he asks me and then looks at my mother. "Carter is about ready to bust down the door." I laugh, and my mother shakes her head. "Can you imagine what he is going to be like when she gives birth?"

"He's going to need to be knocked out. I'll take Lamaze classes, too, just in case," my mother says, and then they look at me and smile. "Let's go," she says, handing me my bouquet. I walk with them out of the room to the door that leads outside. We are getting married at my father's house. I stand with him at the door, and I hear the song for my mother. She turns and kisses me on my cheek. "See you down there," she says and walks down the aisle.

We take our places, and I look down at the ground. "Thank you," I tell my dad, and he looks down and then up at me with tears pooling in his eyes. "Thank you for being the best dad a girl can have." I hold his cheek in my hand. "And thank you for not killing him when I know you wanted to." He laughs now.

"Daddy," I say softly, "take me to my husband." He nods and holds out his arm, and I wrap my hand in the crook of his elbow. The doors open, and I finally see outside. I want to look around, but I can't. The only thing I can see is Carter standing right in front of the big willow tree where I used to swing. The tree my father had planted when I told him it was my favorite tree in the whole world. He stands there in his black tux wearing the biggest smile I have ever seen. He looks at me as I walk down the rose petal pathway. I watch him the whole way, my stomach doing little flips. I swear this child knows when he is near. When I make it to him, my father hands me over to Carter who thanks him and then looks at me.

"You are so beautiful," he says and then kisses me softly on the lips, causing the officiant to clear his throat.

"It's not that part yet," he says, and the whole crowd chuckles while Carter just shrugs. We go with traditional vows, and when he slips on the eternity band, he grabs my face and kisses me again, making the officiant speak up.

"She's mine. I can kiss her anytime I want to," Carter tells the man, and he just laughs.

I finally slip the black gold band on his finger, and this time, the officiant finally says, "You may now kiss your bride." He puts a hand around my waist and kisses me, and everyone cheers for us. I turn around and walk back down the aisle. This time, I'm on the arm of my husband.

We take more pictures than I've ever taken in my whole life, and that night, Jessica finally makes her way to us. "Thank you so much for having us," she says, looking over at Tyler. "It was beautiful."

"Thank you for coming," I say, and then she looks over at Carter.

"I just published the story." She's wearing a huge smile on her face. "Congratulations," she says, and they both walk away.

"What is that all about?" I ask him, and he brings out his phone. His screen saver is the picture of me lying on the couch holding my belly. He types in something and then hands it to me. I read the title right over a picture of us at the altar right when we were announced husband and wife.

How Hollywood's Prince nabbed the role of a lifetime . . . as a husband and a father.

"Come on, wife," he says, taking my hand, "it's time to consummate our marriage." I throw my head back and laugh, reminding him that that horse has already left the barn. He picks me up and carries me inside and has his wicked way with me all night long anyway.

EPILOGUE ONE

Carter

THE SOUND OF CRYING fills the baby monitor, and I look over to see that she is moving in her crib. Her legs are moving up and down, and her hands are in fists over her head. I smile, thinking she has as much patience as I do.

She came into the world three months ago screaming and didn't settle down until she got her mother's breast. Only then did her eyes open and she looked around. I was a mess, to say the least. Seeing Erin in pain while she bounced on a fucking ball was the worst time of my life. But then she became a warrior and gave birth to my nine pound, five ounce baby girl we called Annabella. I still call her little one. The nursery started out neutral since we didn't know the baby's sex, but slowly, pink things started to appear. I walk over to the crib, and her feet and arms are going nuts.

"Hey there, little one," I say, and she stops crying. "What is all the fuss about?" I grab the bottle that Erin left me right before she walked into the bedroom to do her glam stuff. I grab my phone and snap a picture of her, wondering if I can put another picture of her on my Instagram. When the press finally found out we were expecting, I did it with a picture of us on the beach. Me sitting with Erin in the middle of my legs and both our hands on her stomach with the caption.

"Dreams really do come true."

Then once a week, I would post things about being a dad. It was brilliant, as Sylvia said, because my popularity went through the roof, and people kept following just to keep up with our journey.

Walking to the rocking chair, she starts to fuss again, and when I finally cradle her and put the nipple into her mouth, she settles down. Her tongue moves it out of her mouth. "Sorry, little one, this is the best you are going to get." She looks at me with her huge blue eyes, and she just starts sucking. "Momma is getting ready," I tell her, and she just looks at me. "Tonight is the movie premiere." I smile at her. "Grandpa says we don't have to watch the movie." She looks at me and takes in all my words as though I'm telling her all the secrets in the world.

"Momma is having a hard time leaving you. She got Grandma to fly in to make sure you are okay." She finishes the bottle, and I put her over my shoulder and start to rub her back and then burp her. Once she burps, she starts to fuss and cry again. "Don't tell me you're still hungry," I ask her, and she stretches in my arms. I walk to our bedroom, and I hear the blow dryer going, and when I step foot into the bathroom, I'm met with two women working on my wife. My wife, the best thing that has ever happened to me.

"There she is," I tell our daughter. Turning her in my arms, I hold her around her waist and under her bum. "There's the source of all your food." Erin looks over at us, her robe is off her shoulders and her hair is being curled while a woman does her eyes. "See how beautiful she is." I kiss her head and tell her, and she smiles.

"Is that my girl?" Erin says, and Annabella turns her head to look at her, and she smiles and then looks around. "Did she eat?"

"Just finished the bottle, but I don't think it'll be enough to tide her over," I tell her, and I suddenly want all these people to get out of our house. I want it just the three of us, the way it's supposed to be. The way it always is. Ryan tried to get us to have a nanny, but Erin and I both squashed that idea.

"That was three ounces in that bottle," she says, mystified.

"She's growing," I tell her and look in the mirror and see that she is drifting off to sleep while I rock her side to side. "What time is your mom coming?"

"Dad just said that he is picking her up in ten minutes so maybe forty minutes," she says, and then she closes her eyes when the girl needs to put shadow on her.

"Go put her down, Carter," she demands me, but I don't move. I just watch my wife. "She already has the habit of falling asleep on your chest every night." I shrug and gently turn my girl around and place her on my chest. I walk to the bed and place her in the little crib we have in the room. She moves her hands when I put her down. I place my hand on her chest, and she falls back asleep.

When my mother-in-law comes in, she goes straight for Annabella. I'm about to tell her not to wake her, but she lets out a little whimper. My girl doesn't like anyone over either as she fusses. "Go get dressed." She shoos me away while she and Ryan sit on the couch and cradle their granddaughter.

I walk back into the room and see that Erin is by herself now. She still has her robe on over her shoulders. "Is Mom here?" she asks, and I walk to her and untie the robe and slowly open it, seeing that she is naked under. "We don't have time for this." She pushes my hands away, but I can't help it. She was perfect before, but after having Annabella, her body is more perfect. Is it possible? I didn't think so, and she hates it that her hips are rounder and her breasts are fuller, but she's just that much more of a knockout. I thought once we were parents, the sex would slow down, but it's been the opposite for both of us. "The car is picking us up in thirty minutes, and you haven't showered yet." My hand comes up to cup her breast, rolling her nipple. "Carter."

"I can be fast," I tell her, dropping my shorts and letting my cock out. "Five minutes." I turn her around, putting her back to the vanity counter.

"I just did my makeup," she whispers. I kiss her

neck. "The door isn't closed." Her eyes close while I open her legs and move her closer to the edge, having her ass almost hanging off.

"I locked our door," I tell her, grabbing my cock in one hand and rubbing it down and then slowly pushing in. Fuck, she's always ready. She went on the pill as soon as she gave birth to Annabella, and I'm trying to prove that it's not as effective by getting her pregnant. I mean, if she can get pregnant with us using condoms, then she can with the pill. She moans, and I have to cover her mouth to keep her parents from hearing us. "Shh," I tell her, not stopping from fucking her as fast as I can. Her legs wrap around my hips, and she gets wetter, her pussy tightening, and I know she's almost there. We've mastered making it happen in less than three minutes with a newborn.

"I'm going to come," she says breathlessly, her back arching, and she comes quietly with her eyes on me. As soon as I know she's done, I plant myself all the way in her and come. I don't move and neither does she. "That has to be a record," she says now, kissing the underneath of my jaw. "Two minutes."

"Can we not point that out?" I say, slipping out of her and spinning to turn the shower on. "Ever?"

She throws her head back and laughs, then gets up to clean herself. "I'm going to get dressed and go down and feed your daughter," she says, and I nod as she walks into the walk-in closet to get dressed. Twenty minutes later, I'm walking down the stairs, and I head to the family room. "There he is," Erin says, and I look at her with my daughter in her arms. "The car is here, and I just finished feeding her." She turns and hands Annabella to her mother, and I look back and see Ryan coming out of the bathroom in his own suit. I turn around when I hear heels clicking on the floor. She is wearing a one-shoulder black dress that hugs all her curves, coming to her mid-thigh and then it is sheer until her knees.

"The sooner we leave, the sooner we get back," I tell them and grab my wife's hand and walk out the door. We get into the car, and when we get to the red carpet, Ryan gets out first, and then slowly, she gets out. When I get out, the fans go wild. "I'll be right back," I tell her, and she nods, holding her clutch in her hand. I walk across the street to sign some autographs and take some pictures. When I walk back over, I see that Erin is talking to Tyler, and he smiles at her.

"Don't you have your own wife to talk to?" I joke with him, and he just smiles.

"She's home," he says. "I just can't stop trying to knock her up." He shrugs, and I just laugh.

"I know that problem," I say, and Erin gasps, looking at me. "It's like a challenge."

She shakes her head, and Tyler tells me he is going to see me in there. He walks the red carpet and poses for pictures but doesn't stop to talk to any of the reporters. "Shall we?" Erin says, and I grab her hand in mine, and we walk the red carpet. She tells me which reporters to stop and talk to. She still works for Hillcrest but only for me. It was a compromise we both agreed to. I didn't want her to work, and she didn't want to stop working.

In the end, we both win.

"Carter," the male reporter greets me. "Great seeing you." I nod at him. "What do you think about the buzz going around that this role is going to have you winning the Oscar?"

I shake my head. "I try not to get swept up in all the social media rumors. I already have the best award waiting for me at home," I say, mentioning Annabella.

What a difference a year makes. This time last year, I was a shell of a man living an empty life, and then one day, in a blink of an eye, it changed, and I wouldn't trade it for all the money in the world. I would give all this up just to go home to my girls at night. I bring Erin's hand up to my lips, and she smiles at me. You could give me all the awards in the world and call my name to the stage a million times over and nothing can take the place of that smile. Nothing can take the place of being proud to be by her side, proud to be Annabella's dad. But most of all, proud of the man she made me become.

EPILOGUE TWO

Erin

Six months later . . .

"IS SHE OKAY?" I ask my husband, who comes into our bedroom, and I hear my daughter in the monitor calling him.

"Da da da da da da." I shake my head and look at him. He's beaming, and it's not just because he is sweeping through all the award shows. No, he's beaming because our daughter's first words were da da.

"I have to get ready." He comes to me and kisses my neck. "I wish we could skip tonight," he says, and I shake my head. "We could order Chinese." He tries to get me to change my mind, but there is no way in hell I'm letting him get out of the Academy Awards when he's up for best actor in a motion picture. The day the nominations were announced, we were going on a night of not sleeping. Annabella was teething, and I swear he looked like someone was stabbing him each time she cried.

"I am going in the guest room to get ready," I tell him, and he looks at me. "Or else you'll destroy my hair."

"I can restrain myself, you know." He pulls his shorts down, and I see his cock is already semi-hard just waiting for the word. I shake my head. "Go get ready." I point at the shower and walk out of the room. Stopping in the nursery, I see my mother on the floor with our baby girl as she drools.

"She is so in love with her father, it's scary," my mother says, and she leans forward and kisses Annabella's neck, causing her to shriek. "Go get dressed."

I walk to the guest room and see the gown hanging on the hanger. I look at the rose gold gown and touch the beading. It's his big night, and I am so proud of him. I drop the robe and then slip into the chiffon gown. "Mom!" I shout for her, and she comes in with Annabella in her arms. "I need you to zip me." She just smiles, putting Annabella down, and then comes over and zips me in. The gown molds every curve and drops down between my breasts. It goes tight until my knees and then hangs down to the floor.

"The train is amazing," my mother says of the train that starts at my shoulders and then hangs down.

"Do I look the part?" I ask her, turning and taking myself in. I pinned one side of my hair up and then let the rest fall down in curls.

"Babe." I hear Carter call me, and I pick up my girl, and she smiles at me, showing me her two teeth.

I walk out of the room, the swishing of the gown all around me, and I see my husband looking handsome in his black velour tux. "Da da da," Annabella says when she sees him, and when I'm close enough, she tries to pitch herself forward.

"There is my queen," he says, kissing my cheek. "And my princess." He tosses her in the air, and she screams with glee.

We walk down the steps together, and my father snaps a picture of the three of us. Annabella in tights with roses on them and a shirt that says "Dada's prize." My mother put on a cream-colored headband with a huge bow on it, and I'm surprised she hasn't ripped it off.

"We have to get going," my father says and walks over to my mother and kisses her on the cheek and then kisses Annabella. My mother has now moved to California, and she lives in Carter's house on the beach. There was no way to keep her away, and my father is thriving in it. "See you later," he says, and I have to think that he will eventually get his head out of his own ass and just see what is in front of him. They are both still in love, and nothing is keeping them from being together.

"Good luck, guys," she says, walking out with us and waving at us as we make our way to the awards.

"Do you have a speech?" my father asks him, and he just shakes his head. "Winging it? We all know what happened last time," he jokes. When Carter got up on stage at the Golden Globes and was at a loss for words, his speech was all about Annabella and her spit-up stories and the all-nighters that she makes him pull.

We sit in the limo line, and I breathe in and out. Counting to ten, I try to get myself to simmer down because I'm so nervous for him. It takes forty minutes for us to be let out, and the crowd goes wild when he gets out and waves.

Kellie and Brian walk up to us, and she kisses his cheek. She wrote the song for the movie soundtrack, and she is also up for an award tonight. Her husband beams with pride by her side. I walk to step away from Carter so he can take his own pictures, but I know he won't let go. We walk in and take our seat in the front row, and I sit between my father and my husband. Kellie ends up winning the Oscar for the best song, and the crowd goes wild . . . and then it's time for the best actor award.

"I'm so proud of you, regardless of who wins," I whisper to him when they introduce him and play a little clip of the movie.

I hold his hand in mine, squeezing it when the presenter says, "And the Oscar goes to . . ." They take the paper out of the envelope, and I sit here, waiting for his name. "Carter Johnson."

I jump out of my chair, and he hugs me. "I love you so much," I tell him, and he kisses my neck and doesn't let me go. "You have to go and get your award." He smiles at me, kissing my lips. "But before you go, challenge completed," I tell him, and he looks at me with huge eyes and then looks down at my stomach, and I just nod. He shakes my father's hand and takes the steps two by two until he holds the Oscar in his hand and steps to the mic.

"My wife told me in the car to prepare a speech, but I said I'm going to wing it," he says, looking down at the gilded man in his hand. "That might not have been my best choice since I am coming up at a complete blank right now." I shake my head, and he laughs. "I want to thank Ivan for pushing me to the point where I thought I was going to break." He names the key people on the film. "To Ryan, who gave me a shot even though everything was stacked against me and everyone told him not to." I look over at my father, who just laughs. "To Annabella, being your father is the best role I could ever have," he says, beaming with pride and a huge smile. "And finally, to the woman who gave me everything that you could possibly give a person. Erin"—he looks at me—"you are the best thing that has ever happened to me, and you make me want to be a better man. I love you," he says just as the music starts. They are ushering him to the side stage, but he doesn't go. Instead, he comes down the stairs and grabs my hand and hands my father the Oscar and then looks at him with just a nod. He pulls me to the side where it's semi-quiet and then leans in. "Are you really pregnant?" he asks me, and I smile.

"I took a test this morning," I tell him. "I missed a pill last month and then I tried to double up, but you know you and your swimmers."

"They are Olympians," he says of his sperm, and I

laugh.

"Can you go and do your interviews so we can go and get something to eat?" I ask and then he gets down on his knees and kisses my stomach.

"Hey there, little one number two," he says, "it's me. Everyone calls me the Hollywood prince, but to you, I'm just Dad."

The End

ACKNOWLEDGMENTS

My Husband: Thank you for being by my side through this whole thing. I love you!

My Kids: Matteo, Michael, and Erica, thank you for sharing me with this book world!

Rachel: You are my blurb bitch. Whether you wear sloths or bats I still love you. Thank you for writing every single blurb without reading the book!

Beta girls: Teressa, Lori, Natasha M, Lori, Sandy, Yolanda, Yamina, Sarah and Melissa. Thank you for cheering me on and begging for more. Sarah Carter loves you!

Madison Maniacs: This little group went from two people to so much more and I can't thank you guys enough. This group is my go to, my safe place.

Dani: Every single day you are there answering questions and holding my hand for that I thank you from the bottom of my heart.

BLOGGERS. THANK YOU FOR TAKING A CHANCE ON ME. You give so much of yourself effortlessly and you are the voice that we can't do this without.

And Lastly and most importantly to YOU the reader, without you none of this would be real. So thank you for reading!